MEET ME UNDER THE NORTHERN LIGHTS

MANDY BAGGOT

B
Boldwood

First published in Great Britain in 2025 by Boldwood Books Ltd.

Copyright © Mandy Baggot, 2025

Cover Design by Alexandra Allden

Cover Images: Shutterstock

A CIP catalogue record for this book is available from the British Library.

Paperback ISBN 978-1-83678-236-0

Large Print ISBN 978-1-83678-237-7

Hardback ISBN 978-1-83678-235-3

Trade Paperback ISBN 978-1-80635-309-5

Ebook ISBN 978-1-83678-238-4

Kindle ISBN 978-1-83678-239-1

Audio CD ISBN 978-1-83678-230-8

MP3 CD ISBN 978-1-83678-231-5

Digital audio download ISBN 978-1-83678-234-6

This book is printed on certified sustainable paper. Boldwood Books is dedicated to putting sustainability at the heart of our business. For more information please visit https://www.boldwoodbooks.com/about-us/sustainability/

Boldwood Books Ltd, 23 Bowerdean Street, London, SW6 3TN

www.boldwoodbooks.com

For Robin.
Thank you for our amazing trip to Iceland that gave me all the inspiration for Chloe and Gunnar's story!

1

WINCHESTER CHRISTMAS MARKET,
WINCHESTER, HAMPSHIRE, UK

'Why does mulled wine taste so superior to wine that isn't hot?' Kat Jenkins smacked her lips together and gave an exaggerated eyeroll.

'Because it's freezing?' Chloe Bellamy offered, stamping her Ugg-clad feet to will life into her soles.

'No, it's the cinnamon... meeting the cloves... and saying a big how do you do and Merry Christmas to the beautifully warm alcohol.'

Kat had said the sentence like she was on stage playing a part in her am-dram group and then she gurgle-giggled and Chloe noticed exactly how rosy her friend's cheeks were. At least one of them had body parts that were warm. Because Winchester was freezing tonight, even amid these cosy-looking wooden huts all lit up with fairy lights beneath the magnificent cathedral. It was so cold Chloe was wearing Michael's university scarf around her neck. She hadn't even known it was still on the coat hooks until it had revealed itself, draped over the hood of her warmest padded jacket. What it was still doing there when it was almost nine months since its owner had departed carrying everything else he owned in a cardboard box/old suitcase combo, she didn't really know. As soon as those test results had come in, two years together had disintegrated more rapidly than a potted Christmas fir on Boxing Day...

'Aren't you having any?' Kat asked, mid-slurp.

She shook her head. 'Not tonight.'

'Oh, don't be one of those pre-Christmas detoxers. I don't get that at all. Deny yourself life's greatest pleasures when they're all around you, then go crazy from the twenty-fifth to some time before Valentine's Day when self-loathing hits.' She inhaled. 'I say skip the self-loathing and never, ever skip anything that tastes so good you wouldn't mind if you actually turned into it.'

And now Chloe was wondering what life would be like if she had to continue it as a sausage roll...

'I can't drink in case I get "the phone call" and have to drive,' she said, eyes drifting to a chalet stall dishing out ladles full of delicious-smelling hot chocolate.

'Honestly it feels like the whole "the phone call" scenario has been going on longer than the pregnancy. Actually, make that longer than an elephant's pregnancy.'

'Michelle is due on Christmas Day.'

'How very nativity. Do John Lewis do little gift stockings of frankincense?'

Chloe shook her head. OK, it was far from ideal having spent the past eight months with a boss who went from caring to cataclysmic in 0.5 seconds such were her hormones, but Michelle was doing a brave thing, having a baby at forty-two. And, as tough as the situation was for Chloe to be part of, Michelle had been so good to her since she had joined the events company – Celebratey. She had done the smaller events right at the beginning – made actual cow-pat cakes with farm-loving five-year-olds, modelled balloons at the pro-bono gigs for goodwill mentions on socials – now she had risen quickly through the ranks to be Michelle's go-to girl. Any moment now, maybe even like the King's New Year's Honours, Chloe was hopeful to get the fully-fledged 'partner' offer. It wasn't like she had anything else to invest her money in right now.

'I don't know why you don't like Michelle,' Chloe said, stamping her boots a bit more.

'You do know why I don't like Michelle,' Kat answered. She blew at her mulled wine.

'Honestly, Kat, how can you hold a grudge about one tiny incident?'

'She tipped guacamole on me!'

'She didn't tip it on you. It was an accident.'

'She flicked her fork at me!'

'She flicked it in the air! You know how animated she gets when she talks. It wasn't deliberate.'

Kat huffed, breath visible. 'I don't know why I'm trying to get you to see my side of things. You're Team Michelle no matter what.'

'I'm not,' Chloe said. 'But, also I wasn't under the impression that my friendships were in competition with each other.'

Kat whipped her head around. 'Oh, so she's your friend now, not just your boss?'

Was Michelle her friend as well as her boss? Well, it was difficult to have that kind of multifaceted relationship when someone had to be the authority figure, the one in charge. And Chloe didn't really confide in Michelle like she confided in Kat. Michelle didn't even know all the details of what had happened between her and Michael. In fact, Michelle didn't know *any* of the details of what had happened between her and Michael. And, come to think of it, Michelle hadn't actually ever asked...

Then it struck her. This wasn't anything to do with Michelle.

Kat was just in a mood. And Kat only behaved like this when a certain person was on her mind. 'Kat, has your mother invited herself for Christmas Day?'

'Oh my God! So now you think I'm hating on your friend, Michelle, because my mother has invited herself for Christmas Day!' Kat exclaimed.

Chloe waited, watching Kat and briefly tuning out the carol music rising in the frosty air. A hard task when they were being accompanied by a very out of tune trumpet...

'OK!' Kat bellowed. 'So my mother's invited herself for Christmas Day!'

The exclamation was so loud children turned away from the sugared doughnut stand to look.

'And now I can feel a panic attack coming on! I need a paper bag! I need... something!'

Before Chloe could do anything, Kat downed the rest of her mulled wine in one great glug and started to breathe, open-mouthed like she was auditioning for a lead role of a ferocious dragon.

'It's going to be OK,' Chloe said, hand on Kat's back now, gently patting. Although, Kat's mother, Rula, was a force to be reckoned with. She was the kind of woman who knew what the word 'no' was, because she used it a lot herself, but when it came to recognising its meaning with regard to others, it fell out of her personal dictionary.

'It's not going to be OK,' Kat answered, all breathy like she'd swallowed mouthwash that had taken a layer of skin from her tongue. 'She will criticise everything. From the garland on the front door – too much greenery, Katherine, not enough berries; the turkey – I find it can be a particularly dry meat if it's not cooked just right; to the King's speech – does he look a bit peaky to you or is it your television? I thought his cancer had all cleared up.'

'Kat—'

'And you know she never stops. Last year I spent an hour in the bathroom pretending to have constipation just so I could get some peace.'

'Why don't you tell her to stop criticising?' Chloe asked. 'Stop' had to work better than 'no', right?

'And have her criticise my inability to accept criticism?'

Chloe's phone began to ring. A dart of panic hit when she saw the screen. 'It's Michelle.'

'Ugh, trust Guac One to interrupt in my time of need!'

'It could be the baby,' Chloe reminded. She answered. 'Hello.'

'Where are you?' Michelle said abruptly.

'I'm just at the Christmas market and—'

'OK, good. So, you need to get home and pack a bag.'

Chloe's heart started to race. It was the baby. It was too early. Weeks too early. But she needed to be calm like she always was. She was the woman who'd learned magic from YouTube in sixteen minutes when an international conjuror hadn't shown...

'OK, well, my bag is already packed and you said the private hospital has a high-end kind-of Just Eat option so—'

'What do you mean your bag is already packed? I know you're good, Chloe, great even, but you're not a mind-reader surely.'

'My bag's been packed since the start of the second trimester. I'm sure I told you that.' She had definitely told Michelle that. She told Michelle everything she was on top of so Michelle knew she was consistent, reliable, not about to jump ship any time soon... Much better to tell your boss these things rather than the fact your long-term boyfriend left you because you were medically deficient.

'Oh my God! Chloe!'

'Is it a contraction?! How far apart are they? I am leaving, right now!'

She didn't get more than a few steps away from a gesticulating Kat before Michelle spoke again.

'I'm not in labour, Chloe!'

Chloe stopped, unexpectedly jostling someone in the queue for smoky bratwursts. 'What?'

'I'm not in labour! I have a few weeks to go yet and the head is less fully engaged than Milo during the NCT classes.'

Now Chloe didn't understand at all. 'But what bag are we talking about if it's not my not-the-daddy-but-the-work-baddie bag for the birth?'

'A bag that you can fit warm clothes in. Very warm clothes. Along with all the ingenuity I know you have, and all the savvy entrepreneurship I've passed along.'

'I don't think there's a bag big enough for all that savviness, Michelle.'

'Cute, Chloe. But seriously, you can't fuck this up.'

Chloe didn't even know what 'this' was. Only that it wasn't being there with Michelle and Milo as their newborn slithered down the birth canal. Kat was looking at her now, probably wondering what was going down on the call.

'You're going to Iceland. Tomorrow.'

Iceland the supermarket. Michelle had to mean Iceland the supermarket. She tried to speak but quickly realised she was struggling even to draw breath and that smoky sausage aroma in the air wasn't aiding inhalation.

'Remember Lincoln?'

The place? A car? Biscuits?

'I—'

'Chloe, have you caught my baby brain? Lincoln Sinclair! The CEO of Sinclairz Chairs.'

Sinclairz Chairs was a global company that made chairs guaranteed to support every sinew of you and realign your spine or you got your money back. Chloe had been sceptical of how this guarantee was activated without every customer getting a before and after MRI scan, but it seemed there was barely a household or office without one of the Sinclairz chairs in residence. And Michelle and Chloe had met Lincoln Sinclair at a mother and baby expo in Birmingham that Chloe remembered more for devouring three Big Mac meals after what felt like the longest, most exposure therapy day ever and crying into her king-sized bed, than she did for the CEO's nursing chair.

'Chloe!'

Chloe inhaled. 'Yes, Lincoln Sinclair, I remember.'

'He wants us to pitch for a huge event for Sinclairz Chairs' tenth anniversary next December.'

'O-K.' And he wanted catering from Iceland? From what Chloe could remember, Lincoln Sinclair was definitely more a Waitrose man than an Iceland man. Marks and Spencer's good sushi at the very least.

'So, your flight is tomorrow morning. I know it's last minute, but it has to be now, otherwise how are we going to know what kind of thing there is for a CEO and his troops to do? He wants festive and fabulous in Reykjavik and he is going to pay whoever gets the job – that means potentially us – a very pretty sum to organise everything. And the most brilliant thing is... you speak Icelandic, so you are going to be able to negotiate everything in the native tongue and get the best price.'

Icelandic. Reykjavik. Not the home of cut-price pizzas and Mayflower curry sauce. Iceland the country. And finally, having never had to face the reality of her embellished CV before, her lies were coming back to haunt her. She couldn't speak Icelandic! She had no ties, language or otherwise, with the country in the Arctic Circle! And now, right when she was ready to throw even more than everything into her career, exactly when she was poised to leap onto a partnership offer she knew had to be coming, she was about to be exposed as a fraud in the worst way. She had to confess, quickly. Hope that Michelle soon becoming a mother had softened her ball-breaker attitude just a tad. She opened her mouth to speak.

'I mean, Chloe, this is such a huge opportunity for us! Potentially organising an event for Sinclairz Chairs! *The* Sinclairz Chairs! Their anniversary celebration at Christmas time, in Iceland. And do you know how many influential people Lincoln knows? If we win this and then go on to do it brilliantly we could be talking business with people who have been to royal garden parties or... on Graham Norton's sofa.'

'Great!'

That was the word she had chosen? One word. Not the many words she should be saying that explained how she didn't know Icelandic!

'Are you excited? Because I am so excited! More excited about this than having to dilate ten centimetres in a few weeks if I'm honest, but don't tell Milo that! I wish I could go! But, Chloe, I know you are going to do just as good a job as I would, better with your linguistic skills, even. So, I will put everything you need to know in an email and...'

As Michelle carried on wrapping up, Chloe looked to Kat who was coming closer, new steaming paper cups in her hand. This time she was not going to refuse the mulled wine. What did 'no' mean again?

2

CHLOE'S APARTMENT, WINCHESTER

'Repeat after me... *halló.*'

It was almost 10 p.m. now and Chloe was rolling and stuffing jumpers, jackets and anything she possessed that was going to battle with high minus figures into a bag. The bag – budget airline size complaint (just) – was currently looking like the scattered-style racks of TK Maxx and Kat was trying to teach her Icelandic from Google Translate as Duolingo apparently didn't do Icelandic!

'I've got that down, Kat. It's basically the same as English.' In one hand she had skiing salopettes she had bought for a fancy-dress party, but never worn. In the other she had leg-warmers bought for an Eighties night, which she sadly had worn and there were photos to prove it.

'Ooo, OK, let's move on to something spicier... how about "do you have wine?"'

Kat had moved on to something spicier an hour ago when they had arrived back from the Christmas market – the old and very-out-of-date bottle of Captain Morgan's spiced gold rum that Michael had obviously left as well as that university scarf. Kat had found it in the gaming cupboard Chloe hadn't even opened since Michael had left. It used to contain a PS5 and games ranging from warfare to tending to plants – none of which Chloe had ever really understood the fascination with. Now it contained dust and rum apparently. Maybe it was a metaphor for something…

'Do you have wine?' Kat repeated, loudly.

Chloe looked at the salopettes. What was she thinking? She threw them to one side. 'I don't have wine. That's why you're drinking that old stuff.'

'No! How do you say "do you have wine" in Icelandic?'

'I have no idea!' Chloe exclaimed, picking up her hairdryer. 'Because I don't know Icelandic! And you know this is your fault, don't you? Because it was you who told me to write that I could speak Icelandic on my CV in the first place!'

She'd met Kat right before she'd applied for the job with Celebratey. They'd bonded over berating a queue-jumper at the local supermarket and had become firm friends from the off. And, as Chloe had moved to Winchester for Michael, it had been good to establish something in the city for herself. The reason for the move had been a fabulous tech job Michael couldn't turn down and then, suddenly, miraculously even, when things had deteriorated between them, another unput-downable opportunity had arisen in Manchester. Who knew there were so many 'life-changing' career moments in program-ming? Winchester might not have been Chloe's own destination of choice back then, but now it was the place where she was making waves in the event-planning world and she was staying for herself and her career. Those were good solid things she knew she could count on. Good solid things that weren't deter-mined by her poor-quality eggs and sporadic ovulation.

'Chloe! You can't blame me!'

'I can!'

'I also suggested you added stilt-walking and that you played basketball at Olympic level.'

'See! You remember! You know it was you.' The yellow beanie or the black beanie? She threw both on the heap.

'And you got the job!' Kat reminded, slurping her drink. 'The job you love! The job you loved more than Michael!'

Chloe froze like she was perhaps already in Iceland being turned into an ice statue. 'Why would you say that? I loved Michael. It was Michael who left me, remember?'

'I know, I wasn't saying that you didn't love him, just that you really love your job and you got the job and you're going on a work trip for the job you love and—'

'And I obviously didn't love Michael enough? Perhaps that's why we couldn't have children together. Maybe it was nothing to do with the quality of my eggs but more to do with the quality of my heart!'

'Chloe, I didn't mean that at all! I take it back. It was a thoughtless stupid comment and I'm an idiot and my karma will be my mother visiting, trust me.'

Chloe swallowed the knot in her throat. Was it true that she had loved her job more than she'd loved Michael? She remembered working super hard to make a vital first impression with Michelle in the beginning but, when she and Michael had decided to try to have a baby she had been so incredibly happy, focussed on making it happen. She had always wanted a family and they both had great solid career foundations with good incomes and the apartment they had renovated had a second bedroom perfect for a nursery. Practicalities. The next steps on the relationship travelator. Not deep, soul-searing love? Was Kat right?

She wanted to cry. All the feelings were there, trying to

bubble up into existence but... she didn't cry. Not any more. What was the point of tears? It didn't change anything. And, whether she was too work-focussed or not, the facts were that Michael had looked at her differently from the minute the doctor had told them the news. Next he had held her differently. Then they had made love less often until, not at all. Finally, everything drifted like an untethered boat, until there was just the husk of what they had been together. And no one wanted a future based on a loveless shell, empty except for a pile of broken hopes and dreams. Chloe dropped to the bed, the cabin bag tipping to the left and shedding its contents onto the duvet cover.

'Chlo,' Kat said, diving onto the bed next to her and putting an arm around her shoulders. 'I'm so sorry.'

'It's fine,' she answered. 'I expect Michael's seeing someone else now. Someone who doesn't take Pinterest to bed with them.'

'You think he'll be seeing someone else? Already? No, I wouldn't have thought so.'

'It's almost nine months since he left.' The irony.

'Is it?'

She nodded. 'But, you know, I used to count in days not months so, I'm healing.'

'I know,' Kat said, hugging her close, breath like she'd spent all day at a bar. 'And you know what Instagram says is great for healing?'

'Collagen cream?'

'No.'

'Hair straighteners that turn into curlers that turn into an air-fryer?'

'That one is on my Christmas list! But no.' She squeezed Chloe's shoulder. 'Travel. New experiences. Doing something last minute.'

'Like learning a language I've told people I already know.'

'Chlo, so what if you don't know Icelandic. You're not fazed by anything!' Kat reminded. 'You have the world at your feet! An amazing opportunity to boss this Sinclairz Chairs thing and claim that partner position. And who gives a crap what Michael is doing with whoever he's doing it with! Michael who?'

Chloe nodded. Kat was right. It didn't matter if she didn't know Icelandic. Everyone spoke English, right? It was a minor detail. A small one-line incision in her practically glowing resumé. Her career meant more to her than ever. Her career had never let her down. Her career had never made her return a Mamas and Papas gift card for a refund...

'OK,' Chloe said, standing up. 'OK, I need to get all this stuff into this bag and then I need to get to sleep before I need to get up again and get to the airport.'

'Right,' Kat said, standing too and clapping her hands together. 'And it's "*áttu vín*".'

'What?'

'*Áttu vín*. The Icelandic for "do you have wine".'

'OK,' Chloe said, smiling. 'I will say it to the very first person I meet.'

3

GUNNAR'S HOME, THE OUTSKIRTS OF REYKJAVIK

'Gunnar! There is time! Come out!'

A bang on the window with the end of an ice hockey stick made Gunnar Eriksson spill his carefully curated coffee into the small saucer. Frustration bit and he raised his eyes to the kitchen window ready to admonish ten-year-old Magnús who was yelling at him from the front garden of their wooden home. But there was that wide-mouthed grin, those large clear blue eyes so full of enthusiasm and vivre for life despite everything he had been through. How could he be mad at someone who was looking like a poster child for idyllic Icelandic living?

'Five minutes.' Gunnar held his hand up to indicate the number.

'You give in to that boy too much.'

Gunnar turned around and saw he had been joined by Hildur, the third person who lived here in their mismatch of 'family'. She had paused by the table, as if knowing he would be studying her gait the moment she made a move.

'You give in to him more,' Gunnar answered, eyes still on Hildur. 'You made *kleinur* again yesterday.' He should know because he had eaten two pieces of the vanilla-flavoured fried dough himself.

'I like making *kleinur*. It has nothing to do with Magnús.'

'Would you like coffee?' Gunnar asked her. 'I have some right here.'

'No,' she answered, standing still. 'I can make my own.'

'O-K,' Gunnar said, gaze unmoved.

'Did you not say you were going to play hockey with Magnús?'

'In five minutes.'

'Then drink your coffee,' Hildur told him.

'Your hip is hurting.'

'No.'

'Then why are you not walking to the coffee machine?'

'Because you are standing right there in my way.'

Gunnar side-stepped quickly, indicated the freed-up space.

She moved immediately, faster than she should, but it wasn't fooling him. He could see she was in pain and that meant one thing was certain, she was not taking her medication again.

'How many days?' Gunnar asked without preamble.

'Until Christmas? Gunnar, we have a calendar stuck to the refrigerator.'

'You know what I am asking.'

She reached for the countertop with nimble fingers, the skin blanching as they took her weight. 'When Magnús's winter school show is?'

'We can play guessing games if you like, Hildur, but it will change nothing.'

'Then we are wasting time when I could be drinking coffee and you could be playing hockey with that boy who will perhaps break an arm unless you tell him to slow down.'

'How long have you not been taking your medication? How long—'

Hildur interrupted by pressing a button on the coffee machine, sparking it into noisy life, and turning to face him, triumph shining on her lined cheeks. By the time her drink was made and she raised the cup to her pursed lips, he knew that particular conversation was over for now.

'It is going to get warmer from tomorrow,' Hildur remarked. 'An Icelandic heatwave in December.'

Gunnar laughed. 'Are you crazy? The TV has told me the complete opposite this morning. Temperatures diving. Icy fog—'

Hildur tutted. 'You still believe more in a man stood in front of a map with raincloud shapes than you do in the *huldufólk*.'

The damn *huldufólk*. Hildur seemed to think Icelandic elves ruled the land more than the government. He might spend a certain portion of his working life embellishing folk stories of old for the tourists, but he didn't believe a word of it.

'I believe in the science of nature.'

'And how many times have you seen the science of nature arrive when no one with all their complex computers and machines has predicted it?'

He couldn't deny the force of the weather on this island, the extremes were unprecedented, but he also didn't believe it had anything to do with elves. Because the tragedies he had witnessed, the loss that Magnús had had to bear, could surely not be ordained by any kind of spirits or goblins. They had to be down to terrible coincidence, accidents not directed by anything or anyone, except perhaps the anatomy of the Earth.

'You will come to Magnús's Christmas show this time?' Hildur asked.

Gunnar looked at his watch. 'Is that the time? I need to get to work.'

'Gunnar!' Hildur admonished as he went to the coat stand and began to put on his coat. Where were his hat and gloves?

'You said yourself that I need to play quickly with Magnús before he damages himself and then I have to get to work.' He saw his hat on the countertop. He moved to get it and that's when Hildur took hold of his jacket with the force of a thousand elves…

'You cannot let what happened to you as a boy starve you or Magnús from what happens in the future.'

Gunnar shook his head. 'I do not know what you are talking about.'

'You are trying to avoid the Christmas show like you have avoided the Christmas show every year since that night.'

Gunnar laughed. It was a terrible play act. 'You think I am avoiding the Christmas show? Where children eat too much candy then perform songs tunelessly until some of them are sick? Why would I want to avoid that?' He eyerolled. Pointlessly.

'Therapy,' Hildur whispered. 'That is what the *huldufólk* tell me is needed.'

'Perhaps the *huldufólk* could go to the show,' Gunnar suggested. 'Do you think there will be enough seats for all of them?'

Hildur let go of his coat and snarled. 'You know better than to make fun of folklore, Gunnar Eriksson.'

'The only thing I know right at this moment is I do not want Magnús breaking our windows with a puck or his stick if I do not join him.'

Hildur didn't respond, turned her attention back to her coffee, her weight balanced more on her left hip than her right. She was a force of nature herself, but he knew she was getting older, vulnerability unavoidably evident and still there was that feeling he always got, not wanting to disappoint.

'Shall I cook dinner tonight? Get some cod?'

'Do not worry on my account. I might watch the television. Learn something from the people standing by the maps with their cloud drawings.'

Hildur was annoyed. She always got like this but, given the day, she would cool off, maybe. One thing was certain though, there was no point trying to continue the conversation. He put his hat on his head and strode towards the front door.

* * *

'You have been longer than five minutes! I can count and you gave me a watch for my birthday, remember?'

Magnús skidded up to him on the frozen ground Gunnar had made into a makeshift hockey rink with two small nets, one at each end. You couldn't wear skates but, when the tarmac was as icy as it was today, trainers slid almost as well. But it wasn't the boy's footwear Gunnar was looking at.

'Magnús, your nose is bleeding! How did that happen?'

'What?'

Straightaway the boy ran a sleeve across his face, streaking his sweater with red.

'Magnús! Now you will have to change!'

Why had he said that? What did a sweatshirt matter when the boy's nose was streaming blood now and his skin was suddenly getting pale.

'It is... in my mouth,' Magnús said.

'It is OK. Come! We will go inside and we will fix it.' He put an arm around the boy's shoulders but before they could get back to the door a voice broke into the freezing air.

'I have a towel! I see the blood!'

Gunnar looked up to see Hildur rushing from the house in

her thin woollen dress, no coat, with slippers on her feet. What was she thinking?

'Hildur! Do not come out here! The ice is—'

His words were lost to the air as the old woman fell to the ground.

4

REYKJAVIK AIRPORT, ICELAND

Chloe had one beanie on her head, one in each pocket of the coat she was wearing and two coats under her left arm, her right arm controlling her overfilled cabin case. Somehow, amid the chaos of outfits on her bed, Kat had stretched out like a human steamroller over the lid of the case until the zips were as close to meeting as they could be and the grand stretching/straining/manhandling the pull along the track was soon completed. But, if Chloe was honest, she didn't 100 per cent know what items were in there or not. What she did know though was if she didn't get an update from Michelle soon, she might not have anywhere booked to stay…

She stopped wheeling her case, put the coats down on top and stood next to a sign that said 'Exit to Iceland'. She checked her phone. Signal. At last. And three missed calls from Michelle. She didn't waste time checking any other notifications, she called her boss.

'Hello.'

'Michelle, I—'

'Sorry, this is Gretchen. Michelle cannot come to the phone right now. She is under blanket.'

'What?' Chloe asked. What did that mean? And was 'under blanket' some maternity terminology she wasn't familiar with?

There was some background noise, shuffling, grumbling, then a shriek until...

'Chloe? Is that you?'

Michelle.

'Yes, I—'

'I thought a pregnancy massage would be relaxing, but Gretchen has me trapped under a blanket like she's a kidnapper and I need Liam Neeson on speed-dial. It's traumatic rather than therapeutic and she hasn't even touched me yet!'

'Deep breaths, remember. For stress. Panting for when the time comes.'

'I'll be panting before that if she doesn't turn the heating down in here! But, give me good news. Are you there yet?'

Chloe looked around at the walkways of Reykjavik airport – soft glittering festive lights and the frantic bustle of travel co-existing. 'Yes. I'm here. The plane was on time and everything was OK and—'

'OK great! So that's the good news! The bad news is... I haven't been able to book you a hotel.'

Chloe's stomach dropped. In an unfamiliar country, no idea where she was going or what she was doing, it was definitely bad news. What did she do now?

'But there were a couple of places on Airbnb when I looked earlier, I just didn't have time to finish before this torture appointment and I thought, with your knowledge of the local language, you'd be better off booking yourself.'

Chloe closed her eyes and breathed deep. Why, oh why, had she ever agreed to embellishing her CV with that statement about speaking Icelandic?! And why was it coming back to bite her in the arse when she really needed to stay on top of her professional game to prove to Michelle she was more than capable partner-material. But, thinking again, what better way to prove her prowess by taking this on the chin and making it work. She needed to keep her tone buoyant.

'Not a problem.'

'I know it's not a problem, Chloe,' Michelle said straight back. 'Because you're the best employee I've ever had. You're 100 per cent reliable. Unlike the contraception that got me into this situation.'

Being likened to a pregnancy wasn't quite giving the 'take a stake in the business' vibes she'd been hoping for. Still...

'And I need to land this Sinclairz Chairs event and for it then to be the best event we've ever handled. Better than that actually! Because this could elevate us so significantly people could be saying Celebratey in the same breath as Dress Code.'

Dress Code was one of the biggest event management companies in London and Chloe knew that was Michelle's ultimate aim – growth in all areas and having Celebratey be the go-to for VIPs planning any kind of party. And the first step towards that was apparently on her shoulders.

'No worries,' Chloe said, moving her actual shoulders a little and wondering if she should get her laptop out here and now and reserve an Airbnb or wait until she was on a transfer bus Michelle had booked her on and use that time.

'I have no worries about you excelling, Chloe. What I do have plenty of worries about are my pelvic floor collapsing or dehydrating under this heated blanket.'

'Well, at least you know Iceland is safe in my hands.' Why had she said that?

'Aww, say that again but in Icelandic. I want to hear your accent.'

Chloe felt like her heart had stopped and all the blood rushed to her head. What?! Help! She was torn between making fake noises and pretending the connection was bad and just hanging up. Could she do that? Could she just hang up, pretend the call had been severed by technology? An airport announcement saved her.

'Oh, Michelle, that means my bus is going to leave soon. I have to go. I'll call you later. Enjoy the blanket.' She ended the call and pocketed her phone. Where did these buses depart from?

* * *

'Please, Erik. You know I would not ask if it was not an emergency.'

Gunnar was one beat away from grabbing his boss, Erik's jacket and making him pay more attention to him than the pastry he had in his hand and was stuffing into his face.

'This is so good.' He smacked his lips.

'Erik! Listen to me! Hildur is at the hospital. I cannot drive the south coast tour today. Let me take the airport shuttles. Thor is OK with changing.'

'Thor does not have the same quality of reviews as you do, Gunnar.' More teeth were sunk into the food, steam rising from his hot breath.

'I know,' Gunnar said. 'But it's one day. I have to go back to the hospital before five.'

'The hospital closes at five?'

Gunnar shook his head. 'No, but—'

'Then there is no problem.' Erik went to turn away and that's when Gunnar reached out, but not for the jacket, for the pastry. He snatched it from his boss's hand and held it hostage in the air.

'Gunnar! Give that to me!'

'No. Not until you agree to give me the airport runs today. One day, Erik. I have never asked before and it is highly unlikely that I will ever ask again... maybe. And this is Hildur. Hildur who makes you soup for your birthday every year and—'

'Gunnar! I have a business to run. I need the best tour guide on the most expensive tours, you know this and—'

'One day, Erik! One tour! So I can collect Hildur from the hospital where hopefully she will not be coming out in a wheelchair or in a cast!'

A flat heavy hand came down on Gunnar's shoulder and a smiling Thor appeared over his shoulder.

'I am on Bus 101,' Thor said. 'I have not done this for so long. It is a Christmas gift from you, Gunnar.'

'See, Erik,' Gunnar continued. 'Everything is set. Thor is happier than I have seen him in months and as soon as you nod you can have your pastry back.'

'This is not in my planner for today!' Erik moaned, leaping a little for the pastry.

'Plans change, Erik. That is the nature of life.' Gunnar swallowed. 'And you know we cannot interfere with the nature of life. That would be going against the *huldúfolk*.'

'Sshh!' Erik exclaimed, hands over his ears. 'Do not talk about the *huldúfolk*.'

'I need to go to my bus now, yes?' Thor said, still all grins.

'Yes,' Gunnar said. 'You go now, Thor.'

'I have not said yes!' Erik exclaimed.

'*Huldúfolk*! *Huldúfolk*!' Gunnar chanted.

'Stop!'

'I will take care of everyone on the airport shuttles. I will even be nice to the annoying ones with their bags that are too large and the ones with all the questions when it is so early.'

'Give me my pastry! Thor is already on your bus, so I guess I have no choice.'

'There is always a choice, Erik. But, know you made the right one.' Gunnar handed him the pastry. 'And you have done a good deed for Hildur. I will be sure to tell her!' He was backing away before Erik decided to fire him. Although, with tourists here for the ultimate Icelandic winter experience in the run up to Christmas, he very much doubted his boss could afford to do that. 'And I will take the greatest care as always. I will not be too heavy on the brakes even when the tourists stand up when they are not meant to. I will treat them like they are porcelain. Or large boxes of fragile eggs. Nothing broken or even cracked.'

'Erik! There is a problem with this bus.'

The shout from another driver had his boss distracted and Erik turned away, going towards the next morning crisis.

Satisfied he was in the clear for this shift change, Gunnar whipped around, and that's when the collision happened…

5

Chloe had a mouth full of thick padded jacket and a hand full of what felt like icy grit. Everything was suddenly spinning and she couldn't work out quite which way up she was or what had even happened. Cold. Cold was infiltrating her fast. The ground. She was definitely on the ground. Or, at least, some of her was. The rest of her was on a padded jacket apparently...

'I do not know which one of us should move to make this better.'

A man's voice. A man's jacket she still had in her mouth. She needed to end that.

'You are Icelandic? You do not speak English?'

Before Chloe could say anything else he was talking fast in words she definitely did not understand and both of them were still, somehow lying on the ground. There was only one thing she could think to say...

'*Attú vín?*'

'*Hvao?*'

She had asked if he had wine! Why had she said that?!

'Sorry, I do speak English and, I think, if you just move your right leg a bit I can move my arm and—'

He did as she asked and, with a bit of to-ing and fro-ing, like some crazy version of Twister, she was able to get to her feet and realise that quite a lot of her felt sore.

'You are OK?' he asked.

She had to be OK. Michelle was depending on her. She looked up at the man she had been half-mounted on and observed him for the first time. Tall. Broad. Hair the colour of corn, not super long but long enough to be poking out from underneath a beanie. The bluest eyes...

'I'm OK,' she answered.

Hot air came fast from his mouth as he exhaled in what seemed like deep relief. He said something – presumably in his native tongue.

'What does that mean?' Chloe asked.

'It means I am happy you are OK.'

'That's a direct translation? Of what you just said?'

'You do speak Icelandic?'

'No, just a gut feeling that you swore.'

'Really?' Those blue eyes widened as he looked directly at her, got bluer still somehow. It started to get intense like he was challenging her on what she was going to say next. She liked a challenge.

'Really,' she said, matching his gaze.

And that's when time seemed to really slow right down and everything going on around the outside area of the airport – the travellers rolling suitcases, the engines of the buses – became smaller, quieter, insignificant to whatever was happening across the icy air.

'OK,' he said finally. 'Where do you go? Into Reykjavik?'

'Yes, I am booked on a bus at—'

'OK, you will come with me.'

'Wait. What?'

'Fast,' he said, reaching out and taking her arm. 'You will come fast.'

Chloe swallowed as all the connotations of that sentence hit her as severely as the current wind chill. Where was her suitcase? Why was she letting a man guide her to who knew where?

'Stop,' she said, trainers skidding on the ground as she forced them both to a halt.

'Listen, I know this is not the situation anybody wants but if my boss knows that you fell into me and—'

'That I fell into you?'

'Your voice is very too loud now,' he whispered. 'Here in Iceland we like quiet.'

'If you think this is my voice being loud then Iceland really isn't ready,' Chloe said louder than before.

'OK, OK, it's just I have not had the best beginning to today and—'

'Funnily enough, neither have I,' Chloe interrupted.

'OK, well, we can swap our disastrous day stories on my bus. Is this your suitcase?'

She turned around, remembering that yes, she had luggage, and she also did not yet have somewhere to stay and all this distraction was not helping her towards her current goal.

'Yes,' she answered, taking steps to retrieve it.

'Let me,' the man said, reaching it before her.

'It's fine,' Chloe said, fingers on the handle.

'I insist. We do not want any more accidents and the road, it is icy.'

'Well, I fell over you, not because of the ice so I will take my case and take my chances.'

Chloe yanked at her luggage and that's when it burst like an overfilled water balloon, everything she had crammed in there in a frenzy last night spilling out over the ground. She yelped. Definitely too loud for Iceland.

'OK. We go now.'

And before Chloe could do or say anything else, this stranger who said he had a bus, destination not quite known, was picking up all her clothing.

6

BUS TO REYKJAVIK

Gunnar never let anyone sit on the seat nearest to his driving space apart from the tour guide. If tourists sat there they wanted to chat, ask him about road signs, restaurant recommendations, attractions they should not miss. They always seemed to forget that driving in Iceland was sometimes treacherous, even for those who were used to navigating it. But this woman didn't seem like a normal tourist. She was dressed like one: coat, hat over dark brown hair, too many clothes in too small a case but right now, instead of looking out of the window through the cold light drizzle, taking in the sights, she was typing furiously on a laptop. He hoped she wasn't making a complaint about him or leaving a one-star review on Tripadvisor. There was only one way to find out...

'What do you do?' Gunnar asked, concentration back on the road.

'What?'

'Your work on your computer.'

'Oh, I'm not working right now. I'm trying to book somewhere to stay.'

'What? You have come to Reykjavik in December with nowhere to stay?'

'It wasn't exactly my choice.'

'What? Someone is forcing you to be here?' He took a side glance at her, checking her expression.

She laughed. 'Whoa, keep your eyes on the road. Nothing dramatic or dark romantasy. I would have been sure to whisper a safe word already.'

'Well,' Gunnar said. 'You did ask me if I had wine very early in the morning.'

'Yes, well, that is Duolingo's fault. Or rather the lack of Duolingo.' She let out an irritated sigh. 'This apartment has gone! It was there and available last night.'

'Many other people with last minute plans they have been forced into like you,' he suggested, putting on the indicator and moving across a roundabout.

'You're quite judgemental, aren't you?' she said.

He didn't need to see to know she was looking at him. He could feel it. But her accusation wasn't true. He could feel the tension of the morning sitting on his shoulders still though. Magnús's nosebleed had been nothing compared to Hildur's fall and the trip to the hospital. And there was still no word about the X-ray...

'I am sorry that you feel that way.'

She laughed. 'Oh my God. You know those kinds of "apologies" aren't really apologies at all. In fact, they undermine people's feelings.'

And despite the noise of the coach's engine, her voice was sailing free for any of the nearest travellers to hear.

'You called me judgemental,' he reminded.

'OK, perhaps I should have said "critical" instead. My apologies.' She groaned again.

'What is wrong? Does it hurt to say sorry?'

'No, another Airbnb place evaporating before my eyes because I'm wasting my time spatting with you.' It sounded like she hit some keys on the laptop.

'Apologies but not my fault.' Silence prevailed and he glanced her way. 'You would like some help to find a place?'

'Do you know someone who would be helpful? Someone who wouldn't knock into me like I'm a bowling pin and burst my suitcase too.'

He smiled. 'I did repack your case.'

'Badly.'

'Well, if you find somewhere to stay you will be unpacking it again very soon.'

This was a different conversation to what he was used to should the bus be full and someone had to take this 'jump' seat. He couldn't deny he was enjoying it.

'So, do you?' the woman asked.

'Do I what?'

'Know someone helpful that will know somewhere I can stay for a week or so.'

'I can be helpful to you in that way,' Gunnar answered. 'What do you look for? One room to sleep?'

'By myself, buddy.'

'I meant, one room or an apartment?'

'I'm... not sure.'

'So much forward-planning has gone into your visit here. Are you even sure you are at the correct destination?'

'This is Ireland, right?'

He turned his head to her deadpan response only to be faced with an expression that said he had fallen into her humour trap. He turned back. 'I know of a place. When we get to the centre, before I start to pick up people to go back to the airport I will make a phone call.'

'Really? Because looking at this screen while we are travelling is making me feel a bit sick.'

'Then you should stop doing that.' There was nothing he hated more than people throwing up on his bus. 'I am sure my friend's place will be available.'

'How sure?'

'Sure enough that you should stop looking at your computer and not be sick. Join the other travellers in gazing at the scenery.'

'Half of them are asleep,' she answered.

He heard the lid of her computer close and sensed her sit forward.

'What's your name?' she asked.

'Why?'

'O-K. That's a bit defensive for someone who claims he can help me find a place to stay.'

She was right. Why was he being like this? Because he had other things on his mind? He needed to try to temporarily forget about Hildur. She was being looked after, and he had secured an earlier finish.

'I am Gunnar,' he told her. 'Gunnar Eriksson. But, if you are writing a lower than five stars review for my driving, my name is Olga Petersson.'

'Gunnar Eriksson,' she repeated.

He stole a glance at her. 'Are you writing it down?'

'For my review later.'

He smiled. 'Shall I spell Olga for you?'

'Not necessary.'

'And you?' he asked. 'What is your name?'

'Why?'

He smirked at this, but he was ready. 'To put on the accident forms if my back starts to hurt and the company must make a claim.'

'And now you will never know my name.'

He laughed loudly, so much so that a passenger gave a snort like they were waking up from hibernation. He never usually laughed on this airport run. 'OK, then I will call you *krúttio*.'

'What does that mean? Is it an insult?'

'Shh, *krúttio mitt*. It is not long now.'

7

REYKJAVIK

Chloe was standing in a car park, below the towering presence of a magnificent-looking church, its spire layering up towards the ice-blue sky. There were quite a number of people taking photos of the church and the statue of a man in front of it. Was this her first Icelandic attraction? Should it be put on an itinerary for the Sinclairz Chairs event? She shivered, debating getting her phone out to look on Google Maps for the name of this church. And where had Olga gone? Gunnar. He said his name was Gunnar.

She looked for him amid the crowd. He shouldn't be hard to spot. Tall, late-twenties/early-thirties, navy-blue coat and matching beanie. Except... most people seemed to fit that category, as though how they were dressed was some kind of winter uniform.

'Hello, *krúttio mitt.*'

Chloe jumped as Gunnar popped up from behind her, breath visible in the air. She'd googled this phrase, *krúttio mitt.* It meant 'my sweetie'. She kind of liked it...

'Take care,' he said. 'All these jumps and dives you take... the ground is icy. We do not want more accidents.'

'You made me jump!' she exclaimed.

'And you must keep yourself calm when I tell you that my friend's place is not free.'

Her heart dropped. Sadly, probably stupidly, she had been counting on this working out. What was she going to do now?

'But, there is another place,' Gunnar said. 'A friend of my friend has a smaller apartment. His friends were coming to stay there, but now they are not.'

'Why?' Chloe asked, suspicion coating her tone.

'Why what?'

'Why are this friend of a friend's friends not coming to stay any more.'

Gunnar frowned like the question she had asked was the trickiest conundrum. 'I do not know. I did not ask. Do you want me to call him back and say you do not want this place?'

'No,' Chloe said quickly. 'No, don't do that.' She sighed. 'Just, tell me it's... not a dungeon.'

'Oh,' Gunnar said, shaking his head. 'I did not realise. You did not tell me you had such very specific requirements.'

'What?'

He laughed then. 'I am a good person. I do not know people who have dungeons. Do you?'

'Well, there's the royal family for a start,' Chloe answered. 'Not that I know them personally. OK, never mind, just give me the address and is there a key I collect or something?'

'Yes,' Gunnar answered. 'I will take you to it now. It is on the way of turning around and driving people back to the airport.'

'OK, great. Oh, so... how much is it to rent? And do I have to pay in the Icelandic money because I don't have any of that so—'

'You have no *króna*?'

He had said it like it was against the law not to have any in her possession. Was it? She really didn't want to add getting arrested to today's itinerary. 'No. I mean, can I get some? From a cashpoint?'

He nodded. 'Yes, but there will be a fee.'

She had the company card. She could do that. 'OK, so how much is the not-dungeon to rent?'

'I do not know,' Gunnar said.

'What?'

'My friend's friend just said his place was available. I did not talk in details.' He sighed. 'But, you know, I am sure the space has been paid for so—'

'It's fine,' Chloe said with a shiver as the cold suddenly got to her. 'Th... thank you.'

'Ah, it almost sounded like it was difficult for you to say.'

'It's just the cold.' She straightened herself. 'Thank you.'

* * *

'I am sorry for this chaos on the bus.'

He couldn't believe it. Only two minutes from their stop at *Hallgrímskirkja* Church and one of his passengers had thrown up. Fortunately, most of it had gone into an impressively sturdy pig-emblazoned carrier bag from the Bónus supermarket he kept for such eventualities. However, his braking at the first alert of the sickness had meant a rucksack had fallen from the overhead storage and hit another passenger. Today was not going his way at all. But, after that distraction, he felt no guilt for having to make a stop at this apartment.

'Oh, it's OK. I thought you handled both situations really well. I don't think any low reviews could come from it. Definitely not from me anyway.'

He nodded. 'OK, so, this is the apartment. I do not know what it is like, but my friend has texted me a code for the key safe. It is...' He checked the screen of his phone then whispered, '1234.'

'Are you serious?'

'Sshh, we do not want the passengers on the bus to hear the special code.'

He watched the woman looking at the front door of the place and the small black box attached to the door. It didn't look much from the outside, but Henrik had assured him it was definitely a few grades up from a dungeon. She opened the lid of the box and began to turn the dials to the appropriate numbers. Once they were set the key was released.

'Thank you, again, for your help. I will definitely not sue you for knocking me over or badly repacking my case.'

He smiled. 'Do you need me to come in? Light the flaming torches in the dungeon.'

'I think I'll be good.'

'OK, well, enjoy but...' He was hesitant. Why was he hesitant? Then...

'I should give you my phone number,' he said.

'O-K.'

'Not in a strange way,' he continued.

'A strange way?'

Why was he starting to feel hot? It was minus temperatures. He rarely felt hot, even when it had actually made it over twenty degrees here in the summer...

'In case there is a problem and you need...' What was he saying?

'A bus?'

He nodded. 'Exactly.'

'And your number, is it 1234?'

He smiled as she took her phone from her coat pocket and he recited the number.

'OK, Olga,' she said. 'I have that saved now.'

'Good. Then I will leave you to settle in.'

'And meet the other prisoners disorganised for their holidays chained to the brickwork.'

'Yes,' he answered. 'So, *bless*.'

'Bless? Really?'

He smiled. 'It means goodbye. In Icelandic.'

'Really? Or is this a trick?'

'You are very suspicious of everything.'

'I prefer the word "cautious".'

He nodded. 'OK, well, I need to get back to my bus before anyone else has time to be sick.' He turned towards the vehicle parked at the edge of the road only a few steps away. The sooner this shift was over, the sooner he could get back to the people who relied on him.

'Just a second,' the woman said.

He stopped in his tracks, then turned to face her again.

'Chloe,' she introduced herself. 'My name. It's Chloe.'

He smiled and held out his hand. 'It is nice to meet you.'

She put her hand in his. 'You too.'

And now he needed to let go. Because something he hadn't felt in a long long time was sliding through him like a sharp ice skate on a clean rink. He dropped her hand like it was hot lava and waved his in the air.

'*Bless*.'

8

The apartment was about as far from dungeon-esque as a penthouse suite in a luxury hotel. It was large, bright and airy despite Iceland's infamous lack of hours of daylight and there were views of the city including the church she had been stood outside earlier. There was a bright blue sofa in the living area, a small dining table now housing her laptop, a modern kitchenette and a large bed next to an almost spa-like bathroom with luxury tiles and fluffy towels. Chloe couldn't have been happier that the friends of the friend of a friend had cancelled, as it was a grade up from anything she had looked at online. There was even fast Wi-Fi, once she had entered the code – 12345678910...

The first connection she made, when she finally sat down, was to Kat.

'Hi, Kat.'

'Oh, thank God! I've been worried sick. Your location has been in the sea for the past two hours. I checked the plane, and started to think about the possibility of your phone having been stolen or you having been kidnapped or jailed for having overweight luggage—'

'I texted you when I landed,' Chloe said, leaning back on the sofa and starting to realise how incredibly tired she was.

'Objection, your Honour, someone texted me from your phone,' Kat said.

'Have you been reading those kinds of books again?'

'Sooo, tell me about Iceland and don't leave anything out. I'm currently choosing between sushi or a sandwich but really wanting a festive pasty.'

Chloe laughed. 'I've only been here in the centre for about an hour. I've made a coffee, I haven't even unpacked the over-sized luggage.'

'Do you have a great hotel? I bet Michelle has made sure you have a great hotel!'

'Actually no,' Chloe said. 'But I have a great apartment thanks to a helpful bus driver.'

'What? Tell me more! Was he hot? And blond? Aren't they all blond in Iceland? Like Vikings!'

Chloe recalled Gunnar and immediately there was a little fizzy fusion in her chest like she'd swallowed one too many Love Hearts sweets... That was weird. He was good-looking. Tall. Definitely blond...

'You're not saying anything!' Kat yelled. 'Shit! This is something!'

'You've knocked over the sushi?'

'No! You're not saying anything about this bus driver. That's what you do when you like someone! You pretend they don't exist.'

Chloe laughed. 'I don't do that.'

'You did that with Jonah when I organised the dinner party,' Kat continued.

Chloe swallowed and sat up a little. She had been to a few dinner parties at Kat's where her friend had tried her hardest to set her up with guys those first couple of months after Michael had left but her heart hadn't been in it. Her libido hadn't even been in it…

'Kat, I went quiet with Jonah because he was terrifying.'

'He was sweet!'

'Kat, he built miniature homes out of ice cream sticks.'

'For the ants in his garden! Like I said, sweet!'

Chloe shook her head. 'Remind me never to let you near my dating apps.'

There was an intake of breath from the other end of the line and Chloe wanted to pull back the sentence she'd just let escape without proper thought. She got up from the sofa, put both hands around the coffee cup. This conversation was definitely going to need pacing not standing still.

'You're on dating apps!' Kat exclaimed. 'I might get sushi *and* the sandwich.'

'I'm not on them… not really.'

'When I suggested it, you acted like I was trying to get you matched with Luigi Mangione.'

'Because I wasn't ready then.' And she knew for sure, having swiped right and left – mainly left – that she still wasn't ready now.

'I can't believe you kept this from me! I could have helped with your profile! Wait, did Michelle help with your profile?'

Chloe walked towards a patio door she hadn't noticed before. It led out onto a small decked balcony. She was already unlocking the door, needing the air.

'No, and why did you say "Michelle" like you were saying "Gargamel".'

'Have you been on dates?'

'No,' Chloe said.

'Not one?'

'I said no.'

'Well, did you at least talk to some guys?'

'A couple.'

'A couple? What, like polyamorously?'

'No! Not like that. Two guys. Three maybe.'

'And you didn't tell me?'

'There was nothing to tell, Kat, honestly.'

'But we tell each other everything. Or, at least, I tell you everything.'

The reason she hadn't told Kat was because Kat would have become more invested in the matches than Chloe herself. And it had taken a lot for Chloe to even add a profile. Those icon choices – have kids, want kids – had been mocking her from the very beginning. But, in the end, the chats just hadn't been enough of a connection...

'I do tell you everything, Kat, just, with this, it was something I felt I had to do on my own. Just to, I don't know, do something other than work. And it didn't last long. It's over now.'

There was a sniff over the phone line. Had she really upset her friend?

'Kat? Are you OK?'

'Yup, just pausing by the festive candle section before I self-checkout. Who knew chocolate and bayberry was a thing? So... redeem yourself quickly. Tell me everything; tell me about this bus driver!'

Chloe looked out over the rooftops, only the spire of the church towering above her. It was cold but the chill was fresh and it was making her feel immediately more calm and collected, despite winging this trip every step of the way so far.

'He's good-looking,' Chloe said, recalling that her first view of Gunnar had been from literally sitting on him.

'You said that!'

'But, it was strange, we just had...' What had it been? Chat? Connection? Or was it just all circumstantial? He had knocked her over and he was driving the bus she was getting on and he really didn't want her putting a bad review online.

'Banter?' Kat offered.

'Bit strong. Bit *Love Island*. And I will probably never see him again.'

'You mean you didn't swap Instas?'

'No but... he did give me his phone number.'

'What? Now I have dropped the sushi!'

'It was only in case something went wrong with this apartment.' She breathed in the cold air until her nostrils burned from it and she wished she had brought her coat out with her. He had given her his number just in case, right? She would have noticed if he had been fully flirting with her in any way, wouldn't she? Or was she so far removed from anything like that she possibly wouldn't have been able to tell...

'You've been in Iceland a few hours and you already have a guy's number,' Kat said. 'Way to go.'

Way to go. Yes, she had a long way to go, and she needed to focus on what she had come here to do. It was time to research Reykjavik like it had never been researched before. And, as if the phone could read her thoughts, a vibration told her a message had come through. She took the phone away from her ear and saw it was from Michelle.

'Kat, I have to go, I will—'

'Call me later and tell me everything? Console me about having to order three kinds of different stuffing because Mother can't decide if she likes walnuts or not but definitely likes cranberries and, well, sage and onion is always a must.'

'I will definitely call you later and console you. Bye, Kat.'

'Bye!'

Chloe took a moment on the balcony, letting the chill embrace her for a minute longer and then she read Michelle's text.

> Weather in Iceland cloudy for the next few days. Have booked you on a boat trip to see the Northern Lights TONIGHT. Details in an email.

It seemed like some of her itinerary had already been decided.

9

GUNNAR'S HOME, THE OUTSKIRTS OF REYKJAVIK

'Take care,' Gunnar said. 'Swing out your other leg first.'

He couldn't believe this. Almost half past six in the evening and they were just getting home from the hospital with Hildur sporting a boot brace. Thankfully her damaged ankle was only a buckle break, but it still meant reduced mobility for weeks and, because of her age, it might take longer to heal.

'It makes you look like a hockey goalkeeper,' Magnús commented. He was already out of the vehicle, carrying his school bag, his sports kit and the oversized woollen handbag Hildur always seemed to have to have with her constantly.

'Do you think?' Hildur said, wiggling the injured leg.

'Stop moving it unnecessarily, Hildur!' Gunnar exclaimed. 'How is it meant to heal if you do not help? Take my arm.'

'Stop this fussing. I was able to walk from the hospital bed to the car. Why do you not think I can walk to our own front door?' Hildur grabbed the side of the car, looking ready to haul herself out.

'Because, only a few hours ago, you came out of our front door and fell down the steps,' Gunnar reminded her.

'Because of the ice. Not because I am old and incapable.'

'And the ice is still here so, until it warms up, I will be helping you to and from the house.'

'Gunnar, I—'

'And there will be no discussion about it,' he interrupted boldly.

'It sounds the same as my homework,' Magnús said, sighing.

It took more grumbling and resistance to get Hildur from the car and inside but, finally, she was resting in her favourite chair with the footrest up and her bad leg elevated as they had been instructed at the hospital.

'I will make you a coffee,' Magnús announced, bounding from Hildur's side to the kitchen worktop.

'I will make the coffee,' Gunnar said. 'You, Magnús, will do your homework.'

'Right now?' the boy moaned. 'I wanted to practice hockey.'

'Magnús, there is no light and do you not see how the conditions can easily hurt people if we do not take care?'

'Gunnar,' Hildur said, tutting. 'Do not mollycoddle the boy on my account. What is life if we are all wrapped up in padded protection suits unable to do the things we want to do?'

'I agree with Hildur,' Magnús said, nodding, his blond hair flopping over his forehead.

'No one is going outside in the dark right now!'

He hadn't meant to raise his voice quite to that level, but no one seemed to be listening to him. And it seemed they both wanted to take part in pursuits that were set to cause them injury or add to his already full life schedule or both. He went to say something else, but was interrupted by the ringing of his mobile phone. He took it from his pocket and answered.

'*Halló.*'

'Gunnar, it is Erik.'

His boss. This was not good news. Immediately he was on edge and then, just as quickly also distracted by Magnús getting cups down to make coffee.

'Is everything OK?' he asked Erik.

'I need you to work tonight,' came the reply.

'What?'

'I know it is short notice. But Björn's wife has gone into labour.'

Gunnar sighed. 'Is there no one else?'

'Is there no one else, what? To be with Björn's wife while she has their baby?'

'No!' Gunnar said, immediately. 'Not that. I meant no one else that you can ask to do... whatever it is you are asking me to do.' He didn't even know what it was yet. The evening trip to the Blue Lagoon? No, that would have departed already.

'Gunnar, everyone else is out on trips. If you had stayed with the south coast tour, you would have been out too, but you are not. And that is why I am asking you.'

It was a fair point. He watched Magnús drop a mug onto the countertop and the boy looked to him then held the mug aloft to prove it was unharmed.

'I need you to crew the Northern Lights boat tour.'

'What? Tonight?' Gunnar looked at his watch. The tour set off at 9 p.m. from the harbour and it was now creeping closer to seven. He had to make food for the family and he had really wanted to go through Magnús's maths with him...

'Yes, tonight! I said this already! And, Gunnar, this is not a request. If I do not have the required number of crew then the boat cannot go out for safety reasons. And I have a full boat because the night is clear and for the next three or four nights it is expected to be cloudy and you know what that means.'

Gunnar did know what that meant. If the visibility was poor

there was little to no chance of seeing the Northern Lights and the boat trips were cancelled.

'Erik, Hildur has broken her ankle.'

'What?'

'No, Gunnar! You do not use me as an excuse for anything! Give that phone to me!' Hildur shouted, wriggling around in her chair and looking like she was about to leap from it.

'Stay where you are!' Gunnar shouted.

'Are you shouting at me?' Erik asked from the phone.

Hildur was one shimmy away from getting out of her chair and Gunnar raced across the room to stop her. 'I said stay there!'

'Gunnar! I will remind you that I am your superior and—'

'Erik, I am not talking to you, OK?'

There was a crash from the kitchen. He didn't need to look to know Magnús had dropped and broken the mug.

'Gunnar, I need you at the harbour by eight and, I do not want to do this, but if you are not there on time, I will have to give you an official warning.'

He swallowed, a little shocked. But there wasn't time to dwell, he had to respond.

'I will be there,' Gunnar said, his hand on Hildur's arm, gently holding her in place in the chair.

He needed every job he could get. What other choice did he have?

10

REYKJAVIK HARBOUR

If Chloe thought it was cold standing on the little balcony at the apartment, it was nothing compared to the freezing temperatures that had suddenly descended close to the water here at Reykjavik harbour. After getting her ticket from inside the main building Chloe was now waiting beside a large blue and white boat, shivering even in the many layers she'd wrapped herself up in. But the pretty setting was worth the chill. Fairy lights were strung over the roof apexes of the buildings nearest the water, making them look like cosy festive cabins, the lights reflecting off the water. She had taken photos already and she was also making notes on her phone. But would 'cosy Christmas' be the right vibe for a Sinclairz Chairs event? From what information Chloe had gleaned from the internet about Lincoln Sinclair, he liked the finer things in life. This boat, from what Chloe could gather, was about to be full to its capacity with tourists who were being dropped off in a variety of different vehicles – large buses, smaller minibuses, taxis. She made a note to see if there were smaller boat trips they could rent privately for the sole use of Sinclairz Chairs. And then she put her phone away and sought solace for her sore fingers in her gloves, just as a member of staff called everyone forward, presumably to embark.

Getting on board was via a slightly shaky bridge/ramp affair that seemed to have actual ice on it and, as the staff encouraged passengers to get on with care and hold the handrails, Chloe felt a buzzing on her side. Her phone. Tearing a glove off with her teeth, she slipped her hand into her pocket and took her phone out. Michelle.

'Hi, Michelle.'

'Please tell me you're on the Northern Lights boat trip.'

'Yes. Of course. I'm just getting on board now. And I emailed you about it.'

'I know you emailed me about it, but that was hours ago. And I've had to deal with heated blankets and Milo insisting I take some other baby-bearing necessity supplement some chil-drearing guru at his office has insisted is going to turn our baby into a cross between Gandhi and Isaac Newton. And it tastes like sheep urine. And do not ask how I know that but just know that I had a very traumatic childhood.'

'Breathe, Michelle, remember?'

Michelle usually thrived living on the edge of controlled chaos, but the pregnancy seemed to be bringing out a different kind of energy. And apparently concern that Chloe wasn't going to be able to manage this task without constant phone support.

'Is it beautifully cold there?' Michelle asked, finally sounding like she wasn't one inhale away from hyperventilation.

'It's definitely cold,' Chloe agreed, stepping forward and trying to catch up with the other passengers mounting the upper ramp.

'I miss the cold,' Michelle said like 'the cold' was a family member. 'I mean it's still cold here in the UK but if I set foot outside without an outfit that doesn't meet a fifteen TOG rating,

Milo reacts like I'm about to do a bungee jump. Which is on a restricted list he keeps pinned to the fridge by the way.'

'Has he still banned cheese?'

'Yes! And not just the soft cheese! The same "guru" at work told him that all cheese is going to basically make our baby crave saturated fat from the moment he or she appears!'

Chloe stepped towards the door of the boat. 'You know that your pregnancy should be your experience, right? Not anyone else's.'

Chloe swallowed. Had she read that somewhere? One of the posters in the waiting room of the gynae department where there was no segregation. Waiting for test results with all that hope in her heart but reality nibbling away, sandwiched between happily pregnant women waiting for their next pre-booked scan, hands cupped around their bumps. There was silence from the other end of the phone until:

'Do you know,' Michelle said suddenly. 'Not one person has said that to me yet. And they've said absolutely millions of other things.'

Chloe took a breath and paused by the entrance, looking to the clear dark sky. 'Michelle, what you're doing is a lot. Pregnancy is a lot. Running your own super successful business is a lot. Don't ever underestimate what you're doing and what it's taking out of you.'

'Sometimes I wish Milo had taken it out of me,' Michelle answered. 'But here we are.'

Chloe tightened her core. She knew Michelle didn't mean it. Chloe also knew Michelle had no idea how much her pregnancy arc impacted her because she had never told her own story. It changed things when people knew. Michelle would overthink every thought, comment or conversation, tiptoeing around like Chloe's heart was made of glass. Yes, she had been fragile. Yes, sometimes the realisation crept over her firm enough to need time to pause and acknowledge it all over again. But, for the most part, she was resilient, toughened now. And the very last thing she wanted was her experience to ruin anyone else's. She was recovered. Right?

'Anyway,' Michelle said. 'I should not be micro-managing you. You are my right-hand woman, unflappable, dependable, indestructible—'

'And culpable if I don't get the pitch for this event perfect.'

'But what could go wrong, right?' Michelle asked. 'You speak the Icelandic lingo.'

'I need to get on the boat now,' Chloe said quickly. 'I will let you know how it all goes.'

'The same with my sheep piss shake. Bye.'

Chloe ended the call, pocketed her phone and was just about to put her glove back on when there was a queue surge and she found herself being barrelled through the door of the boat and arriving on board at pace.

And then, suddenly, she was covered in coffee.

11

'This was not my fault. You walked into me and...' Gunnar stopped talking, his now empty cardboard cup of coffee still in his hand, as he looked at the woman wearing the contents down her coat. 'Chloe.'

'But, honestly, you may as well call me Americano, Olga! I'm covered in it!'

'I see,' he answered, rather pathetically even he had to admit. 'And there is some on the floor. Listen, everybody!' He was using his outside instructional voice now. 'Please take care coming through the door until this is cleaned up!' He took Chloe's arm and led her away from the spillage. 'Sit here. I will be back.' He patted the edge of a bench next to a set of stairs going upwards.

He was going to get some paper towels to mop the floor up with and then he was going to think about how to clean coffee from a coat that unfortunately wasn't black. Why was everything going wrong today? Why couldn't he just have some plain, no-drama routine?

With the spill on the floor cleaned, a plastic bottle in his hands, he went to turn his attention to Chloe and her coat but when he looked back to the bench she was gone. There was only one place she could be. Without thinking too hard, he headed towards the door to the ladies toilets.

'What the hell are you doing?' Chloe erupted as he rushed into the small space.

'I could ask you the same question,' he said. She had her coat off and the large stain down the front was being held under running water. 'Is that hand soap you have on there?'

'What else is there?'

'It will not work with that. Here.' Before she could suggest any alternative, he had squeezed from the bottle he was holding and bright blue liquid squirted on to the coat.

'Oh my God, you've made it worse!'

'Give it to me,' Gunnar said, hands on her coat.

'No! You're actually insane.' She tugged the coat back.

He let go. 'OK but, I am being honest with you. This liquid is very good. In Iceland we put it on any stain and it is like magic. Just rub it into the fabric and the blue will disappear and the foam will start and you will see the coffee go away.'

He almost breathed a sigh of relief when she worked the detergent into the material and it started to lift the brown as he'd described.

'See, it is working,' he said.

'Lucky for you,' Chloe answered. 'I was drafting the one-star review of this trip in my head already.'

'Really?' Gunnar exclaimed. 'On a trip to see Iceland's most famous sight, you would give one star before the boat has left the harbour? Because of an accident?'

She turned the tap off and drew out the portion of her coat that was wet. Instinctively, he pulled some paper towels from the dispenser and began to dab the damp.

'A lot of accidents seem to happen when you're around,' she remarked. 'What are you doing here anyway?'

'I am working.' He smiled, still dabbing her coat. 'It is nice to see you too.'

She laughed. 'I did not say it was nice to see you.'

'But you will think it. Now that I have saved your coat with the washing liquid and... when I buy you a drink to apologise.'

Why had he said that? And buying a woman a drink when he was working and on a very fine line with Erik wasn't wise either. Suddenly the small bathroom felt even smaller as he realised how close together they were standing. He stopped wiping at the coat, inched back. What was she going to say?

'*Áttu vín*?' she asked.

He laughed. 'Yes, there is wine.'

'OK,' she replied. 'You'll get me a glass of red wine and then you can tell me everything there is to know about the Northern Lights so I can make notes for the event I'm hopefully going to be organising.'

'Ah, well, there is full commentary from one of my colleagues.'

'And it feels like there are hundreds of people on here who will be talking over it. I also saw selfie sticks and I was hopeful they had died out by now.'

He laughed. 'OK, then you should find a seat at the back of the boat. It is quieter there. I will get wine and, as long as I am not in charge of the lifeboats, I will station myself there too.'

'OK, Jack Dawson.'

'You say this because I mention lifeboats or because of my hair?'

'Because I'm just an ill-prepared girl, down on her luck, hoping my prior introduction to you will help me survive the night if we hit an iceberg.' She smiled, with her eyes as well as her mouth.

Suddenly Gunnar felt hot and he knew it wasn't his thermal coat but the eye contact. What was happening to him? He should look away...

The door of the bathroom suddenly burst open and he jumped a little as two women tried to barrel through in a flurry of coats, hats and scarves and 'sorrys'.

'Excuse me,' Gunnar said to everyone, shifting towards the door. He was going to get out before any questions as to why he was in the ladies toilets could be asked.

12

The back of the boat was only slightly quieter than the large upstairs deck filled with passengers, but it had a spectacular view of the harbourside including a building that looked like a mirrored work of art, sparkling and reflecting all the colours. Chloe had settled herself, leaning against the rail at one side, overlooking the rear. And the temperature had definitely dropped since she had emerged from inside, so much so that she had decided to leave voice notes to herself rather than take her gloves off and tap the screen with soon-to-be numb fingers.

'...beautifully cold, Michelle, but we will have to make sure everyone is wrapped up warm. Cosy blankets provided? Some of those furry hats that look like bedded-down cats? The harbour area is kind of cute cabiney on one side and then very chic on the other with this stand-out building that looks like mirrors and—'

'That is Harpa.'

Chloe jumped at the sound of the voice and then there was a plastic cup of wine in her orbit. It was Gunnar.

'Harpa?' she queried.

'Please, take the wine. If I am seen with it I could be fired.'

She pocketed her phone and took the cup from him. 'Thank you.'

'So, Harpa, it is the building over there. A new, but iconic landmark, at the centre of our cultural city. It is home to our orchestra and our opera and it is a world-class concert hall with state-of-the-art acoustic technology.'

'Spoken like a true tour guide.'

'Ah, well, it is not usual for my job to be here tonight but there was an iceberg warning so...'

It took Chloe a millisecond to realise he was joking with her and she doffed him on the arm. 'Very funny.'

He laughed. 'Sorry.'

'Careful, it almost sounded like you meant it. And I know how apologies come hard for you.' She took a sip of the wine. 'Mmm, this is nice.'

'Of course,' Gunnar said. 'Everything we serve in Iceland is of the best quality.'

'Particularly the views. Stunning.'

She had meant the harbour, but she felt her cheeks deepening in colour as she looked at Gunnar. She'd felt similar in that tiny bathroom and it was both disconcerting and unfamiliar. And she was here to do a job.

'That is why people come here from all around the globe. These views and the views you will be seeing in the sky. With hope.'

'Hope?' she queried.

'Yes,' he whispered, head leaning a little closer. 'Seeing the Northern Lights in Iceland, it is not guaranteed how some people think.'

'No?'

'It is a weather phenomenon. Nothing about the weather is guaranteed and here it is no different.'

Chloe took her phone from her pocket and spoke into it. 'We need to consider the weather carefully when we are planning the itinerary. Clear skies.' She looked at Gunnar. 'Clear skies, right?'

'Clear skies are best,' he said, speaking into the phone like he thought he was on a live call. 'But you can still see with light cloud cover and sometimes it makes for a unique experience. Who am I speaking to?'

Chloe laughed. 'Just my phone. I'm making voice notes to send to my boss about this trip and all the other things I'm going to be doing here to put together ideas for an event next Christmas time.'

'Your job is to make events for other people to enjoy?'

She nodded. 'Yes. And usually I'm far more organised than this, but research needed to be done at this time of year because the event is next December so...'

'Here you are.'

'Yes, here I am.'

And then, engines engaged, the boat crept forward into the inky sea and everyone 'oohed' in anticipation of what was to come.

'Thank you again for the apartment,' Chloe said as the vessel moved away from those waterside lights.

'It is OK?' he asked.

'Oh, it's more than OK, it's wonderful. Have you never been inside?'

'The friend of my friend, I do not know him.'

'Well, it's perfect. Cosy yet spacious and the shower is insanely good. If I hadn't had to rush to get here for this trip I would have spent a lot longer in there.'

'I did not hear that.'

'What?'

'Water is very important in Iceland. We look after it the way it has always looked after us.'

And now she felt like she'd suggested flying around the world and back again for fun in a private jet.

'Sorry,' Gunnar said. 'I should be telling you that Iceland is all about indulgence. For your luxury event you are organising.'

'No,' Chloe said straight away. 'I mean, yes, I am organising a luxury event, but our client needs to be mindful of those kinds of ecological impacts.' She mused for a second. 'Maybe that's exactly what I could build into it. Prove that luxury doesn't have to cost the Earth.'

'Turn on your voice recorder,' Gunnar urged.

She pressed the icon on her phone screen and he leaned forward towards it.

'Luxury does not have to cost the Earth,' he said.

'Making sure that whatever we do with the event we can carbon offset. It should be a treat for the staff and, of course, a celebration, but something to give back to Iceland and the planet in general,' Chloe said.

'Sshh!'

Chloe whipped her head around and was face to face with a slightly cross-looking woman and realised she had been talking over the start of the commentary. 'Sorry.'

'Come.'

Gunnar had taken her arm and was leading her over to the other side of the craft. He ducked under a roped off area and pulled her under too.

'Is this the VIP section?' Chloe asked as they arrived on a lower level that seemed to be one slim metal plank fixed to the side of the boat, no cover, just more ropes and misty port-

holes, a hopefully sturdy metal barrier separating them from
the sea.

'This is usually the OIP section.' He smiled. 'Only Icelandic
Persons section. But, I am in charge of this side of the boat so I
say it is OK.'

'What are you actually in charge of here? Apart from stain
removal from coats?'

'Well, I do not do this trip often but there has to be the right
number of crew for safety reasons and tonight I come here
because a colleague has to be at the hospital.'

'Oh, wow, he has been in an accident?'

'No. It is his wife.'

'She has been in an accident?'

'No. She is having a baby.'

And there it was. That sucker punch Chloe didn't always see
coming. Suddenly she didn't feel so recovered. It was like she
had taken a blow to the chest but she immediately, hopefully
subtly, drew in her core and took a sip of the wine. She could
handle this. It was someone she didn't know having a child like
people all over the world had children every second of every day.
Just like Michelle was and she had coped with watching her
bump grow daily for months. But what to say? Did she need to
say anything? Maybe change the subject...

'Whales,' Chloe blurted out.

'What?'

'Are there whales here, you know, that we might see tonight
as well as the Northern Lights?'

'It is best to look for whales in the daylight,' Gunnar told her.
'There are trips from Reykjavik but the best place to visit would
be Husavik in the north of the island.' He smiled. 'Do you want
to speak into your phone, so you remember?'

* * *

Chloe did as he had suggested and then she started taking some photos of the lights as they left the harbour behind and headed out into the real open water. He had noticed the change in her demeanour when he had mentioned the childbirth though. He had also picked up how she had tried her best to hide it, visibly, quietly setting her shoulders straight, sipping her drink, quietening. His mother had always said he had been born with a 'sense of sense', which made absolutely no sense to him growing up. But gradually, as he grew older and, after she had passed away, he had started to realise what she meant. It was tuning in to the conversation of body language, someone's vibe, not what they were saying but what they were displaying, usually without knowing it.

'You enjoy your work?' he asked her. 'Making the events.'

'I do,' she said, nodding. Genuine. Demeanour brightened.

'And you travel often for this?'

She shook her head. 'Not usually so much. Definitely not ever this last minute or without somewhere to stay, but this job could be the biggest chance the company has had to be recognised nationally and perhaps start to think about international opportunities.'

'Wow, you are passionate about your business.'

'Oh, well, it's not my business.'

'You would one day like it to be?'

He was watching her expression. She was stood side-on, half facing the water, half facing him, her breath visible in the air, appearing to think deeply.

'Not the whole business,' she said. 'But a share of it, definitely. How about you?'

She looked directly at him then.

'Me?' he said. He was so surprised at her question the word came out half laugh, half shock.

'What's funny?'

'I just drive coaches. That's it.'

'I don't think you should be so dismissive. I mean, today you not only aided an English woman in need with somewhere to stay, you dealt with tourist questions and puking and now you're crewing a Northern Lights boat and reminding me to be water savvy and helping with voice notes. I mean, that's basically business boot camp.'

'*Krúttio mitt*, you are making me sound like I have... what is it they say? Main character energy.'

'Well, everyone should have main character energy in their own story, no?'

She was looking at him as if she was waiting for him to contradict her. He could. With more than enough reasons why he was only a prop guy, not a leading man, in his life. He was always now a reactor to situations, not a controller of them.

Instead of answering, he pointed to the sky. 'Look. Any minute now the *aurora borealis* will begin.'

13

Chloe was lost for words, eyes on the sky, wrapped up in the wonder of the light show above her. It was indescribable and just couldn't be picked up accurately on a photograph. She'd tried to capture it, after Gunnar had been radioed to go to the upper deck, but all that had come out was grainy grey pixelated nothingness. OK, it was only a camera phone, but to get nothing at all was horrendously disappointing. In the end she had given up, decided to look with only her eyes and just indulge and enjoy this precious possibly-once-in-a-lifetime occurrence.

'Have you taken photos?'

It was Gunnar, back at her side again.

'No.'

'No?' he queried, looking at her like her answer made her immediately suspicious. 'That is all anyone is doing on the upper deck.'

'Well, I tried but you can't really capture how beautiful it is.'

'Give me your phone,' Gunnar said, taking off his gloves and holding out his hand.

'I did try. Nothing worked.'

'I heard you. So, give your phone to me.'

'You think you can make it work?'

'Shall I say it again for your voice notes?'

He was still holding out his hand, so she unlocked her mobile and passed it to him.

'OK, so you have to turn your light settings right the way down.' He pressed on the screen of her phone then held it up to the sky.

'But that looks too dark,' Chloe said. 'Nothing will come out.'

'Do you not trust me? This very capable main character crewing the boat?'

She laughed. 'OK.'

He snapped a few pictures then turned the screen to show her. What she saw was a vast difference to anything she had captured.

'They are not perfect. They would be better with a good quality camera but—'

'No!' Chloe said straight off. 'No, these are great!' She swiped to view the others. 'So good.'

'But, now you have something to show with your notes, you should just look. Because the lights, they change quickly.'

He was absolutely right about that. In the time she had been observing the sky she had seen so many different colours – green, white and even the brightest fiery red. The direction of the light show varied also – parts horizontal, others vertical, strips like a rainbow waterfall.

'It is said that if you make a wish on the lights, it will come true,' Gunnar told her.

Chloe laughed. 'I am sure they say that at every single tourist site the whole world over.'

'You do not believe that parts of the world can be more enchanted than others?'

'Enchanted? I don't think I've heard that word since I got read a bedtime story.'

'Ah, that is because you do not believe,' Gunnar said, leaning his back against the railing as the boat continued to sail gently forward. 'And if you do not believe then there is no point making a wish.'

'Wait,' Chloe said. 'I didn't say I didn't believe.'

'You do not need to say. I have been told.'

'What?'

'Yes,' he said, nodding. He cupped his ear. 'What is that you say? Ah, yes, yes I agree.'

Chloe shook her head. 'I don't know why I am even going to ask this because if there's one thing I don't believe then it's this but... who are you talking to?'

He was still cupping his ear like he was listening to the universe. 'Yes, I agree with that also. Maybe, because she does not believe in enchantment she must never know.'

'OK, that's OK, you can keep your voices in your head to yourself. I'll get a psych ward on standby.'

Gunnar gasped. 'Voices in my head! You insult the *huldufólk*!'

'The what?'

He took her arm and led her further along the walkway until they were poised over the water at the very centre of the boat.

'We must whisper,' he whispered. 'So they do not hear.'

'O-K.'

'More quiet.'

'OK,' she whispered.

'So, here in Iceland there is the... *huldufólk*.' He looked over his shoulder like someone or something was about to rise out of the sea and take him.

'And that means?' Chloe asked.

'Do not tell the government, but it is the *huldufólk* who are really in charge of things around here. They are supernatural beings that live in nature.'

'Like... ghosts?' Chloe queried.

'More like... elves.'

She laughed out loud. 'Elves aren't supernatural beings. They're... well... OK, I don't know what they are, possibly because they only exist in fairy tales and—'

Suddenly a gloved finger was pressed to her lips and she was eye to eye with Gunnar. Those blue eyes. Bright, clear blue eyes. She went to open her mouth, resist the material resting against her lips but then:

'Sshh. You think the *huldufólk* are a joke?' he asked. 'In Iceland we take them very seriously and it is not right to insult them while we are on the sea and under the Northern Lights; both of these things they have deep connections to.'

Chloe said nothing, just kept their gaze fixed together somewhat in challenge.

'So, if I take my finger away will you pledge to suspend your disbelief until we get back to dry land? It would not be good for me if how you feel about the *huldufólk* made them angry and endangered all the other passengers and crew and—'

'Alright!' Chloe said, the word muffled against his finger.

He took away his finger. 'So, now, we will both make a wish on the lights.'

'Do we have to link hands and close our eyes too?'

The second the words were out of Chloe's mouth she wanted to retract them. Why had she said that?

'Yes,' Gunnar answered. 'That is exactly what we must do. And before the lights begin to fade.'

Before she could say or do anything more, Gunnar had taken her hand in his and interlinked their fingers. Even with gloves preventing skin-on-skin contact the connection felt as achingly familiar as it felt alien. She closed her eyes. Wishes. She had wanted to believe in those many moons ago, but it was all fiction. Her wish had been to have a baby. Have a baby with Michael. She'd been ready to settle down, start a family. Her genetics – inarguable science not anything mystical – had ended that dream and then ended that relationship. Her life was taking a different path now – a career one – and she only had one thing to wish for. That partnership opportunity with the business.

Gunnar spoke some words in Icelandic and Chloe opened her eyes.

'What did you say? Because you shouldn't speak your wish, everyone knows that.'

'I thought you did not believe in wishes,' Gunnar answered.

'Aren't you meant to be whispering that, so the elves don't hear?'

He smiled. 'I was not revealing my wish. I was giving thanks. Keeping the elves happy.'

'And are they?'

'Are they what?'

'Happy.'

'Did you make your wish?' he asked her.

'Yes,' she answered.

'Then they are happy.'

'What about your wish?' she asked him.

For some reason her sentence seemed to hang in the air between them like it was part of the light show, heavy yet somehow illuminated. Then static noise broke the air, Icelandic coming from Gunnar's radio, startling them both.

'I have to go,' Gunnar said. 'I am needed.'

'Yes, OK. Very good.'

Very good? Where had that come from?

'OK,' Gunnar said. 'Enjoy the rest of the lights.'

It was only when he went to walk away that Chloe realised they were still holding hands.

'Oh, sorry, I don't know—' She stopped her awkward sentence as they broke apart and, for some reason, put her gloved hand under her armpit.

'My fault,' Gunnar answered. 'Bye.'

And then he was gone.

14

Everyone came off the boat on such an absolute high from having seen the Northern Lights that they needed to rapidly be reminded that the ramp was slippery, as was the ground. And in the few hours they had been out at sea, Reykjavik had got even colder. Chloe shivered as she left the harbourside behind and began the walk back to her apartment. It had been nice pacing it out down here, looking at the Christmas lights, following the route on Google Maps, but now it was a lot colder she wasn't relishing the fifteen minutes whatsoever. And it really was slippery, her fake Uggs could confirm.

She took a breath and instantly regretted it as it felt like shards of actual ice were suddenly in her throat. Focus on your footsteps. Avoid parts of the path that look shiny.

A loud car horn almost had her falling from the pavement into the road. She clutched her coat, teeth chattering as the vehicle stopped alongside her and every kidnapping scenario she'd ever read about ran through her mind.

'Come, get in my car.'

Wow, this one wasn't messing around with any distraction techniques of sweets or cute puppies.

'*Krúttio mitt!*'

At that phrase she realised she also recognised the voice. Gunnar. She turned to look at the vehicle – not a car but some kind of four-by-four – and he had the window down, and was calling to her.

'You are walking back to the apartment?' he asked.

'Y-y-y-es.' God, she couldn't even say one word without her teeth chattering.

'Get in the car. I will take you.'

'I'm f-f-fine, honestly. It's not that far.'

'I know exactly how far it is. Get in.'

At that second a biting wind that seemed to swirl around and up got right under Chloe's padded coat. It made the decision for her. She pulled the door handle and clambered up into the truck.

'I am sorry for the mess,' Gunnar said, putting the window up.

Chloe looked to the floor of where she had put her feet. Were those ice skates? Her teeth were juddering so much now she couldn't form words. As if sensing her cold, the blowers inside the car were raised in speed, and hot air soon began to filter into the space as Gunnar pulled the truck away.

'You... do... ice skating?' she said, feeling coming back in her lips a bit.

'A little,' he said. 'Sometimes. But, I am not training for the Olympics.'

She smiled. 'OK. The last time I did ice skating I pretended I hurt my foot so I could leave the rink and go and eat bratwurst.'

He frowned. 'Why pretend? Why did you not just leave the rink and get the sausages?'

That was a very good question. The answer was because Michael had bought the apparently 'very expensive' tickets and created this 'double-date' scenario with his boss and his wife even though Chloe could barely stand up in the boots let alone waltz around the rink like Jayne Torvill. Saying no hadn't been an option she thought she was allowed to consider. And that felt pathetic. And she was going to share none of those memories with Gunnar.

'I definitely should have done that,' she answered. 'I had to carry on the pretence for a week, limping and taking twice as long over the stairs.'

'You did not like it that much? To skate?'

'It wasn't that I didn't like it,' she said. 'Just that I wasn't very good at it. I expect, living here, you are very good at it.'

'In Iceland a pair of ice skates is made for every baby that is born, their name imprinted on the leather.'

'Really?' she asked, looking at him.

He laughed then, loud and hard. Sexy.

'No, I joke with you. But there are plenty of lakes to skate on and a stadium, and ice hockey is very popular now.'

'Popular enough that you have skates ready to go in your car.'

'Well, they are not mine.' He paused. 'They... belong to someone else. I am... looking after them.'

He sounded awkward. Almost like he was keeping some kind of secret. Without realising it, her eyes began a reconnaissance of the rest of the cab of the truck. A half-empty bag of sweets. A travel mug. Some kind of design in metalwork hanging from the rear-view mirror...

'Did you enjoy the boat trip?' he asked.

'Yes. It was very good. But the Northern Lights stole the show.'

He nodded as he drove. 'It was a great display tonight.'

'Lots of five-star reviews for you.'

'I can only hope.'

'Well, I think the stain on my coat is gone so no loss of rating from me.'

'Thank you.'

He pulled the vehicle to a stop and Chloe saw they were outside the door to her apartment already. She had left a lamp on and it was glowing through the window reminding her that warm and cosy was only a few steps away.

'Thank you, Gunnar. For the ride back.'

'It is no problem. It is on my way home.'

'You live in the city?'

'Just outside. Where there are more ice skating opportunities and less hotels.'

She didn't know what else to say. Why didn't she know what else to say? Why was her mouth dry and her stomach rustling like there was a hamster living inside it?

'So, I do not know if a visit to the south of the island was something you had thought about for your event, but, if you think it would be, you can call me, let me know.' Gunnar cleared his throat. 'I drive the coach.'

'Oh, OK, that sounds interesting.'

'We go to the black sand beach and the village of Vik and... well, the itinerary is on the website.'

'OK. Thank you. I will look at that.'

'OK.'

'Good.'

And now they were just looking at each other, his clear, blue eyes matching hers and Chloe felt this sensation she couldn't remember feeling for such a long time. Sexual tension. It was chemistry. The seconds were drawing out, longer and longer until she grabbed at the door handle and propelled herself out of the door.

'Thanks again! Goodnight!'

She didn't wait to hear any reply. Instead, she pushed the door closed and headed to the apartment.

15

GUNNAR'S TRUCK, OUTSKIRTS OF REYKJAVIK

'Do you have your maths homework?' Gunnar asked the next morning as he drove, rushing like he did every day.

'Are you talking to me or to Magnús?' Hildur piped up from the back.

'Yes, Gunnar,' Magnús replied, a piece of toast in his mouth.

'Why are you driving so fast?' Hildur asked.

'Because we are late,' he answered. 'Or we will be late if I do not drive fast.'

'Or we will not arrive at all if we skid on the ice and fall into the path of something bigger than us,' Hildur stated.

'Your leg is hurting from my driving speed?' Gunnar asked her, looking at her in the rear-view mirror.

'My leg is fine. I do not know why I have to go to the community centre today, I would be fine on my own at home.'

'We discussed this, Hildur,' he said, sighing. 'It is only for a few days until you are more used to the boot.'

'And in that few days my mind will be more damaged than my ankle through boredom of the talk of old people.'

'I like the people at the community centre,' Magnús piped up. 'They give me sweets.'

'Because the old people cannot eat the sweets, they stick to their fake teeth.'

Gunnar hadn't slept very well. He didn't know whether it was the airport runs or the extra work on the Northern Lights trip that night or what had happened with Chloe. He internally shook himself. What was he thinking? Nothing had happened. But, whatever nothing had happened it was weighing on him.

'Magnús, you have dropped toast!' Gunnar exclaimed.

Magnús shrugged.

'Magnús! Pick it up! And you cannot leave your skates in the car all the time!'

'Why are you shouting, Gunnar?' Hildur asked.

'I am not shouting. I do not like mess, you know this. And there is mess in this car, there is mess in the house, and no one else seems to care.'

Now he really had shouted and his passengers were as quiet as he had ever known them. He needed to lift his mood. He needed to stop wondering what might have happened if he had leaned a little towards Chloe before she left the truck last night...

'I know what this is,' Hildur announced as they drove up to some traffic lights. 'This is how he always is when Christmas is arriving, Magnús,' Hildur said.

'You are right,' Magnús agreed. 'It is like he is afraid of Santa Claus.'

'And all the reindeer,' Hildur added with a throaty laugh.

'And my school show,' Magnús continued.

What? Had Hildur said anything to Magnús about that? No, she wouldn't have. Gunnar swallowed as the memories of his own school Christmas show and the night he lost his father came back to him. What was supposed to be the happiest of ends to the year, excitement about Christmas coming for all the children, had been the beginning of his family's demise...

'I am not scared of the school show,' Gunnar said as firmly as he could manage. 'Or Santa Claus and the reindeer.'

'Then why have you not bought a ticket?' Magnús asked.

'The tickets are on sale?' he queried fast.

'Gunnar,' Hildur said. 'I have told you this for the past two weeks. They also need volunteers to help finish making the sets and—'

'I will buy a ticket,' Gunnar interrupted as the lights changed and he drove through them.

'Really?' Magnús exclaimed, definite surprise in his voice.

'If you give the boy some *króna* he can buy the ticket today,' Hildur stated.

'You are not coming?' Gunnar asked her.

'I already have my ticket. But maybe you need a second one?'

He glanced into the rear-view mirror and caught the old woman's eye. What was with that expression on her face?

Within a few minutes he was pulling up outside the school and Magnús was halfway out of the car door before he could stop him.

'Magnús,' Gunnar said. 'Here, take the *króna* for the ticket for the Christmas show.' He pulled a note from his wallet and passed it to the boy.

'And I can put you down to help with painting the set?' Magnús asked him, all wide light blue eyes not so dissimilar to his.

'Magnús, I do not know if I can commit to doing that. Work is busy right now and—'

His answer was the slamming of the truck door, anger and frustration rippling with the metalwork as it vibrated. Gunnar was already removing his seatbelt, ready to leap from the truck and tell the boy his behaviour was not acceptable until...

'Leave him,' Hildur ordered. 'He will calm down. It is hard for him. All the other children having parents.'

'That is not an excuse for life, Hildur. We all have to make the best out of our individual situations.'

'Or bury them and pretend they have never happened? Would that be better?'

'I did not say that,' he answered. 'But slamming doors does not solve things either.'

'He is a young boy who lost everything. There are no rule-books for that,' Hildur reminded him.

Gunnar looked out of the window, watching Magnús striding towards the school building, backpack swinging from one arm, coat falling off his shoulder until it almost dragged on the ground. It was true he had been through so much in his ten years. It seemed almost impossible that it was three years ago that Gunnar had plucked him from the ferocious lava trail that had claimed the lives of his parents. No one really knew exactly how it had happened. Eruptions here occurred more often than ever, but they weren't yet catastrophic, not claiming lives thanks to good management and warnings from the authorities. Yet that was no comfort to a boy who had cried every night as he relived his parents falling into a bubbling fissure.

Gunnar pulled the car away from the kerb, refocussing on dropping off his next passenger.

'So,' Hildur began. 'If it is not Santa Claus and the reindeer you are scared of, and you say it is not the Christmas show, then there is only one reason for your mood this morning.'

'Only having time for one coffee?' he asked.

'This is how you were when you first met Kirstin.'

As if the universe was reacting to what Hildur had said, the car in front of them braked suddenly and Gunnar was left having to do exactly the same to avoid a collision.

Hildur gave a moan from the back seat.

'Hildur, you are OK?' he asked.

'Yes, but I am not so certain about the tomatoes.'

'I do not care about the tomatoes. I care that you have not injured your leg any more.'

'And you are now using concern for me to brush away what I said about Kirstin.'

He put the truck into first gear and pulled away again. Kirstin. The last woman he had dropped his guard for. The woman who left the moment he told her he was a guardian to a small boy and lived with an octogenarian. He didn't know why he had foolishly thought Kirstin was different, would understand and accept. Maybe because he thought she had genuinely cared for him like he had started to care for her. In the end she had taken a different job, one that took her away from Iceland and quickly out of his life.

'There is nothing to brush away,' Gunnar said. 'Kirstin lives in Denmark now.' He could say her name. He could deal with reality and facts. No emotion necessary.

'I know. I have Facebook.'

Gunnar knew Hildur had Facebook, as did he, but he didn't know that she had kept in touch with what Kirstin was doing. He didn't. They were no longer online friends either. What was the point of keeping any kind of connection? It had been over a year now.

'So, there is no new Kirstin?' Hildur asked like 'Kirstin' was an iPhone model.

'No.'

'No one?'

'No,' he repeated. 'Except...'

'Except?'

Why had he said 'except'? There was nothing. Chloe was someone he had bumped into a few times, a customer he had helped, a tourist he had given information to, except... argh, damn that word!

'It is none of my business, of course,' Hildur said when he made no response. 'But, as much as you do for that boy and for me, you have to make time for more than work for yourself, Gunnar.'

'I think we have had this conversation before,' Gunnar answered.

'And we will continue to have this conversation until you believe,' Hildur said.

'Like with the *huldufólk*?'

'Ah! At last! You bring them up yourself so they are real to you now!'

Gunnar shook his head, taking a left turn towards the community centre. 'Now, the minibus will pick you up at six and Magnús is going to his friend's for dinner and I will pick him up when I have finished with the tour.'

'Do you want me to make you something to eat?' Hildur asked as he pulled to a stop.

'No!' Gunnar said immediately. 'No, Hildur, you do nothing but rest your foot. I will take care of the food. OK?'

There was no response and he turned his head to look into the back seat of the car.

'We have some tomatoes that are not squashed,' Hildur announced, two large fruits in her hands.

'I will help you get out of the car,' he said, undoing his seat-belt, ready to get out.

'You will not,' Hildur said. 'I have to learn.' She opened the door. 'And tonight, with dinner, you can tell me more about the "except".'

He should have known that nothing would get past Hildur.

16

REYKJAVIK

'So, is your location accurate now, on the maps?'

It was Kat on the phone, it was almost lunchtime and Chloe had taken the short walk from the apartment into downtown Reykjavik. There were brightly painted buildings, shops selling all manner of Nordic knitwear, Christmas decorations hanging from arches, huts with wares in baskets outside. It was a festive shopping paradise.

'I presume so,' Chloe answered. 'But I haven't checked. Where does it say I am?'

'I don't know the name of the street but you're quite near something called Rok.'

Chloe looked to her left and there was the building. With its wooden façade, it seemed like a high-end restaurant, and peering through the window, Chloe could see the tables were set for service, presumably for the evening. 'Yes.'

'And it's not open, that's annoying. Because I'm starving.'

It took several seconds for what Kat had said to sink in. And still, how did she know...

'Surprise!'

Kat's voice was no longer coming out of Chloe's phone; it was closer, very close. And when Chloe turned around there was her friend on the street, right in front of her. Chloe's mouth hung open in absolute shock.

'Oh, Chlo! I know! A shock, right? But a good shock? Please say it's a good shock, because I can absolutely get in a taxi, go back to the airport and go home again if this is too much and—'

Chloe stole the rest of her friend's words as she embraced her hard, hugging her tight. 'I can't believe you're here! How are you here?' She let her go to look at her again.

'Well, there's this thing called "air travel", I'm pretty sure you're familiar with it and used it yourself very recently... God, I got on a plane early this morning and flew to Iceland without telling anyone!' Kat slapped her gloved hands to either side of her face. 'I'm a maniac!'

'You didn't tell anyone? What about work?'

'Oh my God! What time is it? Should I be there right now?'

Chloe knew Kat could be erratic in nature, but usually that involved spontaneous evening plans, not leaving the country without booking annual leave. 'Kat!'

'I'm kidding! Well, not really, I sent an email. I just thought I am under an incredible amount of stress and my mother is going to give me even more stress and I haven't been out of the country since we all booked with Ryanair vouchers after Covid and, I don't know, Iceland sounded so cool and you said you had a sofa, right? Please tell me I wasn't wrong about that because otherwise I'll be trying to find a coach driver who can help me find somewhere to stay!' She suddenly inhaled and it sounded like it had come from the very depths of her. She put her hands to her woollen hat. 'I'm crazy, aren't I? I'm actually crazy!'

'No!' Chloe said fast. She bundled Kat up in another big hug, holding her tight and rocking her from side to side. 'Not at all. I can't believe you're here.'

'You keep saying that,' Kat said. 'You don't keep saying you're pleased I'm here.'

'Of course I'm pleased!' She *was* pleased, it was just so unexpected and she couldn't help thinking that it was quite the quick decision and was there more to it than just Iceland sounding like a cool place for her friend to visit. But, she was overthinking now so she smiled at her friend. 'Kat, if I had even thought it would be something that could have happened I would have invited you myself but your work is always so busy and your mother—'

'Please, I can't talk about that woman right now. Not without something strong sat in front of me. The Icelandic equivalent of vodka or a Viking, I don't mind which.'

'O-K.'

'But, I don't want to get in the way of your work stuff, obviously, because I know Michelle will have you running around like an events fairy godmother, jumping through festive hoops while she incubates "Prada" or whatever name they settled on.'

'It was never Prada,' Chloe said, shaking her head. 'You know that.'

'Balenciaga?'

'No.'

'Kendrick?'

'Kat.'

'Lamar?'

'Stop it.'

'OK, OK.' Kat inhaled again and spread her arms wide. 'Wow, I'm in Iceland!'

'Yes, you are,' Chloe said, smiling. 'Let's go and get a coffee.'

17

DÜRÜM, REYKJAVIK

Coffee hadn't been enough and, in the name of research, as well as the cold, Chloe and Kat had bundled into a cosy café on a street called *Laugavegur* and ordered fish and chips.

'It's a bit British, isn't it? To have fish and chips. I feel like a travel fraud and I've only been in the country a few hours,' Kat said, steaming crispy batter on her fork.

'Actually no,' Chloe replied. 'Fish and chips is one of the things to have here and this is so good!'

'Good enough for Sinclairz Chairs?' Kat asked, pushing a forkful of battered, flaky white deliciousness into her mouth.

'Not sure about that,' Chloe said. 'In fact I'm not 100 per cent sure what Sinclairz Chairs are looking for apart from this location.'

She'd asked Michelle, in two emails now, if she could have a vague idea what Sinclairz Chairs were looking for. Ultimate luxury? More traditional? A mix of the two? Or completely different itineraries – one more relaxed: spa/lagoon, cocktails – the other higher intensity experiences: dog sledding, glacier walks. Right now she was hedging her bets and looking into getting as many ideas as she could to put together entirely differing proposals if she had to.

'Michelle a bit light on the details?' Kat asked her. 'All "go, go, go" and then "wait, what are we actually doing"?'

Chloe felt her shoulders tighten, almost defensively. 'I wouldn't put it quite like that. She does have a lot on her mind at the moment.'

'Or rather a lot in her uterus.'

'Kat!'

'Well, I don't think you see how much she relies on you to make her business run like clockwork.'

'That's my job,' Chloe reminded her.

'I know. But I also know from experience how people in a position of power can use others' expertise to bolster themselves without giving credit where credit is due.'

'Michelle appreciates my diligence. She's always telling me that.'

'But does she tell anyone else? No,' Kat answered for herself. 'Because if she did there's no doubt in my mind that you would be headhunted for another bigger, more esteemed company. You know that, right?'

'I think you underestimate how well thought of Celebratey is. Lincoln Sinclair wouldn't just give this opportunity to anybody.'

'But you're still pitching. It's still a bit of a competition.'

'I know.'

'And you should also know that it's you who has shaped that company since you joined it.'

'Well, I've done what I can and—'

'And Michelle can't do without you and it's time she realised that.'

'I know, which is why I'm going to mention buying in to the

business and maybe becoming a partner. As soon as the baby is born. Well, you know, not as soon as the baby's born because that would be a bit rude and—'

'What's rude is that woman thinking you have no other options and taking advantage of that.'

Kat said the last sentence with so much ferocity, conversations between other customers ceased and attention was definitely focussed on them. Chloe put down her knife and fork and took a sip from her water glass. Kat was always harsh about Michelle, she knew this, but amid the harshness was there an element of truth?

'Sorry,' Kat said to Chloe. Then she smiled an apology to the couple sat closest to them who went back to their own meals.

'It's OK. You always tell me exactly how you see things.'

'I know, but sometimes I could tone it down a notch. And I know you're not stupid, you know Michelle takes advantage of your loyalty.'

Now it felt like the water was souring in her mouth. Did Michelle actually really take advantage of her?

'Chlo, you know that, right? We talked about it the night she made you hunt down a needle and thread like it was a task on *The Apprentice* because she couldn't possibly give a speech at the entrepreneurs' dinner with a loose hem.'

'That was so long ago,' Chloe answered. 'And I didn't mind.'

'Like you didn't mind dropping everything to come to Iceland?'

'It's my job,' Chloe reminded her. 'And she's trusted me with the groundwork for this big opportunity. And it's not like I have any social life to let go of. Present company excepted, and you're here now so...'

'I just want Michelle to value what you do a little bit more, that's all,' Kat said, tone a bit softer. 'Because you do so much for the company and I think, sometimes, you do it because you think there's nothing else for you. There, I've said it.'

Chloe swallowed, sat back in her chair. 'What do you mean?'

'Oh, Chlo, I just... I don't know... sometimes I think maybe you hold on so tight to your job with Michelle because it's like a lifebuoy. Now hear me out because I know what you're going to say and—'

'I'm going to say this is more to do with you wanting me to date than it is to do with my career. And you're doing this, Kat, like you always do, because your mum is stressing you out and no one but me in your friendship circle is single now that Harriet has got together with Justin.'

Kat was shaking her head. 'And now you're deflecting like you always do when you tell me anything I say is because I need you to date. When really it's because you can't see Michelle's flaws, because you're clinging on too tightly to a job you're doing so you don't have to stop and think and come to terms with Michael leaving.'

Now the whole restaurant was silent apart from the background festive music that was at complete odds with the atmosphere in the room. Chloe got to her feet.

'I'm just going to the toilet.'

'Chloe, don't go. I shouldn't have said—'

But Chloe left the table not caring about whatever Kat had to say next.

18

Chloe took a deep breath of the crisp, cold air and hoped it would work magic to her heated-up temperament. She shouldn't have let Kat's line of questioning get to her. Why had she done that? Because there were elements of truth to it? She swallowed, watching tourists coming out of the Icewear store, bulging totes full of knitwear. Baggage. Like she was carrying? She sighed. She knew she had unaddressed issues to work through, she was trying to work through them by literally working through them.

'Please come back and finish the fish and chips.'

It was Kat, at her shoulder, looking like she might burst into tears.

'I will,' Chloe said. 'Just, give me a minute.'

'I'm an idiot,' Kat said. 'But you know that. I don't think, I just say, and sometimes I could do with a muzzle.'

'Well maybe a muzzle is a little far but—'

'Don't be nice to me, I don't deserve it. I've got on a plane here without asking you if it was OK and now I'm here I'm pushing my agendas probably because my mother does that to me and how awful is that?!'

'It's OK,' Chloe said, putting a hand on her friend's shoulder. 'It's really not.'

'And, maybe, just maybe... you have a point.' She sighed. 'Perhaps I have been burying myself in work to forget about... everything.'

'Which is totally understandable,' Kat said. 'I mean, I tend to bury myself in Häagen-Dazs and other people's problems apparently. We all have our coping mechanisms. But, you know, I just want you to be happy and if working for Michelle makes you happy then it's not my business to make you question that,' Kat said.

'Working *with* Michelle,' Chloe said. 'That's what I want, remember? The partnership.'

'Then that's the plan,' Kat said, winding an arm around her shoulders. 'Your plan. Not something I've bitch-talked to you about. And I am here now to help you create this perfect Christmas celebration party/whatever it is for Sinclairz Chairs.'

'OK,' Chloe said, taking a deep breath and refocussing.

With minimal input from Michelle it was going to be down to her to pull something out of the bag that was going to wow her boss and the boss of the chair business, something that was going to elevate her to that piece of company ownership pie.

'So, what is the plan? Apart from me paying for this lunch to make up for being a total cow.'

She had a few places in Reykjavik she had noted down for this afternoon – the Sun Voyager sculpture, the *Arnarhóll* statue – but after that she didn't know.

'Let's go and finish our food, then we will brainstorm,' Chloe said.

'And I'd better call work,' Kat said, clapping her gloved hands together. 'Check they got my email. It's a bit reckless of me, isn't it? Let's hope I don't get fired. I need the cash for all the Nordic knitwear I've had my eye on since I arrived.'

'Gift bags,' Chloe said, pointing a finger into the air. 'We could suggest gift bags for all the Sinclairz celebration attendees – a mix of luxury and traditional. Something woollen. Or something kooky.'

Huldufólk. She thought about Gunnar. Him talking about the mysterious hidden people. Him looking at her so intensely from the driver's seat of his truck last night. What trip did he say he did? Something about the south coast...

'So, how do I wangle an invite to this festive celebration if you get the job?' Kat asked, breaking into Chloe's thoughts.

'Well,' Chloe said. 'If you get fired from your job, you could apply to Sinclairz Chairs and—'

Kat slapped Chloe's arm good-naturedly. 'Stop!'

'Come on,' Chloe urged, glad the air had been cleared. 'Before they think we're not coming back.'

19

GUNNAR'S HOME, THE OUTSKIRTS OF REYKJAVIK

'So, how was your tour today?' Hildur asked Gunnar as they sat down to eat later that evening.

The last thing he really wanted was conversation. The south coast tour was one of the longest day trips the company he worked for did and it had been a gruelling one today. His eyes were tired from driving and his ears were ringing from the fault there had been in the coach speaker system that had hummed and buzzed through some of his commentary.

'It was fine,' he replied, pushing spiced green beans into his mouth. He knew these weren't from the freezer. He also knew that it meant while he had been in the shower, Hildur had not been resting but had prepared them to go with the chicken he had put in the oven for them both. Apparently full from a home-cooked meal made by his friend's mother, Magnús had skulked to his bedroom the second Gunnar had asked if he had done his homework while he was there.

'Was anyone sick?' Hildur asked.

'Hildur! We are eating!'

'I do not know why I ask the question. Every trip someone is sick.'

He swallowed a mouthful of green beans and took a sip of his water. 'How was the community centre?'

'No one died,' Hildur announced. 'Although I very much wanted to when they decided to play Christmas bingo.'

'You like bingo.'

'Not when I am forced to wear a hat like *Jolasveiner*.'

Gunnar couldn't help but laugh. It had nothing to do with Hildur not wanting to be festive and don the attire of the Icelandic Yule Lads, Hildur didn't like hats in any shape or form.

'And everyone there is so very old. It is a wonder there are not as many deaths as you have passengers being sick into carrier bags.'

'Hildur! We are still eating!'

'Then it is time to change the topic of conversation,' Hildur announced, cutting into her chicken. 'We will now talk about the "except" yes?'

Gunnar should have known Hildur wouldn't forget their train of talk from that morning and she was a master at manipulating the conversation to go her way. He would tell her something. As little as possible to satisfy her curiosity.

'There is nothing to tell. A tourist I helped find some accommodation for.'

'That is not your job.'

'No,' Gunnar agreed. 'But, you know, I made a call and Fridrik knew a place and I helped Chloe out.'

'Ah! She has a name!' Hildur exclaimed like having a name was a miracle.

'And she was on the Northern Lights boat trip last night. That is it. Nothing else to tell.' He focussed back on his meal.

'Nothing to tell,' Hildur repeated. 'Except your face is now more red than a hat of a Yule Lad.'

'It is not,' he said, feeling heat creep into his cheeks.

'So, when do you see her again? Chloe?' Hildur asked, her expression nothing short of the kind of gleeful she got when she was winning an argument with one of their neighbours.

'I do not see her again.'

'Why not?'

'Why would I?' he asked. 'She is a tourist. She is here to plan an event for her job.'

'An event here in Iceland?' Hildur asked.

'Yes.'

'Then she is a tourist who is coming back!'

Gunnar shook his head and was glad when his mobile phone rang from its position on the countertop and he could get up from the table.

'Maybe that is Chloe. Wanting to see you again,' Hildur said. 'You need to start using that conditioner on your hair again.'

Gunnar looked at the screen on his phone. It wasn't Chloe. It was Magnús's teacher.

'Hello, Mr Almr.'

'Good evening, Mr Eriksson. I am sorry to bother you at home so late.'

'It is OK. There is no problem, is there? With Magnús's schoolwork?' He leaned against the counter, almost bracing himself.

'Not exactly with his work, no,' came the reply.

What did that mean? There was something else? A social problem? Worse?

'Please, Mr Almr, tell me,' Gunnar urged.

'Mr Eriksson, Magnús has not been in school for the past few days. Is he sick?'

Gunnar's stomach dropped. 'What? I... do not understand.'

'So he is not sick?'

'No, he is not sick.' Gunnar put a hand to his head trying to work this out in his mind. How was this possible? 'We... we have had some things going on here. A trip to the hospital. And I have been busy, but I have dropped him at school every day.'

And only tonight he had arranged for someone else's family to collect Magnús from school and look after him until Gunnar had finished work. Had Magnús not been at school today? Had he walked to the outside of school from wherever he had been to be there for his lift? Gunnar's brain was ticking over so many scenarios and none of them were good.

'OK,' Mr Almr said. 'I understand.'

'You do?' Gunnar replied. 'Because I do not. And I am ashamed and embarrassed that I did not know he was not at school.'

Now Hildur's full attention was piqued and the older woman swivelled in her seat like she might be about to try and get up. He signalled to her to stop and she stayed where she was.

'There is no shame, Mr Eriksson and there is no judgement either. All we want at the school is the very best for Magnús and to be able to support him and you.'

Gunnar shook his head. He was a failure. He had taken his eye off the ball. He had thought he could trust Magnús to follow the rules. He should have remembered better what it was like to be his age. 'How long has this been going on?'

'Only this week but...'

There was a 'but'. This was not good.

The teacher continued. 'But there have been a few other concerns we had that might have something to do with Magnús's absence.'

Gunnar did brace himself now. 'Go on.'

'Well, last week, there was an altercation between Magnús and one of his classmates.'

'An altercation?' Gunnar was already thinking the word 'fight' and hoping he was wrong.

'We do not know exactly what happened but both students were dismissive of it when we asked them, shook hands, settled down and—'

'And why did no one tell me about this? I am Magnús's guardian. If there is anything going on I need to be kept informed.'

'Mr Eriksson, at the time we decided it was an incident that needed no further action but, in light of Magnús's absences—'

'And the other boy? Has he been missing from school too?'

'Other boy?'

'The one Magnús had whatever you are calling an "altercation" with. Can we not cut through to the truth? Which one hit the other first?'

Gunnar was caught between feeling defensive and annoyed. Had he had prior knowledge of this he might have been able to better control the situation.

'I am sorry,' Mr Almr said. 'I was not clear. The other student was a girl. But, as I said—'

'What?' Gunnar exclaimed. Now he was nothing but angry. Whatever had happened, Magnús was involved in a verbal or physical situation with a girl!

'Mr Eriksson, I know this may have come as a shock but, really, this call was to—'

'You will leave this with me now,' Gunnar spat. 'I will speak to Magnús, I will find out what is going on, I will make him apologise and accept any punishment that you think is necessary and I will ensure that he is in school tomorrow and every other day after that.'

'Mr Eriksson, if you could wait a—'

'Goodbye, Mr Almr.'

Gunnar ended the call and paced immediately towards the door that led to the bedrooms.

'Gunnar, wait!' Hildur ordered.

He wasn't waiting, not for anything or anyone. He was going to get hold of Magnús and give him the talking-to of his life. How dare he miss school! How dare he lie to him, pretend that everything was normal!

'Gunnar! I said no!'

The door to the corridor slammed shut and somehow there was Hildur, out of her chair, back firm against the door, blocking his path.

'Hildur, you should be sitting down,' Gunnar said.

'So should you,' the woman replied.

'After that phone call?' Gunnar exclaimed. 'Did you know that—'

'I heard enough to figure things out.'

'Then you know I have to speak to Magnús and find out what the hell is going on!'

'Yes,' Hildur agreed, back still pressed against the door. 'Speak to him. Not shout at him.'

'Hildur! He hit a girl!'

'We do not know that yet.'

'He did something that was not right.'

'Maybe.'

Gunnar shook his head. 'He has been absent from school.'

'Weren't we all at one time or another? I know you were. And, me too.'

'Hildur, let me through the door,' Gunnar ordered.

'Not like this,' Hildur told him, voice full of determination. 'Not angry and wanting to shout. What good will that do?'

'It will show Magnús that his behaviour is unacceptable!'

'Will it?' Hildur asked, one eyebrow rising. 'Or will it frighten the boy and make him immediately think that you do not understand and retreat into himself more so that he never opens up to you about what he thinks or how he feels?'

'Hildur.'

'What?'

'If he does not go to school, they will say I cannot cope looking after him and the authorities will look for another family. And... maybe they will be right.'

Gunnar put his hands to his head in exasperation, anger quickly dissipating into frustration.

'Do not say that,' Hildur said. 'That boy clung to you when you rescued him. He did not speak for days. He would not talk to anyone but you. Look how far he has come. And that is down to you.'

Gunnar swallowed, shoulders dropping. He remembered the rescue like it was yesterday, but only when he was made to or it infiltrated his sleep, his subconscious demanding that he process. Moving forward was his choice in dealing with crises. Problem-solve. Don't dwell on the negative. But was that the kind of nurture that was best for Magnús? He had to work to pay for the house, the food, the ice skates; there were not enough hours in the day for any kind of emotional support.

'Whatever has happened,' Hildur continued. 'You must make small steps to uncover it. It is like pulling back many layers of wrapping paper in the game where the parcel is passed. One sheet at a time.'

'Maybe I am not the right person for that,' Gunnar said.

'Gunnar Eriksson,' Hildur admonished. 'You are the only person for that. You were chosen for this.'

He shook his head. 'Please, Hildur, do not make this about the *huldufólk*.'

'I am not talking about the *huldufólk* choosing, Gunnar. I am talking about Magnús. He chose you.'

He had no immediate answer for that. His insides flooded with so many emotions as he realised that, for now, in this moment, Hildur was right.

'What do I do?' It took a second for him to realise that he had said the words aloud. It wasn't Hildur's responsibility. He had taken on the care of Magnús.

'Nothing tonight,' Hildur said, finally stepping away from the door and putting a hand on his shoulder. 'Tomorrow will be a new day. Begin again with a clear head, yes?'

He nodded. 'Yes.'

20

CHLOE'S APARTMENT, REYKJAVIK

'Kat, wake up,' Chloe loud-whispered, giving her friend's arm a bit of a shake.

It was the following morning and Chloe had got little sleep for two reasons. One because Kat snored like a lawnmower and the second because she'd gone online researching the south coast trip and, after extensive looking and checking and thinking about it, she'd booked them on it. Today. In an hour's time.

Kat inhaled like she had woken from a Sleeping Beauty style sleep of years, rising up, eyes wide in shock. 'Is it Christmas?'

'No,' Chloe said, with a laugh. 'You're in Iceland, remember.'

Kat inhaled again. 'Oh, thank God, because I haven't ordered a meat hamper yet.' She yawned then. 'What time is it?'

'It's almost seven,' Chloe said, opening the blind at the window.

'Is that all?' Kat said, flopping back down onto her pillows.

'But, we have to be at the bus station in forty minutes.'

'What?' Kat exclaimed, sitting up again.

'I booked us on a trip. The south coast tour. I think it's something Sinclairz Chairs would enjoy. I just need to find out if there's enough to keep everyone entertained or, if there's not, how we could build in more bespoke activities.'

'Could one of the bespoke activities be napping?' Kat asked, yawning again.

'I know it's early, but I've had no response from Michelle to my last two emails and I don't want to chase her up in case something's wrong. So I'm just getting on with things and if it's not right, or she needs me to do something more specific, she can let me know.'

'Oh, she will,' Kat said. 'She will tell you it's absolutely not what she wanted and you'll have to do things all over again. Like that event for the dog groomers. "Tiny dalmatians on the napkins, Chloe. Not bones. What were you thinking?"'

Sometimes Kat knowing and remembering the specifics of what they'd talked about was a curse not a blessing. But Chloe was well aware of her boss's exacting nature. Michelle could be harsh but she always sought perfection and that was something Chloe admired about her.

'Well,' Chloe said. 'I would rather have something she can pick apart than do nothing and wait for instructions. That's what a potential partner does, right? Uses her initiative.'

'Yes,' Kat agreed. 'I just wish it was initiative that started after seven in the morning.'

'Sorry.'

'But, I am your wing-woman for all things so I will arise and shower quickly and perform whatever bespoke activity I need to to help you with your mission and to help keep my mind off the fact I'm going to have to spend a week playing Trivial Pursuit, eating Jacob's biscuits for cheese selection and pretending I like re-runs of *The Two Ronnies*.'

'Then today will feel like a breeze,' Chloe said, smiling.

'An icy one? Because I need to know if I need to take two hats.'

Chloe's phone started ringing then.

'I'm getting in the shower right now,' Kat said, finally pulling back the covers. 'So if that's Michelle with an alternative plan then whatever we end up doing at least I'll be clean.'

Chloe picked up her phone from where it was charging on the small table. It was Gunnar. And her heart immediately picked up pace. She had called him last night. Convinced herself it was only because it might be easier to book the trip with him than the company website. But he hadn't answered and she hadn't left a voice message. Just a trail of a missed call he was obviously now responding to.

'Hello,' Chloe said.

'Hello, Chloe. Is everything OK with the apartment? I am sorry I did not see your call last night I—'

'Everything's fine,' Chloe broke in. He sounded so concerned she almost regretted not leaving a voicemail. 'Sorry, I shouldn't have called you so late. It was... I was wanting to book onto the south coast tour today.'

'Oh, OK.' His relief was audible.

'But I managed to book on the website. I think. I mean I have a booking number but not a confirmation email so...'

'It is OK,' Gunnar replied. 'I know you, *krúttio mitt*. I will save you the best seat.'

She smiled. 'Actually it's two seats.'

'One for you and one for the *huldufólk*?'

'No, my friend has arrived from England.' She gasped then. 'Sorry, that's OK, isn't it? To have someone else staying in the apartment. I just assumed it would be OK. I should have asked. But, she's, you know, trustworthy too.'

'You worry too much. Relax now. You are about to travel for hours on a coach with little leg room.'

'But heating, right? The website said the coaches have heating.'

'Yes,' Gunnar answered. 'And bags for vomit. You know this.'

'I was trying to forget.'

He laughed. That warm, bubbling, sexy sound... She cleared her throat. 'So, I will see you soon. It leaves at 8 a.m., right?'

'Yes,' he replied. 'And the door closes at seven fifty-nine.'

'O-K.'

'I am just joking,' he said. 'You have until eight-oh-one.'

She laughed. 'Well, in that case, I had better finish packing my bag for the day.'

'Bring snacks,' Gunnar told her.

'What kind?'

'I hear the driver of the south coast tour likes liquorice.'

Chloe laughed again. 'OK. Bye, Olga.'

'*Bless, krúttio mitt.*'

21

GUNNAR'S HOME, THE OUTSKIRTS OF REYKJAVIK

'You are smiling,' Hildur remarked, spooning yoghurt into a bowl as she sat at the table, leg up on the chair opposite. 'It was Chloe.'

'No,' Gunnar said, putting his phone back on charge.

'Gunnar Eriksson. You said her name. I may sometimes be stupid, but I am not deaf.' She grinned, digging the spoon into the yoghurt mound she had made.

'It is nothing,' he said. 'She is coming on the tour today.'

'Oooo,' Hildur said, excitedly.

'Hildur, stop that,' Gunnar said as Magnús burst into the kitchen.

'What is Hildur doing?' Magnús asked, picking up toast from the table.

'Nothing for you to worry about,' Gunnar answered. 'Do you want orange juice?'

He had decided he was going to keep things completely normal with Magnús this morning at home. Then, when they had dropped Hildur off at the community centre he was going to speak to the boy in the truck. The truck had always been a safe space for talking since the first time Magnús had opened up to him after he lost his parents.

'No,' Magnús declined. 'I need to leave, or I will be late.' The boy was already picking up his backpack and heading towards the front door.

'What?' Gunnar said, thrown by this. 'What do you mean late? Late for what?'

'I am meeting Isak. His dad is taking us to school today.'

Magnús was not looking him in the eye. In fact, his whole body language was screaming out 'lie'. Had he performed this act before and Gunnar just hadn't noticed?

'Magnús,' Gunnar said.

'I don't have time to talk. I will get the bus home tonight.' He made strides towards the door, fast. Gunnar moved faster, a bit like Hildur had done last night. He planted his back against the framework.

'Stop,' Gunnar said firmly.

It was enough to catch Magnús off-guard, shoulders rolling forward, head dipping, seeming unsure of his next move.

'I have to go,' the boy said in nothing more than a mumble.

'Magnús,' Gunnar said, softer. 'I know you have not been going to school.'

The boy lifted his head now, showed a flash of defiance. 'I have been going to school. You take me there every day.'

'Do not be smart with me, Magnús. I will say it a different way. You have not been staying in school.'

There was no quick remark to follow just a very blank, emotionless expression now. And then, a shrug.

'You think it does not matter?' Gunnar asked, anger nibbling. 'You have better things to do with your life than get an education?'

Another shrug.

'Magnús,' Hildur called from the table. 'Gunnar is not mad with you, you know. He worries about you. We both worry about you.'

Gunnar was mad. He was just proceeding with caution. He swallowed.

'Magnús, you know if there is something you need to talk to me about then I am here to talk about it with you.'

Magnús said nothing. He was standing completely still, eyes locked on the window behind the kitchen sink. How did you get through to someone who was trying so hard not to let anyone in? He could relate, that was how he had always been in life when he had lost his own parents, but when you were on the receiving end it was frustrating. He racked his brain back to when he had saved Magnús, ran with him over his shoulder to safety...

'OK,' Gunnar said decisively. 'No school today.'

'What?'

It was Magnús and Hildur at the same time.

'Yes. You will come on the coach with me,' Gunnar said, nodding.

'But—'

'There is no more conversation to be had,' Gunnar said. 'So, shall I call Isak's dad and tell him you will not need a ride to school today?'

Magnús said nothing.

'OK, good. That is decided then. Hildur, we will leave in fifteen minutes.'

Hildur sighed and pushed away her yoghurt bowl. 'Can I not go to school with Isak's dad?'

Magnús turned around and headed back towards his room.

'Magnús, be ready. Take a coat. It will be extra cold where we are going.'

His words were lost to the slamming of the door separating the living area from the bedrooms.

'You will take him on your tour?' Hildur asked.

'There is no other choice.' Gunnar's hope was the boy would open up on his coach like he had used to open up in his truck.

'And you will introduce Magnús to Chloe?' Hildur asked. 'Who will also be on the tour.'

Gunnar had not thought about that. And he was not about to start thinking about it now.

'Just be ready to leave in fifteen minutes,' he said, following the same path Magnús had taken to avoid awkward conversation.

22

REYKJAVIK BUS STATION, REYKJAVIK

'So, this coach has heating, right?'

Kat clapped her gloved hands together as she jigged up and down on the spot outside the transportation hub where coaches and minibuses with numbers in the window sat in lines waiting in anticipation. A bit like them.

'Yes,' Chloe said. 'But we can wait inside if it's too cold.' She checked her watch. It was almost five minutes to eight and there was no sign of anything happening with coach number six. Had she read the board wrong?

'No, it's fine. You said it was leaving dead on eight o'clock, right? So I won't have time to turn into a frozen sculpture.'

If, in fact, the coach was going to depart on time. Just as Chloe was mulling over that thought, a truck sped into the parking area. A vehicle she recognised. It wheel-spinned to a halt with screeching brakes.

'God!' Kat exclaimed. 'I know I rushed around the apartment getting ready in a frenzy but tell me I wasn't giving that desperate for this trip.' She laughed. 'I hope the coach driver doesn't drive like that.'

Chloe couldn't help but smile as she watched Gunnar get out of the truck. 'That *is* the coach driver.'

'What?' Kat exclaimed, eyes on the tall figure emerging in front of them. 'Wait... that is your Gunnar?'

Chloe shivered. 'He's not my anything.'

'Yet,' Kat said. 'Because, Chloe, he's sooo fine!'

'Sshh!' Chloe said as Gunnar began walking towards their position. She swallowed as she checked him out anew. She knew he was attractive. But now, as she observed him, there were other attributes she hadn't given him full credit for. He was tall and athletic-looking. And his hair wasn't yet under a hat. It was loose, wavy, dirty-blond. Sexy.

'If you don't want him I might have to unbutton my coat as soon as we get on board. Glad I bought that new push-up bra now.'

'Don't do that,' Chloe found herself blurting out.

Kat grinned. 'Ah! So you do like him!'

'No,' Chloe protested.

'OK,' Kat said. 'That wasn't at all convincing. But, who is the kid? His?'

It was only then that Chloe noticed there was someone walking behind Gunnar. A boy. He was about ten or eleven. Blond hair shorter than Gunnar's but still long enough to flop into his face. He was wearing jeans, a black puffer jacket and a very glum expression. Was this Gunnar's son? Was he married? With someone? Suddenly she was feeling caught off-guard somehow. Except, he had never said he was single. Why would he? They had shared a few conversations and he'd helped clean a stain off her coat. And she wasn't looking for anyone...

But then he waved a hand in greeting and she found herself waving back.

'Aww, cute,' Kat remarked. 'Now introduce us!'

Why was Chloe feeling suddenly nervous? She internally shook herself. She was a soon-to-be partner of a successful event-planning company. She was a business woman with the world at her feet.

'Good morning, *krúttio mitt*,' Gunnar greeted.

'*Halló*,' Chloe answered.

'You are here on time,' Gunnar continued.

'Earlier than you,' she replied.

'And did you bring the snacks?' Gunnar asked.

Chloe gasped. She had completely forgotten about the liquorice.

'I do not know if you can board the coach without this part-payment,' Gunnar said, shaking his head.

'It sounds like we should definitely be punished,' Kat chipped in. '*Halló*. I'm Kat, Chloe's best friend. Or *krutty mid* or whatever you called her that sounded mildly sexual in your accent.'

'Kat!' Chloe exclaimed, her eyes going to the young boy in their presence.

'Magnús, please get the information from Erik inside.'

Gunnar had addressed the boy and, still looking like his world was about to end, the boy headed into the building.

'Sorry,' Chloe apologised. 'Kat had strong coffee before we left the apartment and it makes her brain disconnect from her mouth.'

'Ouch,' Kat said. 'I am here you know. Sooo, you're the man who helped Chloe find a room at the inn.'

'What?' Gunnar asked.

'That was an unnecessary Christmas joke. She means you helped me find somewhere to stay,' Chloe said.

'And helped her take not too bad photos of the Northern

Lights,' Kat added. 'A miracle worker I'd say. It's nice to meet you.' She stuck out her hand.

'It is nice to meet you too,' he said, shaking her hand.

'So, when do we get going and do I have time to go to the toilet?' Kat asked.

'Yes,' Gunnar told her.

'Great! Be back asap.'

And with that Kat headed into the bus station building.

'Sorry to bother you with the phone call last night,' Chloe said. 'I should have just booked on the website and—'

'It is OK. I gave you my number for things like this,' Gunnar answered. 'And I am glad the call was not because the apartment had a problem.'

'No, everything is great and I'm really looking forward to the tour today. It sounds amazing.'

'It is amazing,' Gunnar told her. 'And the coach driver is exceptional. Five-star rating for Tripadvisor.'

Chloe laughed. 'I will be the judge of that. And Kat. She's a harder critic than me.'

'I will try not to make either of you sick.'

'Gunnar.'

It was the boy back, offering some paperwork that Gunnar rapidly took almost as rapidly as he spat out words of Icelandic that saw the boy leave again, heading towards one of the coaches.

'So, is the boy your—'

'Magnús,' Gunnar interrupted. 'Is... on work experience today. I am doing a good deed for a friend.'

'Oh, that's nice,' Chloe said. It *was* nice. 'Will he be in charge of the puking or the driving?'

Gunnar smiled. 'It takes a long time to work towards being

in charge of something, no? This is a premium trip. The trip of all trips.'

'Oh, really?' Chloe said. 'I mean that sounds like quite the promise. Does it come with some kind of money-back guarantee?'

'No,' Gunnar said. 'But, if you do not enjoy the day I will... take you to the Blue Lagoon.'

She'd read about the Blue Lagoon. It was on her visit list. But Gunnar saying it, imagining thermal springs and steam rising into the freezing air as everyone enjoyed drinks and detox face masks, was making her a little bit flustered. Was this intention on his part? An almost 'date' scenario?

'And your friend, of course,' Gunnar added.

Chloe felt her deflation but was quick to cover it up. 'Challenge accepted.'

'OK, *krúttio mitt*. I will prepare the coach now.' He smiled. 'And, just so you know, they do sell liquorice at the first place we stop.'

She smiled. 'I can't wait for this premium trip to start.'

23

ON BOARD GUNNAR'S COACH

'...you will see, if you look out to the left, that there are many horses in Iceland. These horses are unique to our country. Brought here in the ninth and tenth century by Norse settlors, they remain pure bred after more than a thousand years.'

Gunnar waited for the murmured comments of his passengers; a few he could see in the mirror were taking photos. Then he continued.

'No horses are ever imported. And if an Icelandic horse ever leaves the island, it can never, ever return.' He paused for a beat. 'I know this is what we all wished with Donald Trump but here in Iceland with the horses, there are stricter rules than in the American White House.'

The laughs arrived as always.

'So, relax and take in the views of moss-covered lava fields as we continue towards our next stop.'

Satisfied, he focussed on the driving. It was a little misty here but the sun was trying to break the clouds.

'Why am I here and not at school?'

It was Magnús from the jump seat just behind him. He had

been going to wait until lunchtime before he talked to the boy but, as Magnús had started conversation perhaps he should just roll with it.

'You were going to really go to school today?' Gunnar asked.

Silence for a time and then:

'So, my punishment is to come on the coach all day?' Magnús asked.

Gunnar thought for a moment before making his reply. 'This is not a punishment, Magnús. People on this trip have paid to be here, to see the wonderful sights of our great country.'

Magnús sighed. 'I would rather be at school. Just tell me my punishment. I can do it and then we do not have to do whatever this is.'

Gunnar sighed, eyes firmly on the road, mind wondering how this boy had as much smarts as he did. There was only one way forward. He switched on his indicator.

'Why don't you tell me why you hit a girl.'

Gunnar wasn't sure what he heard first. His voice coming over the speaker system and being broadcast to the whole coach or the gasps from his passengers.

'*Skítur!* Shit!'

He had no idea why he had translated the Icelandic into English but all his passengers had heard that too as he desperately tried to turn off the microphone and keep his eyes on the road.

'Listen, everyone! Sshh, listen very carefully!'

Gunnar looked in the rear-view mirror and could see Chloe up from her seat and standing in the centre of the aisle, voice clear, hands beckoning for attention. What was she doing?

Everything got quiet though and all eyes were on her.

'Can you hear that?' Chloe continued. 'It is the whispers of...

the *huldufólk*. The little hidden people that protect Iceland and its legacies.'

Gunnar couldn't help a small quiet laugh escaping his lips. She was using what he had told her to get him out of a fix. No one had ever done anything like that for him before.

'I don't hear anything,' an American voice drawled.

'Argh!' Chloe gasped. 'You can't say that! Because, if you are a disbeliever, who knows what will happen?' She whispered, 'To all of us.'

'I hear something,' another voice said. 'Like a light whistling.'

'Yes!' Chloe said immediately. 'That is it! The *huldufólk*!'

Gunnar clicked the microphone back on. 'And we will be hearing more about the *huldufólk* when we make our stop. So, sit back, relax and let us see if we continue to hear their almost silent whispering.'

In the mirror he saw Chloe retake her seat.

* * *

It was a coffee and comfort break before they reached *Skógafoss* waterfall and Gunnar needed both. He handed Magnús a steaming paper cup as they stood outside the service station with fantastic views the passengers were taking photos of.

'You never let me have coffee,' Magnús said, readily accepting it.

'Well, today I do,' Gunnar said. 'Do not question it.'

Magnús took a sip of his coffee.

'Listen, Magnús, I am sorry for my words coming out on the microphone for everyone to hear.'

Magnús shrugged. 'At least you did not sing. That would have been worse.'

Gunnar drank, let the silence elongate in the hope that...

'I did not hit anyone,' Magnús said.

'OK,' Gunnar replied.

'You do not believe me?'

'I want to, Magnús. But I also believed you were at school this past week.'

'I wanted to tell you but...'

'But?'

'But you are always so busy working and then Hildur fell and—'

'All I am hearing are excuses, Magnús,' Gunnar said.

But what the boy had said about him working a lot was touching a nerve. He knew that, felt responsibility for it, guilt even. And now Magnús had stopped talking, and was burying his head in his coffee. He needed to offer solutions, not still seek to blame. Moving forward from this was what was required.

'Tell me what happened,' Gunnar said.

'Which time?' Magnús asked. 'The time she cut my hair? The time her friends spat on me? Or the time she put dog shit into my locker?'

'What?' Gunnar gasped.

Magnús shrugged. 'I am the boy who should have died along with my parents.'

Gunnar didn't know what to say, but what he did know was his insides were now bubbling like the molten lava from that fateful night. 'Did this girl say that to you?'

'Not only her. But she is the leader.'

'Magnús! Why did you not tell me about this?'

'Because you always tell me to be strong. That problems are not problems unless you make them into some. That fighting does not solve things. That—'

'Stop,' Gunnar said, shaking his head. 'Do not say any more.'

He was feeling that this whole situation was almost entirely of his making. His 'parental' advice had been to hold in emotions and put up with issues? He took a breath, eyes going to the mountain peak in the distance.

'It does not matter,' Magnús said, shrugging. 'It is just how the world is.'

'No,' Gunnar replied immediately. 'If that is how the world is, then that is not how the world should continue to be.' He put a firm hand on the boy's shoulder. 'What the girl said is wrong, Magnús. You know that, right? And all the things she has done, they are wrong too.'

He shrugged again. 'I am different. And they do not like who I am.'

'And if that is true, then that is their problem, not yours,' Gunnar reassured him. 'Everyone is different in some way. If we were all the same then the world would be very boring, no?' He paused. 'Imagine if Hildur was quiet and did not express her opinions!'

A small smile appeared on Magnús's lips. 'She would not be Hildur.'

'Exactly! And you are Magnús, exactly who you are meant to be. Whatever this girl and her friends have been saying is because of their own insecurities about themselves. And it will stop. I will make it stop.' He squeezed Magnús's shoulder.

'I did not hit her, Gunnar,' Magnús said, all big eyes and seriousness. 'But I pushed her... after she kicked me.'

Gunnar gritted his teeth, feeling that pull of both empathy for what Magnús had endured all on his own without coming to him and anger that this bullying had gone on virtually undetected by the school. Their lives weren't perfect, they were unconventional but unconventional did not deserve this kind of disgusting judgement or physical and mental assault.

'I will come into the school tomorrow,' Gunnar said. 'I will speak to Mr Almr.'

'But you have to work and—'

'Magnús, some things are more important than work. No matter what I might have said before.' He sighed. 'And you must never ever think that you cannot come to me with these things. That is what I am here for. I know that I am not your father, or even a good-looking older brother, but I made a pledge to take care of you to the best of my ability.'

'Because there are no orphanages in Iceland,' Magnús stated.

'No, Magnús, that is not why,' Gunnar said. 'It is because I made two promises that night. The first was to continue looking for life until there was absolutely no hope and the second was to protect and care for whatever or whoever was left. We Icelanders are family, it does not matter what form that takes. This girl and her friends need to learn that fact.'

A few moments passed and then Magnús gave a nod.

'OK, so we are agreed,' Gunnar said. 'No more keeping secrets or telling lies to cover things up. Only honesty.'

'I think I can do that,' Magnús said. 'But can you?'

'What?' Gunnar said.

'Do I need to pretend I am here today for work experience?' Magnús asked, a glint in his eye.

Gunnar swallowed, ashamed that he had said that to Chloe and also embarrassed that Magnús had overheard him.

'You do not need to be pretend anything, Magnús,' Gunnar said. 'Except perhaps that you believe in the *huldufólk* for the duration of this trip.'

'Well, perhaps I *do* believe in the *huldufólk*.'

'My God, Hildur, she has got to you.'

24

SKÓGAFOSS WATERFALL

'Oh wow! Wow!'

Kat was shrieking over the noise of the cascading water plummeting down from the sheer rock face still a good few metres away from them. It was a thunderous roar and the spray was soaking them already, despite the distance they still were from it. It was one of the most wonderous things Chloe had ever seen and she was snapping as many photos and taking as many videos as she could get. How could Sinclairz Chairs not be impressed by this? She already had visions of getting some mulled wine and cheese to accompany the cold, wet and wild afterwards.

'It's so powerful,' Kat continued. 'Like how Christian Grey makes Anastasia Steele feel when she's whimpering in a corner.'

Chloe was not going to use that line in her event pitch. 'It's amazing,' she agreed.

'I'm going to get a bit closer,' Kat said. 'Send help if I'm not back in ten minutes in case I get sucked into it.' She laughed. 'No *Fifty Shades* pun intended there.'

Chloe snapped some photos of her friend stomping forward,

facing off with the elements and then she jumped as she realised someone was standing next to her. Gunnar.

'Your friend will get very wet,' he commented.

'Yes,' Chloe agreed.

'She does not care?'

'She's a bit crazy.'

'Like you,' Gunnar said. 'With your breaking the rules of the coach and standing in the middle of the aisle when the vehicle is in motion.'

'Is that the Icelandic way to say thank you for saving your arse?'

'My arse is grateful to you, *krúttio mitt*.' He bowed. 'The *huldufólk* are also very happy about the wonderful story you painted with words.'

'Good,' Chloe said. 'I am hoping this means I will be Icelandically blessed. Perhaps awarded an honorary pass from being cursed for doubting their existence at first.'

'I am certain this will be the case,' he agreed.

'So, I'm going to ask quietly, in front of nobody else and not on loud speaker... what is going on with your friend's son? Did he really hit a girl?'

Gunnar looked over his shoulder and ensured he could see where Magnús was standing, far enough away, looking not at the waterfall but at his phone. He turned back to Chloe. 'No. He did not.'

'That's good,' Chloe said. 'Less for your friend to sort out with the situation. You must be quite close that you know all this is going on with their family.'

Gunnar nodded. 'His father, a close friend, as I think I said. Do you not have close friends you help out?'

'Yes,' Chloe said. 'That crazy woman hellbent on getting as

close to that torrent of water as she can without being water-boarded by it.'

'So you understand,' Gunnar said. 'How important friends are. That they are as important as close family.'

'More important sometimes,' Chloe agreed.

'You have family, Chloe? Parents?'

'No,' she answered. 'My parents died. My mother when I was five. My father when I was twenty.'

'And you have no brothers or sisters?'

'No. How about you?'

'The same.'

'Which parts?'

'All of them. Except my father died first. When I was six. And my mother when I was eighteen. My father had no time to teach me anything. My mother, who had been sick her entire life, taught me everything because she knew I would need it.'

Chloe sighed. 'I don't think I've met anyone as independent as I had to be before.'

He stuck out his hand. 'It is nice to meet you, independent *krúttio mitt*.'

'You too,' Chloe answered.

She put her hand in his and the sensual jolt was like a bolt of lightning from Thor. The urge to retract was strong but the desire to keep holding was greater. Could he feel it too? As she was thinking that, he let go.

'So, you are... completely independent?' he asked, eyes meeting hers.

She swallowed. 'What do you mean?'

'I mean...' he began. 'What do I mean?' He took a breath, vulnerability seeming to get in the way of that initial bravado. 'I mean... even if you enjoy the trip today so I do not have to take you to the Blue Lagoon... would you like to go out somewhere with me some time? If you are... free.'

Her heart was pounding now and all the cold spray the waterfall was providing didn't seem to be bringing the temperature down. If you are free. Was he asking her on a date? She didn't date. It was too difficult and the end result was always going to be the same. Heartache.

'Gosh! I'm soaking! Look at me!'

Chloe was prevented from answering as Kat arrived back, hair dripping wet, water droplets snaking down her face, coat saturated.

'It looks like you turned into the waterfall,' Gunnar said. 'Bravo.' He smiled at them both, professionalism back in place. 'Remember, be back at the coach at half-past.'

And before Chloe could say anything else, Gunnar was walking away.

25

REYNISFJARA BLACK SAND BEACH

This place was somehow a perfect combination of beautiful, wild and rugged. From the black sand on the ground to the towering basalt columns and the sea stacks set against a bright blue sky it was a winter postcard waiting to be admired. And admired it was being, by all the passengers on the south coast tour being noisy, taking videos and getting much too close to the white ferocious froth Gunnar had warned them about. Chloe wondered what it would be like here completely alone, just her and the elements, hearing only the waves and the birds overhead. Then she contemplated how the Sinclairz Chairs group would fit here. Black volcanic sand did not mix with anything pale and she remembered Lincoln Sinclair was very much a cream chinos and Ralph Lauren kind of man...

'What do you think, Kat?' Chloe asked. 'What could I do here for Sinclairz Chairs if we do cheese and mulled wine at the waterfall?'

'Chocolate fondue,' Kat said immediately, picking up a pebble from the beach. 'Or, stack up mini cakes that look like those columns by the cave. Everyone loves cake. Ooo, how about Christmas cake?'

It was too much food and not enough pizzaz. If she was going to convince Michelle that she was partnership material then she needed something as dramatic as this backdrop. Fire.

'What about some dancers doing a traditional dance with fire?' Chloe suggested.

'Oh… fire dancing… oh, I don't know about that,' Kat said, words seeming to get all caught up with each other. She dropped the pebble again.

'Really? Because Iceland is all about fire and ice because of the landscape – the glaciers and the volcanos and—'

'I just, you know, fire dancing, it threw me for a minute. Ignore me.'

Kat was beaming now. Too much overplaying of happiness. And Chloe was suspicious.

'Kat, what's going on? You're hiding something from me.'

'No. No, I'm really not.'

Chloe didn't need to say anything else, she let her expression and the folding of her arms do the talking.

'Ugh! Why did you have to mention fire dancing? I mean, literally anything else and it would have been OK.' She huffed an irritated sigh and let her feet sink into the black sand.

'Whatever it is, just tell me because I can't think of anything you could tell me that is going to ruin this wonderful trip,' Chloe said with utter confidence.

'You mustn't let it, Chloe, OK?'

Now Kat wasn't sounding like whatever she was about to say was not a trivial annoyance at all. She was sounding serious. Chloe pushed her hair back behind her ears and braced externally against the wind and internally for whatever was coming next.

'Just, whatever it is, tell me,' Chloe said.

'OK,' Kat said, taking a big breath. 'So, it's Michael.'

Chloe's heart dropped like it was a boulder being hurled off the top of the cliff they were standing under. 'He's not... died has he?'

'No,' Kat said. 'Not yet.'

'What?!'

'He would if I got my hands on him.'

'Kat, for God's sake! Tell me!'

'You were right, you know. Absolutely right.' She took a deep breath and then blurted it out. 'Michael has a new girlfriend.'

Chloe let that sentence settle, first on the surface and then, after a few milliseconds, she let it creep inside, waited for her mind and her heart to process it. It was fine. It was to be expected. She had expected it. Why wouldn't he have moved on? What else was there to do? Except maybe dwell and be too scared to move on like her...

'OK,' she said in a tone that definitely gave away that she was, in some way, moved by the news. She hated that.

'OK?' Kat clarified, giving Chloe the large eyes seeking confirmation she thought might be detected better if the eyes were made bigger.

'I mean, yes, it's been a while, like I said and—'

'And... Chloe...'

'What?' Chloe asked, heart racing suddenly.

'I'm just going to say it.'

'OK.'

Kat gripped her arm and held on tight. 'She's pregnant.'

And that moment was the moment she realised that it felt like it wasn't just her feet sinking into the black sand, it felt like it was her entire being. Pregnant. Michael had a girlfriend. And Michael's girlfriend was pregnant.

'That's why I'm here, Chloe,' Kat carried on, still holding her. 'It's not because I was stressed about my mother coming for Christmas or whatever else I told you about being disorganised. As soon as I saw the post I prayed you weren't still stalking his social media and I booked a flight and I came so that I could be the one to tell you.'

Pregnant.

'And I know that telling you on a black sand beach surrounded by frankly very annoying fellow coach trip passengers isn't the best thing, but when you said about fire dancing, well, I had to tell you.' Kat took a breath. 'Because that's where they were when they made the grand Instagram announcement. On some beach in Bali with a blazing arch and a fiery flash mob like it was a weird over-produced Addison Rae video.'

Pregnant.

Run.

26

Chloe's heart was pumping hard and her head felt like it might burst as the pressure of a million thoughts all pushed against her skull. She was running up the black sand, boots and the terrain making it heavy work, but she was determined to get as far away from Kat and this revelation as was possible in this moment. Except being utterly determined and focussed about escape was counterintuitive when it came to practicalities. She found herself not caring about her foot placements on the steps upwards, adrenaline surging, hurt powering through her.

'Chloe, you need to slow down.'

A voice. Her subconscious. Telling her what to do. She was absolutely not listening to reason right now.

She stepped faster, feet slipping as she tried two steps at once.

'Chloe, stop.'

It was then she realised it wasn't a voice in her head, it was real. Gunnar.

'Not stopping,' she replied, her breath catching as she carried on rushing up the incline.

'You will stop,' came the reply. 'Because you are not reading the signs that say caution is needed. Because the stone is wet. Because you are on my tour.'

'I don't care about any of those things. Leave me alone.'

She was furious. With Michael. With the world. With herself for letting this news hit her so hard. And then she came to a very abrupt halt. It was like walking straight into a mountain. A mountain with arms that were forcefully holding her in place. She tried to move, wriggle, just breathe, but nothing was working.

'Everything is OK,' Gunnar said, the timbre of his voice low, vibrating through her.

She went to speak, opened her mouth but nothing was coming out. Instead she found herself struggling to breathe, emotion clawing.

'Do not cry.'

It took the words to make her realise that she was actually crying. How could she be crying and not know? What was happening here?

'Be still. For a moment,' Gunnar continued, holding tight.

Be still. Think. Don't think.

It took a few moments before her heart stopped racing and her mind started fighting with the emotional response and winning. She took a deep breath in, solidified her stance, let the chill breeze hit her cheeks.

'OK?' he asked, loosening his hold just a little.

'Yes.' She wasn't. But she was better.

'OK, so, you need to lean forward now,' he said.

'What?' She went to move and then she rocked on her heels.

'Slowly, Chloe.' His hand was at her back fast.

It was then she realised just how close to the edge of the path she was, only a short distance away from the steepest drop.

Then she shook and he didn't wait a second longer, he pulled her towards him harder.

'Breathe,' he ordered. 'Look at me.'

She took a deep breath, and met his intense eyes.

'You want to talk about it?' he asked her, his words more of a whisper of a suggestion. Supportive, encouraging, yet unpressured.

'No,' she answered, shaking her head.

He nodded, accepting. 'You are OK, *krúttio mitt*. Safe now.'

Safe. Mind over heart. Focus.

'I know,' she answered with as much determination as she could muster.

'Good,' he said. 'Very good.'

And still he was holding her... until...

'So, slowly up the steps, yes?' He let go. 'I have to make sure everyone is leaving now so we are on time for the next stop.'

'OK,' she answered. 'Good.'

He nodded. 'Good.'

Without saying anything else she watched him start to make his way back down the incline.

27

SÓLHEIMAJÖKULL GLACIER

If there was one place on his island that helped put life into perspective, it was here at that glacier. Gunnar looked out over the lake at its base, admiring the almost surreal-looking ice formations sadly retreating from what they once were. Yet the view was still as captivating to him now as it had been on his very first visit here with his mother. They had brought a picnic and she had likened the changes of this landscape to life itself. *It seems so immovable, Gunnar, yet it is always moving in some way. Never forget that.* No truer words had ever been spoken.

'Some people are going behind the barrier,' Magnús remarked, pointing.

'Yes,' Gunnar answered. 'They always do. They want the best photographs. The closest they can get.'

'And if they fall into the water?' Magnús asked.

'We will have more room on the coach. You can stretch out, have a sleep while I drive back.'

Magnús raised his eyes.

'I am joking, Magnús. I will rescue them, of course.'

'But, what if you get hurt doing that?' Magnús asked. 'Because they did not follow the rules?'

Gunnar sensed the boy's unease. Just like that, the passengers ducking under the ropes and standing at the edge of the water, he was thinking about his parents and the fight for their survival they did not win.

He put a hand on Magnús's shoulder. 'Magnús, nothing is going to happen to me, OK?'

Magnús shirked off his hand and dropped his head a little like he was embarrassed to confess some kind of fear. Gunnar remembered being his age, how he was stuck in that midway point between childhood and adolescence, not quite being oblivious to the struggles of life but still too young to grasp the full reality of them. Yet, like Magnús, loss had struck too early, meaning that growing up had increased in pace compared to his peers. Gunnar remembered wondering if his life would ever go back to being on the same base level as his friends one day, or if he would forever remain branded by tragedy. That one night when he was six, his mother and the police turning up at school when he was in the Christmas show...

He pointed out at the ice. 'Look, life is like the glacier, Magnús. On the surface, it looks the same, it behaves the same, people come to look and they see what they see. But underneath we know that many changes are happening, changes that we cannot always detect until more time has gone by and other things react to those alterations. Like the climate because of the glacier.'

Magnús sighed. 'I am not a glacier. And school is not the climate.'

'No,' Gunnar agreed. 'Life is the glacier, Magnús, and sometimes we have to change how we view it to protect it. Because it is precious and it is ours and we only get one chance.' He looked at the boy. 'You understand?'

'Not really,' Magnús answered. 'Because it took away my parents.'

'I think,' Gunnar began. 'That when faced with a difficult decision, your parents gave up their chance for their choice.' He put his hand on the boy's shoulder again. 'They chose to protect you.'

He swallowed as memories of that night flooded his mind like the lava had flooded fields, roads, engulfing everything in its path. It had been a reminder of how powerful nature was, how Iceland was governed by that force every single day and had to live alongside such ferocity mixing with all its contrasting beauty.

'Do you think,' Magnús began, 'that they made the right choice?'

The boy's large eyes found his then and Gunnar's heart ached for him and everything he had been through. He squeezed his shoulder tight. 'Yes, Magnús, of course.'

'Even though I have been avoiding school and telling lies and... hid Hildur's knitting needles last year.'

Gunnar shook his head. 'Magnús.'

'What?'

'Your parents would be so proud of you. Look how you have grown! On the hockey team! Doing OK with your maths! Trying to deal with problems independently...'

'I want to be better,' Magnús told him. 'I should be better.' He paused before continuing. 'Because they gave up everything for me.'

'Magnús, your mum and dad would not want you to feel a responsibility for being anything other than exactly who you are. There is no pressure to... go into government or... be the next Alex Ovechkin. They gave you the gift of more time. For you. To just be. That's it. That's all they wanted.'

Magnús nodded. 'OK.'

'OK?'

He nodded again. 'So now you can tell me why you talk funny when you're with the English girl.'

Gunnar's gaze immediately went to Chloe, standing with Kat a few metres ahead of them. 'Well,' he began. 'I am still trying to fully understand that myself.'

28

'This view,' Kat said, phone snapping more photos. 'It's incredible. And I feel like we should all be whispering here. It's like the land that time forgot.'

Chloe knew exactly what Kat meant but it was difficult to think about anything more than what Gunnar had told them on the walk to this spot. Glaciers covered around 11 per cent of Iceland; they were ever-moving, creating different formations and even spectacular ice caves, but the environment was changing here, global warming taking a toll. The vastness of the landscape and the enormity of the worldwide problem did put things into perspective though.

'It's grounding,' Chloe answered. 'Definitely.'

'Aww, Chlo,' Kat said, sliding an arm around Chloe's shoulders. 'How are you feeling now?'

How was she feeling after silently weeping her eyes out on the coach trying to keep a fixed I'm-focussed-on-the-tour-guide's-highly-interesting-ancedotes-and-historical-info expression on her face for the past hour? Exhausted. Demotivated. Inadequate. So she said...

'I'm OK.' She added a nod.

'OK,' Kat said. 'I know that's not true but, you know, that's why I'm here, that's why I came.'

'I know,' Chloe said. 'But, you didn't have to do that.'

In fact, hearing the news when she got back to England after what would hopefully be a successful trip here researching the Sinclairz Chairs event, in the comfort of her own place, with her own time and space to process, would have been a whole lot better. But she knew Kat had acted with the very best of intentions.

'Chlo, I didn't want you to see that. You know, just be on Instagram one day innocently sending me reels about being kidnapped by hot men in leather and then bam there's all this fire and a baby belly in a bikini and pink smoke.'

'It's a girl,' Chloe stated like it made any difference whatsoever.

'It doesn't matter,' Kat said quickly. 'Because it's bound to have Michael's chin, yes?'

'I don't—'

'And it will inherit Michael's passion for Liverpool football club and no one wants that, Chlo.'

'I guess, but—'

'I mean, you've had a lucky escape with all this, honestly,' Kat rattled on. 'And he ate Wotsits like a savage. Licking his fingers, all that orange dust everywhere and—'

'OK, I get it,' Chloe interrupted. 'Let's just enjoy the peace of this place.'

She closed her eyes and took a deep breath in, grounding her boots into the cold, frosted ground and looking out over the lake. None of this was really about Michael or Michael's girlfriend or Michael and his girlfriend's baby. It was about her. She was the one who could never bear a child. She was the odd one out. Although, statistically, she was one of every eight women in the UK struggling with some kind of fertility issue. It didn't make it any easier to know it was a significant problem. Nothing had changed. She opened her eyes, looked out at the ice mounds. Michael was always going to move on. Michael had always had some kind of timer going on his life with set benchmarks to hit. Marriage wasn't important to him, but children were something he had talked about almost from the moment they had started dating. He was just following his path. And that's what she needed to do. That's what she had been doing. Was she really going to let some kind of social media showing-off announcement from her ex undermine everything she had worked so hard to achieve? She had her work. She was here in Iceland on the cusp of getting the promotion of all promotions. Everything was good. No, everything was great. And she needed to embrace it.

'I think Gunnar asked me out,' Chloe said, breaking the silence.

'What?' Kat exclaimed.

She nodded. 'Except I didn't really know what to say and then you came back from the waterfall.'

Kat inhaled, putting her hands to her face. 'Did I bloody ruin it? Why didn't you push me back into the water?'

Chloe smiled. 'I would never do that.'

'If I'd have known I would have pushed myself back into the water. So, you managed to say "yes", right? Before your annoying friend turned up and gate-crashed.'

'No.'

'What? You said "no"?'

'No. And now—'

'You said "and now"? I hope you didn't follow that up with "the end is near".'

'I should have said something,' Chloe said.

'You should have said yes. That is absolutely the only response.'

Chloe shuddered and she knew it wasn't from the cold. It was from feeling that somehow, next to this glacier, Michael's baby news felt like the tip of her personal iceberg, the push she needed to discover what could be beyond the wreckage of that old relationship...

'Should I... say something to him?' Chloe wanted to know. 'Suggest something?'

'Yes!' Kat said. 'Where's that itinerary you've been curating that could fix Sinclairz Chairs up for a whole fortnight here instead of a couple of days?'

Kat began patting her down like she might be carrying actual ancient scrolls of parchment rather than most of it being on her notes app.

'Stop,' she said in a whisper. 'But I was thinking, something casual, just a coffee or—'

'Oh, no, no, no, absolutely not. You have to have an activity!'

'What? Why?'

'Because there is nothing less casual than a "casual" cup of coffee,' Kat continued. 'Think about all the "casual" coffee dates you've been on and tell me I'm wrong.'

Chloe really hadn't got that much experience but she didn't need to recall at all as Kat was already ploughing on...

'You need a date with substance. You don't even need to call it a date but there definitely needs to be activity. Otherwise you're there stirring sugar you don't want into an Americano you also don't want, wondering what small talk is going to see you through until you get to the end of the date and the will-we-won't-we kissing crunch down.'

Now there was so much spinning through Chloe's mind she

was beginning to wonder why she had mentioned it or whether it was really a good idea to go from hearing Michael's news to jumping into a new situation...

'Itinerary!' Kat demanded. 'Where is it?' She wiggled her fingers like she was about to turn into Mr Tickle from *Mr Men*.

'It's on my notes app.'

'Good,' Kat said. 'So share it with me and I will have a suggested evening's activity shaped up in no time.'

It didn't seem like Chloe had given herself any other choice.

29

SELJALANDSFOSS WATERFALL

'...now remember that the staircase is wet. You should take care. And if you want a photograph through the waterfall you must also be careful because the rocks are...' Gunnar stopped talking as most of his passengers raced off to start up the incline. 'I do not know why I give the warnings. As soon as I tell people the waterfall appeared in a Justin Bieber music video they are already getting ready to run.'

'Did it really?' Kat piped up. 'I thought you were lying about that to get the two teenagers to stop yawning.'

'No,' Gunnar said. 'I do not tell lies as part of the trip.'

He swallowed. Except recounting folk tales about the *huldufólk*. Except telling Chloe that Magnús was his friend's son on work experience.

'Can you really walk behind the waterfall?' Chloe asked him.

'Yes. Again, not a lie.'

'Good. So, what are we waiting for?' Kat asked. 'We don't have to run, but I don't want to get in a queue for a photo and find we have to leg it back to the coach before I've got my turn.'

'Magnús, do you want to lead the way?' Gunnar suggested.

'OK,' Magnús agreed, stepping forward.

'Great,' Kat said. 'A fit young man to catch me if I fall.'

'You will not fall if I am leading the way,' Magnús stated.

'I like your confidence,' Kat answered. 'I have less confidence in my shoes however.'

'Magnús,' Gunnar called. 'The tourist way. Not the other way.'

The boy raised his hand in acknowledgement and headed off with Kat at his heels.

'Now I'm intrigued that there are two ways to get to this waterfall,' Chloe remarked. 'What does "the other way" involve?'

'Peril,' Gunnar answered straight away. 'The chance of death. Exactly like when you were running too fast up from the black sand beach.'

'O-K,' Chloe said.

'Sorry,' he said quickly. 'I didn't mean to bring that up.'

'Exactly what the passenger called Richard said when we had that impromptu stop half an hour ago.'

She had ridden over any awkwardness about the situation with humour. He was an idiot for mentioning her running up the steps at *Reynisfjara*. Because it hadn't just been about her taking risks with her speed and her foot placements, it had been about him rushing to her rescue, holding her still before she fell. Close. Too close? Except his sense of sense had told him she was not going to stop even if falling from the cliff was the outcome. He had had to be there.

'I did warn you about the likelihood of sickness on this trip,' he said. 'It is a long day of travel but, the spectacular sights are worth it, no?'

'Oh, definitely,' Chloe agreed with a nod. 'And I think some of them would work for the event I'm organising but, you know, there are other places I need to go and different activities to try out.'

'Yes,' he agreed as they walked. 'So, do you have a shortlist?'

'It's actually a pretty long list.'

He laughed. 'OK.'

'But, I was wondering, if you might have time to... do a couple of the things with me.'

'Oh.'

His heart was racing now, speeding away like someone had attached it to a F1 car flat out from the starting grid. He had put a tentative suggestion of something out there not really expecting anything to come of it and now she was moving with it? Was she? Shit. He had only said one word and it hadn't been 'yes'.

'Sorry,' Gunnar said quickly. 'I mean... what did you have in mind?'

He internally cursed himself for sounding more LinkedIn than Hinge. He needed to work on his rizz. If that's where this was going...

'It's OK, you know, if you don't have time I—'

'No,' he said fast. 'No, tell me your ideas.'

They had reached the foot of the stairs now, could hear the powerful rushing of the water as it came over the cliff.

'Well, I definitely want to try the dog sledding. I think it sounds like something my clients would enjoy.'

'OK,' Gunnar answered.

'You have done that before?'

'Not the way you mean,' he said, putting his hands into the pockets of his coat. 'When I was a kid, myself and my friends, we would try to get the neighbours' dogs to take our go-karts for a ride. We had mixed results. But, dog sledding, the real tours, they are very popular here.'

'So, shall we do it? I mean, it sounds like you have experience in the core concept and Kat, you know, she is not so good with dogs.'

'Really?' he asked.

'Allergic actually,' Chloe added.

'Oh, wow,' Gunnar said, watching her cheeks pink. 'Then it does sound like you need my help.'

'I mean, yes, but I understand that you're busy with work and—'

'Maybe tomorrow evening?' Gunnar suggested. 'After seven? I could pick you up.'

'OK,' Chloe said. 'It sounds like a plan.'

It sounded like a date. And that both scared and excited him at the same time. If it hadn't been for the waterfall mist hitting his cheeks there would definitely be heat there.

'OK, good, *krúttio mitt*. So, let us go to the waterfall now. See how the sunset begins to look.'

And, as he stepped onto the first stair there was something fizzing inside him that suggested he more than liked the idea of dog sledding with the 'except'.

30

KAFFI LOKI

'Don't look at it,' Kat ordered, making a snatch for Chloe's phone across the table at this traditional eatery they were nestled in, not too far away from their apartment.

It was almost nine in the evening now, the south coast tour concluded, everyone tired from the trip but their camera rolls bursting with videos and pictures and Gunnar's tip tray full when she and Kat had disembarked the coach. But now the high of the ending to the tour – a sunset view through the tumbling water of the waterfall – had depleted, Chloe was on Instagram seeing Michael's baby news for herself. And somehow Kat knew exactly what she was looking at.

'It's OK,' Chloe said, sighing. 'I actually don't feel as bad about seeing it as I thought I would.'

'No?'

'No. I mean, yes, seeing him with someone pregnant is a bit weird when we tried for so long to achieve that but, it wasn't meant to be for us.'

For you. It will never be for you. Chloe took a sip of her

water. It was her with the infertility issue, not Michael. She couldn't expect him to abstain from having a family with someone else just to what? Save her feelings? She had had her moment where she had let it soak into her at the black sand beach. Anger. Sadness. Disappointment. Gunnar had saved her from falling headfirst down a ravine. It was time to pick herself back up again.

'Good,' Kat said. 'Because I know, despite what you've been saying. Or, rather, what you haven't been saying, that Michelle's pregnancy hasn't been easy either.'

'That's different,' Chloe answered quickly, picking up a piece of her rye bread with herring.

'Why?'

'Because Michelle's pregnancy is like managing a West End production. It's making sure the right people have the correct roles and that all the props are in place and everything is running to schedule.'

That was exactly how she had dealt with it. It was an event, no different to any of the events the company planned. The only thing that set it apart was the grand finale was going to be a brand new human not fireworks or a huge five-tier cake.

'Good! So we are free from babies now to enjoy this feast of sheep head jelly and fermented shark, yes?'

'Absolutely,' Chloe agreed. 'And I think Sinclairz Chairs would like this traditional menu.'

'It's very cosy here,' Kat agreed. 'And the Christmas decorations are all sparkly and cutesy.' She jammed a piece of bread into her mouth. 'So, did you book the dog sledding yet?'

'I did,' Chloe said. 'Eight o'clock tomorrow night.'

But she was already feeling nervous about it. She wanted to get to know Gunnar better, but should she want to? She was only here for a very limited time. Where was it really going to go?

'I can see your mind working overtime and that needs to stop,' Kat said sternly. 'It doesn't have to be anything serious. It doesn't have to even mean anything. It can just be fun, you know.'

The concept of fun and light and not overthinking sounded good, possibly great, given that she was super busy in the midst of this vital organisational period for the biggest gig of her life. However, the way Kat was selling it almost made Chloe feel that 'fun' and 'nothing serious' was all she could ever aim for. Or was that just her reading too much into things? She took a bite of the mashed fish.

'I mean, let's not forget that the fun stuff, the sexy stuff, the stuff that you get excited about all happens at the beginning of any relationship.' Kat ate more bread then recommenced talking through chews. 'After that's worn off it's trips to Ikea and the gastronomic delights of an extortionately priced pie at a pub that states Marco Pierre White once walked past. No one really wants that. That's why I don't date any more.'

Chloe crunched her face up. 'What do you mean? You have Stephen.'

Kat laughed. 'Stephen and I are friends with benefits. I keep telling you that and you keep forgetting.'

'I don't forget you said that, I just know he has clothes in your wardrobe and he keeps a toothbrush in your bathroom.'

'Because sometimes he stays over.'

'Which is kind of a relationship? I mean, he's the only person that stays over, right?'

'For now,' Kat said, eating some bean salad.

'It's been that way ever since we've known each other.'

Kat shrugged. 'We don't need to put a label on it.'

'And he feels the same?'

'He knows how I feel. Anyway, this conversation isn't about me, it's about you and your new Icelandic hook up.'

Hook up. Was that what it was going to be? Was that what she wanted? Needed?

'So, what do you know about him already?' Kat asked.

What did she know about Gunnar? 'Well, he's an orphan, like me.'

'Things in common! Great! Not that you necessarily need things in common to have an amazing time with someone.'

'No, but, well, it's good to be able to talk with guys about mutual interests.'

'So do you have any? Mutual interests? Apart from eye contact and sexual chemistry?'

She didn't know. She barely knew anything about him. She'd only just met him. She didn't know what music he liked or his favourite colour.

'OK,' Kat said, leaning forward. 'Your eyes are glazing over now. It doesn't matter what you know or don't know. It's new. And that's what dating is all about. The finding out. And you can find out when you're dog sledding.'

Chloe nodded but the conviction that this was at all a good idea was fast fading. And then her phone rang. She saw immediately from the display that it was Michelle.

'Of course it's Michelle, late in the evening when we're having a nice meal,' Kat said, tutting as she got up. 'Just going to the loo.'

Chloe didn't hesitate to answer the call. She was hoping her boss was going to give her some feedback or pointers on the two varying proposals she'd briefly emailed.

'Hello, Michelle. Is everything—'

'Hello, Chloe, I don't have long, but this is very exciting and very important and I want you to rearrange anything you might have arranged already, yes?'

There was only one response Chloe could give. 'Er, yes, OK. What—'

'So, tomorrow one of Lincoln's trusted account managers is going to be in Iceland! Actually in Reykjavik! But only for twenty-four hours and they are going to make some time to meet with you and give their suggestions for the celebration event.'

'O-K,' Chloe said slowly.

It wasn't OK. It didn't feel OK for a few reasons. Why was Michelle needing someone from Sinclairz Chairs to meet with Chloe to make suggestions? Was this person an event planner like she was? Why didn't Michelle trust her competence and skill set? What was with this third-party interference they'd never had before? And they were still only pitching for the job; nothing was confirmed, was it?

'I mean this is amazing, right? Lincoln must be almost absolutely certain he's going to go with us for this event if he wants one of his people to meet with one of my people.'

It didn't feel amazing to Chloe, it felt like someone was needing to oversee her, as if her boss didn't trust her to make these calls. Yes, she had sent Michelle some ideas, asked for a little more detail on whether she should go down the traditional themes route or the high-end festive cocktails being sipped by a steaming thermal spa way, but other than that she was in charge of this, she needed to be in charge of this. And she should spell that out to Michelle.

'Michelle, I mean, it's great that Sinclairz Chairs want to have input from the beginning but that's not usually how we work,' Chloe began. 'I've put together two very loose suggestions for itineraries for events and I just wanted to get your take on—'

'I'll be honest. I haven't had a chance to look at anything you've sent me, Chloe. Because I'm having a baby.'

The last sentence was said like this was akin to captaining a space craft into uncharted galaxies with no other crew and the threat of alien life forms ready to start a battle over a black hole or three. Michelle had always demanded that it was business as usual but now it was a company gamechanger that was going to alter the way they worked.

There was only one way to handle Michelle when she was like this. Flattery.

'I know that,' Chloe said. 'Of course I know that and you are doing such an incredible job of seamlessly growing the next Baroness Brady and handling everything that—'

'So, you're going to meet her and be really nice to her, Chloe, because she's going to be reporting back to Lincoln and I can't tell you how much I want this job.'

Be really nice to her, Chloe. When wasn't she nice? When did she start needing to be told how to behave in business? Her hackles were really starting to raise now.

'I know, Michelle,' Chloe said firmly. 'I want this job too. That's why I dropped everything to fly to—'

'So, bend the expenses account just a little and, as I said, be really nice.'

If she heard the words 'really nice' once more she might vomit. She looked at the glittery angel at the top of the Christmas tree channelling inner peace then opened her mouth to say something but Michelle beat her to it.

'And the fact you speak her language will be the icing on the cake that not even Dress Code will be able to compete with.'

'Her language?' Now there was a lump in Chloe's throat. She

meant the language of business, right? Two people invested in making this event for Sinclairz Chairs the best it could possibly be. Except dread was suddenly drowning her on the inside.

'Icelandic, silly! She's originally from Iceland. And her name is Kirstin.'

Chloe slapped a hand to her mouth to stop the fermented shark escaping.

31

Hildur had cooked again and Gunnar knew he should tell her that keeping off her foot was more important right now than preparing dinner, but for two reasons he said nothing. The first was because Hildur generally never listened to anything that contradicted what she wanted to do. And the second reason was because the *plokkfiskur* – fish stew – was absolutely delicious.

'Is there more?' Magnús asked, eyes wide.

'Magnús,' Hildur said, humour in her tone. 'When I cook there is always more, no?'

Before anything further could be said the boy was up from the table and heading towards the pot on the countertop in the kitchen area.

'The trip was good today?'

Hildur had lowered her voice to ask the question even though Magnús was so busy spooning extra food onto his plate he was oblivious to anything else.

'Yes,' Gunnar answered. 'The weather was not too cold and everyone enjoyed themselves.'

'And the "except"? Did she enjoy herself?'

'Her name is Chloe,' Gunnar reminded her. 'And yes. But the tour is good. Icelandic views are unmatched. There are never any bad reviews about the scenery.'

But, despite Chloe brushing over whatever had happened to her on the black sand beach, he hadn't forgotten how close she had come to falling off that ridge. He had kept calm, like he always tried to, made it seem like nothing, but it hadn't been. He wondered if she would ever tell him what she had been thinking about in that moment…

'And Magnús? Did you manage to speak to him about school?'

Gunnar's eyes went to the boy, piling up food, oblivious to their conversation. He nodded. 'Yes.'

'And?'

'And I will be going to see his teacher tomorrow. I need to make sure that they know the full story and that at the very beginnings of any issues with Magnús they make me aware.'

'Very good,' Hildur said, nodding.

'What is very good?' Magnús asked, sliding back into his seat with a steaming plate of food. 'The fish stew? Or the way Gunnar did not tell you he has a date tomorrow night?'

'What?' both Hildur and Gunnar exclaimed at the very same time.

Gunnar was quick to recover sense and follow the one word up. 'I do not know what you mean. I am simply meeting with Chloe to investigate something for her work. She organises events.'

'Hmm,' Hildur said, a suspicious smile on her face. 'So you will be taking your computer with you?'

'What? No,' Gunnar said. 'She has a computer and—'

'And the kind of "investigations" do not need you to work your fingers.' She gasped. 'With the keyboard at least.'

'Hildur!' Gunnar said warningly, eyes darting to the impressionable boy he was responsible for.

'She seems nice,' Magnús said, gravy falling from his overladen fork.

'Does she?' Hildur asked. 'Tell me more of what she is like. Or maybe, after your "investigations" you can invite her for dinner. I can cook and—'

'No,' Gunnar said firmly as he felt this conversation was getting out of his control. 'No one is coming to dinner and you will not do any more of the cooking while your foot is still broken.'

He knew he shouldn't have raised his voice and both Hildur and Magnús were looking at him like he was scolding them both. He hadn't meant it to come across that way, but he also didn't like the weight Hildur seemed to be putting on his getting to know Chloe.

'My foot,' Hildur said soberly, 'is my foot and I have been taking care of that, and the rest of the things that belong to me, for many many years.' She wriggled in her seat like she was about to get up.

'Hildur, I am—'

'Hildur,' Magnús interrupted. 'Tonight would you like me to get the boxes of Christmas decorations for you to look through? We can decide what to get out for this year and which pieces can go on the tree when Gunnar gets it down.'

He had to marvel at how switched on Magnús was. If there was one thing guaranteed to get Hildur to forget about anything it was the thought of her fingers travelling through the decorations of yesteryear and telling them all the stories of when she was a child.

'I think,' Hildur began, sitting still, 'that you are saying all this to make a distraction.'

OK. That had not worked.

'But,' Hildur continued. 'I am happy to let the conversation change, for now, and indulge in reliving the stories of when I was a child and we made our own festive decorations from wood. If that is what you would both like.'

Gunnar and Magnús exchanged a glance between them. Camaraderie in this moment.

'What I would like is for Brigitta Lundgren's hair to fall out and her face to be covered in spots,' Magnús admitted.

'Magnús!' Gunnar exclaimed.

Hildur paused before replying. 'There is a spell I can teach you for that.'

'Hildur!' Gunnar admonished.

'What? If you do not believe in the art of the mystical then it should not matter to you because you will not think that it can work.' Hildur held a finger in the air. 'Or perhaps I should see if there is a spell for romance?'

Gunnar stood then, pushing back his chair. 'That will not be necessary.' He picked up his bowl.

'Ah! Such confidence! This is good,' Hildur said with a smile and a wink at Magnús.

Gunnar took his bowl to the kitchen sink and looked through the window, out into the cold, dark night speckled with stars. When had his life started to feel chaotic? When had order and calm been replaced by feeling like he was plate-spinning 24/7?

'You know,' Magnús said, bringing his now empty bowl to the kitchen area. 'You could ask Chloe if she wants to come to my Christmas show. I mean, I know I have not been at the last few rehearsals, but I have been working on my lines and my dancing and it is traditional, right? It might help with her work.'

Gunnar turned around and smiled at the boy. 'I am sure

Chloe would like that, Magnús but I do not know how long she stays in Iceland.'

'Then ask,' Magnús said, his eyes locking on Gunnar's. 'Like with my parents. Maybe you need to make your choice.'

Gunnar swallowed, the poignancy hitting him firmly in the chest.

He nodded. 'OK, Magnús, I will ask.'

32

THE ICELAND PHALLOGICAL MUSEUM, REYKJAVIK

It was the next morning and Kat was laughing. 'I'm sorry,' she said. 'This is one of the funniest places I've ever been.'

'Yes,' Chloe responded.

She still wasn't sure why she had agreed to come to the world's only penis museum, only that she had hoped Kat would be distracted and not ask questions as to why she was attempting to do a crash course in Icelandic on her phone.

'What makes someone want to collect these?' Kat continued. 'Because perhaps I shouldn't have been so eager to delete those penis pics I accumulated. I might have been able to call them art and sell them somewhere like this.'

'Yes,' Chloe said.

How did you say 'yes' in Icelandic again? Já. That was one basic word nailed. But you couldn't have conversation with one word alone when you were pretending to be somewhere close to fluent.

'So, which one is your favourite? One of the whales? Or the polar bear?' Kat asked.

'Yes.'

'Chloe!'

'What?'

'It was your idea to come here and it's really weird but oddly entertaining and you aren't paying attention!'

She looked up at her friend, full scrutiny being paid to her now. It was a mistake not to share this information with her best friend. It couldn't get any worse by telling her. Kat would only try to help.

'It's not the penises,' Chloe admitted. 'Although I stand by the idea that this is probably not something to add to the suggested itinerary for Sinclairz Chairs.'

'Is it still the Michael thing because—'

'No,' Chloe said. 'It's the fact the Icelandic language thing is coming back to haunt me.' She felt her chest tighten. It was like all her hopes and dreams for a slice of the company pie were resting on her rib cage, weighing down.

'What's happened?' Kat asked as they made their way towards the café part of the building. 'Is this why you were so quiet after dinner last night?'

Chloe sighed, putting a hand to her chest. 'Michelle has arranged for me to meet someone who she described as something like a trusted advisor of Lincoln Sinclair.'

'O-K.'

'And it's today. It would be now, but I changed the time so I could think... and practice.'

'Spit it out,' Kat demanded. 'Like every person wanted to do when they were faced with the when-they-were-warm penises in this museum!'

'The trusted advisor is Icelandic!' Chloe blurted out. 'And she is expecting me to discuss the celebration event in my fluent Icelandic that I am not fluent in because I lied to Michelle from the very first day I met her, before I met her actually, on email when I attached the CV you made me embellish!'

'Calm down,' Kat said as all eyes belonging to the other people in the café turned to them. 'It's not as bad as you think.'

'It is! No, you're right! It isn't as bad as I think! It's worse!' And she really really didn't want to be losing control in the middle of a museum of dicks.

'Breathe, there's a perfectly simple solution to this,' Kat said, holding her shoulders.

'I can pass A-level Icelandic before I meet her?'

'No, you have someone who speaks Icelandic who can help you. Gunnar.'

It wasn't that she hadn't thought of that. It had been one of her first ideas because she was a natural problem-solver. But she had disregarded it. Because she needed to not rely on someone else to get her out of the hole she had dug that she never in a million years expected to fall into.

She shook her head, pulling a chair out and sitting down at a table. 'I can't ask Gunnar for help.'

'Why not?' Kat asked, sitting too.

'Because we're going out tonight and I'm already nervous about it and all I've done since I arrived here is need his help and I'm not that kind of person.'

'A person who needs help isn't some kind of second-class citizen. It's normal.'

'I don't like it,' Chloe said, still head-shaking. 'It means depending on someone and them knowing that you're depending on them and...'

'And?'

What was she going to follow that up with? Her mind was offering her the answer but voicing that wasn't going to help anyone.

'And the last person you depended on ran away when the going got tough and announced his virility with someone else in an obnoxious Instagram post.' It seemed that Kat had filled in the blanks herself.

'It's not all about Michael.' That was true to some extent. It was much more about her not liking her control being taken away, particularly when it was her own fault it was happening.

'I know,' Kat said. 'But it's because of him you are second-guessing the solution to this issue. You know asking Gunnar is a great option. He can speak the Icelandic and you can... pretend you're ill and can't speak at all. It's the most straightforward way and will absolutely get you out of this predicament without Michelle ever knowing that you don't know Icelandic or until you feel ready to admit to her that you don't.' She looked directly at Chloe then. 'Tell me I'm wrong.'

Kat wasn't wrong. But it was that sense of having to rely on someone to get her out of a fix. She was Little Miss Self-Sufficient these days. Needed to be.

She sighed. 'You're not wrong.'

'Correct. So, all you need to do is call Gunnar and ask for his help. What's the worst that could happen?'

'So many things.'

'But not death,' Kat said, matter-of-factly.

'No,' Chloe said, sighing. 'Not death.'

'Then, you know what to do.'

33

MAGNÚS'S SCHOOL, REYKJAVIK

'Thank you for coming in today, Mr Eriksson.'

Gunnar looked around the principal's office as Magnús soberly followed him inside and Mr Almr greeted them. It took Gunnar right back to when he was a student at this very school. The office was virtually unchanged, apart from a smarter computer and fewer filing cabinets. And it had a certain scent to it. Books, dust and the essence of fear...

'*Halló* Magnús,' Mr Almr said.

'*Halló*,' Magnús answered, a little sheepish.

'OK,' Gunnar said, pulling up a chair, sitting down and urging Magnús to do the same. 'So, let us get to the point of our being here and the misunderstandings that have taken place.'

'Misunderstandings?' Mr Almr asked.

'Yes,' Gunnar continued. 'Because you have only communicated to me that you believe Magnús has hit Brigitta Lundgren and not the fact that Brigitta Lundgren and her friends have been bullying Magnús for quite some time.'

'I do not believe I gave you the girl's name,' Mr Almr said, looking uncomfortable and shifting about in his rotating leather chair.

'And I do not believe that you have adequately looked into the cause of this incident. The root cause. The bullying of Magnús.'

'We take physical bullying very seriously, Mr Eriksson.'

'And what of mental bullying?' Gunnar questioned. 'Telling someone that they are nothing because of where they have come from and how they have been brought up and the fact their parents are dead.'

Gunnar hadn't meant to say the words quite like gunfire, had thought, after sleeping on things, that his anger would have depleted, but there was something about being back in this room that was reminding him of all the times he was told similar by someone who was supposed to be caring for him. Just because some children find study harder than others it should not mean their needs are overlooked, their difficulties thought of as bad behaviour. He had been the boy who had lost his father, lost his way for a while and gone through challenging times feeling different from everyone else.

'This is what has been happening to you, Magnús?' Mr Almr asked, looking at the boy.

Magnús sat stock still, eyes on the floor.

'Magnús,' Gunnar urged. 'There is no shame in admitting that these students hurt you with words. Words can be so much sharper than hitting with fists.'

Finally, Magnús looked up. 'I did not hit her,' he said firmly. 'I pushed her. And Brigitta and her friends have been calling me names and saying horrible things all year. They cut my hair. They used the shit of dogs on my locker.'

Gunnar folded his arms across his chest. 'As I said. For months, Mr Almr. And you call me only to tell me that you think

Magnús has done something very wrong when really the school has failed to protect him.'

'Mr Eriksson, I can assure you, if I had known this was ocurring I would have been able to stop the matter escalating and getting us into the position we are in now. I think that—'

'So what next?' Gunnar interrupted. 'You will speak to these bullies and ensure that Magnús does not have to put up with this any more?'

'I am afraid it is not as simple as that,' Mr Almr said, a heavy sigh leaving his mouth.

'Why not?'

'Because a physical assault has been reported, I have to follow certain procedures and I also have to respect the wishes of the parents of the student with regard to those procedures.'

'Talk straight to me,' Gunnar ordered. 'Stop with the procedures. And when did this reporting of a physical assault happen? It was not what you told me in our phone call.'

'Well,' Mr Almr continued. 'I have tried to de-escalate things, but, the girl's parents, they now wish to take the matter to the police.'

'What? Why? I did not hit her!'

The words had come from Magnús and Gunnar saw the absolute fear in the boy's eyes. This was not going to happen. But Gunnar had to maintain calm. He put a hand on Magnús's shoulder, firm, consoling mixed with solidarity. 'It is OK, Magnús.'

'I am a little surprised that the officer has not contacted you already today. I think—'

'You know what I think?' Gunnar interrupted. 'I think that your school is not the kind of place that Magnús needs to be right now. And that I understand why he has felt he cannot come to you for help and has instead decided to be absent.' He got to his feet.

'Mr Eriksson, Magnús must come to school. It is the law.'

'And, Mr Almr, to feel safe at that school is a matter of human rights.'

The teacher stood too. 'Mr Eriksson, I can—'

'We are leaving now,' Gunnar stated. 'But this is not the end of the discussion. Come on, Magnús.'

'Mr Eriksson, please, we can—'

The teacher's words were lost in the closing of the door and Gunnar's heart was thrumming in his chest as they got out into the slightly less cloying scent of the corridor. He took a breath, could see Magnús shaking next to him.

'What... are we... going to do?' Magnús asked, words juddering, expression speaking of his terror.

'We are going to think,' Gunnar stated, a lot more confidently than he felt. 'And find the solution.'

'I... do not want... to be in trouble... with the police,' Magnús said. 'Brigitta is lying. I have said that I pushed her but I did not do more than that, I swear!'

'Magnús, I will not let anything happen, OK?' His mind was working overtime now. How did they prove the bullying when it would be Magnús's word against the bullies? How did they prove that Magnús pushed and did not hit? And then it came to him. 'Magnús, did anyone see what happened with Brigitta? Does anyone know about the bullying? One of your friends? Anyone else?'

Gunnar looked directly at him, saw his eyes were tearing up with the stress of the situation. He drew the boy closer, put one arm around him. 'Do not worry, Magnús, OK? We will fix this.'

34

THE SUN VOYAGER SCULPTURE, REYKJAVIK

This gleaming sculpture that resembled a Viking long ship was something Chloe was definitely putting on the list for the Sinclairz Chairs event. With its sleek, long metal body and prongs reaching for the sky it was even more beautiful against a fresh, cold, clear mountain backdrop at the waterfront. It was apparently an ode to the sun representing a dream of hope, progress and discovery. And that was exactly what Chloe was aiming to get from this request. When she had the guts to call Gunnar's number. What was she waiting for? A cosmic sign? The *huldufólk* to tell her it was OK? She pressed dial and eventually...

'*Halló.*'

'Oh, Gunnar, it's Chloe.'

'I know,' Gunnar answered. 'Your name comes up on the screen of my phone.'

She was stupid. 'Oh, yes, of course.' She cringed at her own voice sounding so pathetic. But she was desperate for his help.

'You are OK?' he asked. 'It sounds like you are by the sea.'

How did he know that? 'Um, yes, I am actually.'

'I think it sounds very much like you are next to the Sun Voyager sculpture.'

What? Now this was crazy! 'I don't know how you know that.'

He laughed then, the sound that somehow made her feel a whole lot lighter inside every time. Then he replied. 'I can see you. I had to start work later, I am in the office for the boat tours the rest of today. The building just to your left.'

She turned a little, the phone pressed to her ear, searching. Then she saw a figure in the window. A figure who was waving. She raised a hand, waved back.

'I do not know who you are waving at,' Gunnar told her.

'What?' Chloe exclaimed, dropping her hand.

'I am joking with you, *krúttio mitt*. It was me.'

'Oh. OK. Sorry.'

'Something is wrong? Tell me.'

She swallowed. It was time to ask. Beg if she had to. It was either that or she was in danger of losing this precious potentially business-changing opportunity. Say the words.

'I need your help.' It came out grated, unfamiliar, almost painful.

'Tell me,' he said straight away.

It was like those two words had opened the flood gates to all the emotion she was holding in. She released it in a visible rush of cold air. 'I need you to speak Icelandic for me.'

'O-K.'

'And lie for me,' Chloe added.

She looked at the window of the building Gunnar was standing in. She couldn't see his face, only the outline of him, but she could only imagine what he must be thinking.

'I know how that sounds,' Chloe carried on. 'It sounds

terrible and pathetic and deceitful and I'm not usually this kind of person but—'

'Will the lying involve me getting a criminal record?' Gunnar asked her.

'No.'

'And no one dies?'

'The only thing that might die is my career.'

'And we should not make Iceland the place where this happens. Very bad for the tourist board.'

'I have to meet someone from the company I am planning the event for and she thinks I speak Icelandic and it's too late for me to confess that I don't speak the language and if I tell her then my boss, who has probably sold the fact she thinks I speak Icelandic like it's the ability to turn water into wine, will fire me or at the very least she will question everything I've ever told her and I really really need her to trust me right now so I can further my career because my career is honestly all I have.'

She was out of breath now, almost panting into the freezing air, looking out to sea, trying desperately either to ground her thoughts or let them sail out into the ocean and away.

'Chloe,' Gunnar said, his voice drawing her back to the conversation.

'Yes?'

'Look at the window, *krúttio mitt*.'

Chloe turned back to the building, seeking out the space Gunnar had been in. Where was he? And then she saw there was a large white square filling one of the windows.

'Do you see? Can you read it?'

She nodded, the phone pressed against her ear as she said the message written on it out loud. 'Yes.'

'Just tell me when,' he said.

And, suddenly, what had been terrifying her so much didn't feel quite so frightening.

35

GUNNAR'S HOME, THE OUTSKIRTS OF REYKJAVIK

'Stop fussing around me like I am an old woman!'

Hildur shrugged off Gunnar's attempt at assistance as they arrived home later that afternoon from her day at the community centre. He opened the front door and, before he could offer her help to get inside, she had bustled as fast as her leg boot could carry her over the threshold and into the open-plan living area. By the time Gunnar had turned and closed the door, Hildur was standing in the centre of the room with her arms folded across her chest.

'Now, you tell me exactly what is going on with Magnús and the school. Because all this "there is nothing for you to worry about" and "everything has been worked out" are lies you think you have to tell me because you think I am too old.'

Gunnar swallowed. Their conversation in the car had been a stupid attempt to try to pull the wool over Hildur's eyes but for only the right reasons, because he really did not want her to worry.

'Gunnar Eriksson!'

'OK,' Gunnar said quickly. 'But, please, Hildur, let us sit down.'

'No, I have been sitting down all day watching people who are really old in their minds as well as their bodies playing games for children. We will stand.' She tightened the fold of her arms. 'Start talking.'

He nodded, then explained exactly what had happened with Mr Almr and the threat of action from the police. And when he had finished Hildur just stood stoic, as if the information hadn't reached any part of her.

'I see,' Hildur said, finally.

'So, it is a very hard situation and—'

'Where is Magnús this evening?'

'He has hockey practice. He is there. I have checked his location and one of the parents is bringing him back here after.'

'Good,' Hildur said, nodding. 'Now, you will leave this situation with me to deal with.'

'What? No, Hildur,' Gunnar stated firmly. 'Magnús is my responsibility.'

'Nonsense! We are family. When one of us has a problem, it is a problem for all of us. That is the purpose of family. And then we decide which one of us is the best person to solve the problem. I am the eldest, as you are always so quick to point out, and I have decided that I am the best person to fix this.'

'Hildur, no,' Gunnar said, shaking his head. 'I have a plan. Magnús says that there were witnesses to what happened, so I am going to speak to the children, with the parents' consent of course and—'

'Gunnar, did you not hear what I said? You are to leave this problem in my hands.'

He had never heard Hildur sound as utterly full of conviction as she was now. And her blue eyes were almost slicing the air between them. He didn't know what to say. But Hildur didn't even allow him the opportunity.

'You say the girl is Brigitta Lundgren, yes?'

Gunnar nodded. 'Yes, but—'

'OK,' Hildur said. 'So now this conversation is over. And you can tell me what time you are meeting with Chloe.'

'I—'

'You are meeting with Chloe, yes?' Hildur said, finally unfolding her arms.

'Yes, a little earlier. She needs my help with something for her work and—'

'Good,' Hildur said. 'Because I will not let you use anything as an excuse not to take this chance, Gunnar. Not problems with Magnús, not that you have too much work, or you are too tired from work... they are all excuses you make because you are afraid to get your heart broken.'

Now he really wished they were talking about Magnús's school issues. He dropped his eyes to the floor, looked into the swirls of the blue and red patterned rug.

'Look at me, *strákurinn minn*.'

My boy. Gunnar raised his eyes to meet hers.

'If you do not take the chance, you will never know again all the joy that courtship brings. The highest of highs, when just thinking about that person makes the widest smile on your face. When being near them makes your stomach churn and your nerve-endings feel like they are on fire with passion.'

'Hildur—'

'Gunnar, listen to someone who knows, someone who took some of her chances yet is still regretful of those she did not take that could have given her life more laughter, more light.' She reached out and took hold of his arm, squeezing it between her fingers. 'That is the one wonderful thing about the heart, you know. No matter how many times it breaks. With time, it will always, always mend.'

He let the undeniable truth of Hildur's statements sink in. She was right.

'Now, take a shower and choose something nice to wear. I know it is cold but I sense that dressing like you are a yeti is not going to get you anywhere with Chloe.'

Gunnar smiled and enveloped Hildur in a firm hug before she could think about pushing him away... which she quickly did.

'Stop with that nonsense. Always near Christmas everyone thinks they must touch each other all the time.' She shook her head but Gunnar could hear the warmth wrapped around her words. 'Save these actions for Chloe.'

'Hildur,' Gunnar said, retreating for the bathroom. 'It is our first time going out together.'

'And she is not here for long,' Hildur reminded him. 'Do not waste a moment.'

With that advice ringing in his ears, Gunnar nodded and headed for the shower.

36

CENTRE OF REYKJAVIK

Chloe was pacing up and down outside the five-star hotel wondering if she was cold from the steep drop in temperature since she had arrived on the island or if it was down to sheer nerves. The woman she was meeting was going to be here in thirty minutes and Gunnar was supposed to be here already so they could talk through her non-speaking backstory and work out how he could run the meeting without her having to talk in any language at all. All this because she needed to cover up a stupid lie, one she didn't think she'd have to worry about ever again. Was it worth it? Should she come clean now? Or was she too far gone, Kat in her corner, Gunnar on board with the ruse, her partnership possibilities nearly in reach? Before she could think any more she saw Gunnar walking towards her down the icy pavement. And there was that feeling again. That feeling that acknowledged the sheer hot masculinity of the man, his perfectly proportioned stature, his fine jawline, those stunning eyes... Chloe swallowed. She hadn't actually felt this 'lust queasy' for... well, she couldn't quite remember another time.

'Hello, *krúttio mitt*. I am sorry I am late. There was a puffin on my truck.'

Why that had sounded like something sexual to her she didn't know, but it had. And she needed to answer and not look at his lips...

'It's OK.'

'It is not OK,' Gunnar said. 'It had left shit all over the windscreen.'

Chloe laughed and it felt like a release of so much more. 'That's funny.'

'Oh, you think this is funny! This is good,' Gunnar said, smiling. 'Because after I have spoken Icelandic for you, you can help me clean it off before we go to see the dogs.'

'Eww no,' Chloe said straight away.

'And if I make it a condition of me helping you now?' he asked, eyebrow raising.

'Ah, Gunnar, that is the thing with negotiations, once the deal has been agreed there is no more re-aligning the contract. You said you would help me and now you want to add conditions?'

He took a step closer, eyes locked on hers. 'This seems very harsh. No amendments? No time to reconsider? I might have to insist on a cooling off period.'

Cooling off didn't seem to be an option for Chloe with those bright blue glacier-like eyes fixed on hers. It was intense. It was hot.

'I don't think you've paid enough attention to all the clauses. The fine details.'

'No?' he queried, tone pure devilment. 'Then tell me, what did I overlook?'

Chloe's heart was beating in her ears now and it wasn't the nervous energy of knowing she was going to have to lie her way out of a situation in no time at all, it was Gunnar making her feel a certain way on an icy moonlit street that was becoming hotter by the second.

'I think,' Chloe began, inching closer towards him. 'That you might have underestimated my strategy. Maybe from the very beginning.'

'Oh really,' he countered quickly. 'In that case, I feel I need to question why, when we first met, we ended up on top of each other.'

She had no answer, but his words were sizzling between them and all she had to do was move ever so slightly more and...

'Gunnar?'

* * *

That voice saying his name had Gunnar stepping back like he'd been zapped by a Taser. He had to have imagined it, right? Except, when he turned around the truth was right there in front of him. Kirstin.

'Hello,' he replied, the word never having sounded so awkward on his lips. 'Kirstin.' That felt odd too.

'This is so crazy! Isn't it? I am here for one night only and we bump into each other like time has not passed.'

'So crazy, yes.'

He wanted to leave. Or Kirstin to leave. Because he had business to attend to with Chloe and not whatever may or may not have been about to happen on the street between them that had him more flustered than he currently wanted to admit, but an actual, real business meeting.

'Should we hug? I don't know,' Kirstin said. Then: 'We should hug, right?'

Before Gunnar had any chance to do anything else, his ex-girlfriend had put her arms around him and hugged him exactly how she had when they had said goodbye. And then she let go exactly the same way too.

'So, what brings you to town tonight?' Kirstin asked. And then it was like Kirstin only just noticed Chloe standing on the street. 'Oh, *halló.*'

Chloe waved a hand but the expression on her face wasn't a warm and welcoming smile for a new acquaintance, it was panicked, wide eyed and completely directed at him. And she hadn't replied to Kirstin's salutation.

'Kirstin, this is Chloe,' Gunnar introduced.

'Chloe,' Kirstin said, an odd expression suddenly on her face.

Chloe still wasn't saying anything. And that was when the penny finally dropped. Kirstin was who Chloe was meeting. Gunnar was about to have a discussion with his ex-girlfriend about the event Chloe was in charge of planning. How was this possible?

'You are the Chloe I am meeting. From the events company,' Kirstin stated, hand held out for greeting.

Chloe made some kind of throaty noise and nodded. Gunnar needed to stop thinking about his feelings in this situation and start focussing on what he needed to do for Chloe.

'And that is why I am here,' Gunnar told Kirstin in English for Chloe's benefit. 'Unfortunately, Chloe cannot speak today. She has a... virus.'

Chloe shook her head at speed, like if she carried on doing it at that level it might fly off and drop to the ground. Think, Gunnar.

'Sorry,' he said. 'Not a virus, obviously, because it would not be good to spread illness. It is laryngitis, non-contagious, but no speaking.'

'Oh,' Kirstin said. 'That is disappointing.'

She was now looking at Chloe as if she was something potentially hazardous.

'For Chloe it is more than disappointing,' Gunnar stated firmly. 'To unfortunately be unwell. But, she is a professional. There was no way she was going to cancel something so important.'

'But, how will we communicate?' Kirstin asked, frowning like this situation was one of the most complicated she had ever encountered. 'And why are you speaking English?'

Chloe was already pulling her laptop out of her bag.

'Chloe can show you the ideas she has and I can talk you through everything,' Gunnar said as calmly as if this had always been the plan. 'Sorry, I speak English because all day I speak English to the tourists. A habit. And I like to practice. This is OK?'

'I guess it will be—'

'But, let us go inside the hotel,' Gunnar interrupted quickly. 'It is so cold tonight and we do not want Chloe's throat to get any worse, no?'

'Oh, yes, fine,' Kirstin agreed.

'Good,' Gunnar said. 'Please.' He offered out an arm, directing the way almost like one of his coach tours, but as the two women headed in the direction of the entrance he couldn't help wondering what kind of curveball the universe was going to throw him next.

37

INSIDE THE HOTEL, REYKJAVIK

She had to remain mute or her cover would be blown, but Chloe hadn't envisaged exactly how hard it was going to be to run this meeting through Gunnar almost like she was Whoopi Goldberg's medium character in *Ghost*. While Gunnar ordered drinks – paid for by Sinclairz Chairs platinum card that Kirstin had flipped out like it was an all-access pass to everywhere – Chloe hammered at her laptop keyboard writing questions for Gunnar to ask which were all the things she had intended to brief him on in the time they were supposed to have before Kirstin had arrived...

'Two Baileys hot coffee lattes and an Americano.'

The waiter arranged the drinks on the table and Chloe took hers straight away. She needed that shot of creamy alcohol to inject confidence into her gut. The hotel vibe was perfect though – with its glitzy Christmas tree in the bar area they were sitting in and 'big band' festive tunes playing – it was exactly the tone Chloe had envisaged for a glorious Sinclairz Chairs celebration weekend. Taking a much-needed sip of her drink, Chloe then pushed the laptop screen towards Gunnar.

She watched him lean in to read it.

'So... how long have you been working with Sinclairz Chairs?' he asked Kirstin.

He looked at Chloe who nodded.

'Oh, for just over six months now,' Kirstin answered.

'You left the company you were working for before?' Gunnar asked her.

'You knew I was looking for something better. That I wanted to travel.'

'Yes,' Gunnar said. 'I just did not know that you were so interested in top-of-the-range chairs.'

He had remembered what exactly Sinclairz Chairs did. But he was going off piste with the questions now. Just how did they know each other? The initial meet outside had been slightly awkward, like a greeting with someone you didn't particularly like but had to endure or seeing someone you had more than liked at one time before everything changed... She continued to observe.

'I'm in marketing, Gunnar. It's my job to sell anything for whoever I decide to work for whether they are selling something I'm passionate about or not.'

'I remember you said you were passionate about sustainability, so I'm not sure how that fits with the carbon footprint of business air travel. Iceland for one day?'

That question was definitely not on Chloe's list and it sounded like Gunnar was trying to rile Kirstin. That was not what she needed at all.

'I am sure Chloe can tell you that Sinclairz Chairs offset all their carbon emissions and are on course to becoming one of the leading companies in supporting green energy.'

'And does that include flying their best workers and special guests out here to enjoy a weekend of wasting money they could be using to save the planet?'

Chloe slapped a hand to Gunnar's arm and shook her head. What the hell was he saying! This was her job! Her big chance to prove her worth to Michelle!

'You have to live life, Gunnar!' Kirstin exclaimed. 'I actually remember that being a problem for you when we were dating.'

'I know how to live a life, Kirstin. I just don't want my enjoyment to cut short anyone else's. You know... vulnerable ocean life, irreplaceable flora and fauna, that kind of thing.'

They had dated. And they were using her meeting to thrash this out. This was a nightmare! And what were the chances of the person she was meeting being the ex of the very guy she had asked for help. She could almost hear the *huldufólk* laughing and she couldn't let it continue.

'You're actually insane, you know this? You're making it sound like Sinclairz Chairs are going to slay turtles in front of a live audience and drink their blood.'

'I think that is the second stop on the tour after defecating into the natural springs.'

'Stop!' Chloe roared, getting to her feet. 'Please, both of you, just stop!' She swallowed, surprised at her own outburst.

The Christmas music seemed to quieten, the bar person stopped polishing glasses and looked their way and the two tables of customers who were nearest seemed distracted from their dinner-eating. And now Chloe's throat truly did hurt, as did her brain because it was working hard wondering how to salvage this situation as quickly as possible. Perhaps there was only one thing for it. Honesty.

'Sorry,' Chloe said, to the customers. Then: 'I am so sorry, Kirstin. I didn't realise that you knew Gunnar or that there is obviously some kind of communication difficulty between you.'

'Which is not your fault, Chloe,' Kirstin said. 'However, I am now wondering about your communication difficulty. That laryngitis has been cured by a sip of Baileys coffee?'

Chloe sighed. 'OK, let me be straight with you.' She sat down again, lowered her voice. 'I don't have laryngitis.'

'Oh really,' Kirstin said, sounding unsurprised.

'And I don't speak Icelandic either.' She sighed. 'I know my boss, Michelle, told you I did and she didn't lie, she thinks I do speak Icelandic, so the lie is on me.' She took a breath. 'And that's why Gunnar is here, but he's apparently talking and arguing with you in English so, if you don't mind, perhaps we could continue this discussion in my native tongue rather than yours, and make it about the Sinclairz Chairs anniversary event, not whatever Gunnar turned it into. If that's OK with you.'

Chloe picked up her latte cup and took a large swig before putting the cup back down on the table. She hoped it wasn't too late, that her lie and whatever performance Gunnar had put on wasn't going to have scuppered the whole thing.

'OK,' Kirstin said, finally. 'But I only have perhaps thirty more minutes so we should not waste any more time.'

'Fine by me,' Chloe said, tapping some keys on her laptop.

'And it is definitely fine with me,' Gunnar said nodding. He picked up his Americano and headed towards the bar.

'So, Chloe,' Kirstin said. 'Let us start again, yes?'

'Yes,' Chloe said, a sigh of relief leaving her. She held out her hand. 'I'm Chloe and I am really excited to be planning out this event for Sinclairz Chairs. Honestly, it's an honour.'

Kirstin shook her hand. 'It is very nice to meet you. Or, as we say in Icelandic, *gaman að hitta þig.*'

'Yes,' Chloe answered. 'A phrase I am completely unfamiliar with. Let's get started. I have made a short PowerPoint.'

38

Gunnar was working his way through a large bowl of nuts on the bar that didn't really go with the strong, slightly bitter taste of his coffee. Bitter. That was how he was feeling if he was honest. Seeing Kirstin again had thrown him. And, for some reason, everything about her being here had made him angry. Why was she back in Iceland? Why was she here in this moment? Why was she the person that Chloe had to impress? What was the universe trying to get across to him? That Kirstin had moved on and her life was so much better without him in it? That he still had some kind of feelings towards Kirstin or had unresolved resentment about how their relationship had ended? That he wasn't in the right place to consider moving on romantically? Maybe it was some kind of amalgamation of all of those. He took a sip of his coffee, swallowed a few more nuts. He didn't like how he was feeling because there was emotion involved and it was bouncing inside him begging for him to address it instead of his usual game of hide and not ever seek. He glanced over at the table Chloe and Kirstin were sitting at. They were hunched over Chloe's laptop, looking at it, and then there would be talking from each one of them, hand gestures, note taking, now some laughter... He hoped it was going well. And, if it was, that was no thanks to him.

A few minutes later Kirstin was getting to her feet, putting her bag on her shoulder and looking like she was bidding Chloe goodbye. Gunnar sat taller in his seat as Kirstin turned towards him then began making her way over.

'So, Chloe and I have finished our meeting,' Kirstin said once she had reached him.

'It went well?' he asked, palming some more nuts.

'She is a nice person.'

'I know she is a nice person,' Gunnar said. 'That is not what I asked.'

'It's business, Gunnar. Confidential.'

He nodded. 'The same as it always was.'

Kirstin sighed. 'You have not changed.'

'Neither have you.'

'Oh, I disagree. I think I have grown since I left this island and the closed community mindset.'

He nodded. 'It must be nice to have that freedom. To leave whenever you feel like it, see new places, meet new people, think only of yourself.'

'Gunnar, there is no point in us having this conversation. What happened, happened.'

'What happened,' Gunnar stated, 'is that I told you I was responsible for a child and you told me it was over.'

He hadn't meant the words to come out so hard or so loud and he flicked a surreptitious glance over to Chloe who seemed to still be looking at her computer.

Kirstin sighed. 'Gunnar, if you think it was just about that then you're wrong. You knew I wanted to travel, explore my career options and—'

'And there was no reason that you couldn't do that and for us to still carry on. People who care about each other can make anything work if they really want to.'

'If they have the same goals,' Kirstin stated.

'Or have independent goals and want to work towards joint goals also.'

'Sometimes things are just too hard, Gunnar. When people haven't planned for them. When they are dropped on someone unexpectedly.'

He shook his head. 'His name is Magnús, Kirstin. The "thing" that was dropped on you unexpectedly, the "thing" that got too hard. He's just a boy and he needed my help.'

And Gunnar felt as passionately about this now as he always had. Magnús had lost everything in one distressing night and he wasn't about to turn his back on him.

'The trouble is, Gunnar, Magnús was not the issue for me. The issue was you and the fact you did not tell me at the very beginning. That you didn't trust me to know about him.'

He shook his head. 'And look what happened. I was correct.'

'This is pointless,' Kirstin said. 'And it is time for me to go. Take care, Gunnar.' She turned away and then she turned back, facing him again. 'Just, maybe, if things are romantic with Chloe, do not make the same choices again.'

She didn't give him the opportunity to make any reply but headed towards the exit.

Gunnar took another handful of nuts and crunched them hard as what Kirstin had said filtered through his mind. She was surely just telling him that because she felt guilty. Except he knew not being honest about Magnús from the start hadn't been right. He looked to Chloe, packing up her things at the table. He hadn't been honest with her either. He had told her Magnús belonged to a friend...

Chloe looked over to him and gave a small wave. He owed her many truths. Perhaps he owed it to himself too. He waved back.

39

The journey in Gunnar's truck to the location for the dog
sledding had been peppered with nothing but small talk. It was
not at all like the rapport they'd built up, the flirtatious banter
Chloe had also started to get accustomed to. Ordinarily, having
him go off piste and make the beginning of her meeting with
Kirstin super difficult and potentially business-destroying,
would have made her cross, but, from his behaviour at this
moment, she knew there was far more to it. And now, here they
were, about to meet Alaskan husky dogs who were going to drive
them over the snowy terrain. She knew she had sold the idea as
research for Sinclairz Chairs, however she couldn't deny the
thought of it being a date had been appealing. But now...

'Chloe, I am sorry for what happened at the hotel,' Gunnar
said once they had got out of the truck and planted feet on
snow-covered ground. 'I let my shock about Kirstin being here
distract me from the whole reason I was there in the first place.
To help you.'

'It's OK,' she answered.

'No, it is not OK,' Gunnar responded, putting his woollen hat over his head then locking the car door. 'You will accept my apology and you will let me make it up to you with this dog sledding experience. I will use all my negotiating skills to get the best price for your event.'

'You don't need to do that. I can negotiate in English.'

'Come on, you know that I have charm for this work,' he said. 'How I talk about all the folklore on my coach tours.'

'Hmm,' Chloe said. 'I don't think more lying is going to help anything.' She stepped towards the small gathering of people a few metres away but then he crossed her path, moved in front of her, blocking the way.

He inhaled like he was in shock. 'Your faith in the *huldufólk* has been rocked? But you talked so passionately about them before.'

Chloe sighed. 'To get you out of a difficult situation with your microphone. And I had far more success helping you with that than you did with helping me with my meeting.'

He nodded. 'And that is why you will let me help you again now. In fact, there is no more conversation to be had. I insist on it.'

And before she could say anything else to the contrary, Gunnar was striding ahead towards what looked like their guides for the experience.

* * *

Chloe was taking photos. She didn't wholly believe that these dogs were going to be able to pull their sled. Yes, she had seen the videos, but they were dogs, not horses. They also looked way too cute to be able to be strong. However, they were leaping around now, getting ready to be fixed into formation at the front of the large wooden sledge.

'You think the people from Sinclairz Chairs will like this mode of transport?' Gunnar asked her.

'I don't know yet,' she said. 'It will depend on how covered with snow we get and how cold it is.'

'They do not like the cold?' Gunnar asked. 'And they want to come to Iceland?'

'Well, Kirstin did say the focus should be "classy" and "classic".'

'What does that even mean?'

'It means if I can arrange for the dogs to wear cute festive outfits and there to be a smorgasbord of fine cheeses or something traditionally Icelandic, yet not gross, at the end of the trip it may be something they would like to do but...'

'But?' Gunnar asked.

'I don't know,' Chloe said, sighing. 'I get the impression that maybe I've been trying too hard.'

'No,' Gunnar said, shaking his head. 'Do not say that. That is how you are with the job that means so much to you. And that is absolutely the way to be.'

'But what if I'm trying too hard for the wrong reasons?' she asked him as much as she was asking herself. 'What if all the things I'm doing are not really with the client in mind, but with my career aspirations leading the way?'

'Chloe,' Gunnar said seriously. 'This is not the time for doubt.'

'No?'

'No,' he said even more firmly. 'We are here.' He spread his arms and, even in the darkness, you could make out the incredible views of snow-capped mountains, crisp white terrain and all the dogs raring to take them on a winterland adventure. 'In this magnificent place that is so wonderful because of the simplicity, it is unenhanced by anything but nature.'

Chloe swallowed, her gaze going to the view as she took in Gunnar's words. Glitz and glamour, classic and classy wasn't what she thought of when she thought about Iceland. She thought about the power of Mother Earth, the rugged beauty of the landscape, the dramatic waterfalls, the lava fields and the horses, the black sand beach and rock formations. Cocktails and expensive cheese could take place anywhere.

'You're right,' she said. 'If Sinclairz Chairs have chosen Iceland then Iceland needs to be celebrated as much as the chair company's anniversary.' She took a breath. 'And if they don't approve of my vision then...'

'Then?' Gunnar asked.

'Then I will... convince them of my vision,' she stated with utter confidence.

'Yes, *krúttio mitt*.'

'And, if that does not work, I will... reconsider my future at Michelle's firm.'

She gasped, putting her hands to her mouth in shock. What was she saying? The piece of the partnership was her goal. It was all she had been fixated on for so long. Maybe too long? Because shouldn't Michelle have already asked her to step up? Hadn't she proved her worth enough? There was nothing she hadn't done, nothing she hadn't given 100 per cent to. But, perhaps it wasn't partnership with Michelle's firm she wanted, perhaps what she really truly desired was personal career success. Maybe even career success formed by all her own ideas singlehanded...

'New adventures are waiting,' Gunnar told her.

Were they? She looked into his bright eyes and felt solidarity, the thought that she could tell him anything and he would categorically be on her side. It was the strangest feeling when she hadn't known him that long.

Happy barking punctured the air and it brought Chloe back to the moment.

'Come on, *krúttio mitt*, let us ride with the huskies.'

40

'This is crazy!' Chloe screamed, hair flying out from under her hat, her words being whipped away into the cold air.

They were speeding along on the sled, the dogs galloping at a super fast pace over the glistening snow, nothing but ice-white landscape all around like they were a moving centrepiece on a celebration cake.

'This is much better than any fast car!' Gunnar yelled back, bumping beside her.

'So much better!' she laughed. 'And less environmental impact!'

'The air is fresh! The sky is clear! There is no one else around! It is like we have the whole of Iceland just for us!'

His words sent delicious shivers shooting down her back. Iceland was so beautiful. It was so steeped in the tales of ancient times, with a rich history of how everything came to be here, yet, right now, Chloe was feeling that its pure simplicity was firing off thoughts of only new beginnings.

'Stop thinking, *krúttio mitt*,' Gunnar ordered. 'I can hear your head over the yelping of the dogs and the sled against the snow.'

How did he do that? Know that she was churning things over?

'You go quiet,' Gunnar continued as if he had read her mind. 'And your shoulders drop.'

Yes, their bodies were pretty close together and cosy in this sledge, wrapped up in their thick coats and tucked in under a waterproof blanket like burritos. Him mentioning her shoulders highlighted the fact their bodies were tight against each other. And suddenly this sleigh ride was feeling the exact opposite of chilly. She needed a distraction from that...

'So, Kirstin was your girlfriend?'

Now the quiet was from Gunnar not immediately responding and Chloe wondered if her choice of distraction conversation had been a step too far.

'Yes,' he answered finally. 'We were together for around six months. It was a while ago now.'

'So a surprise to see her,' Chloe stated.

'A shock,' Gunnar admitted. 'In that situation of her being the person you needed to speak to. That I needed to speak to for you.'

'I am sorry about that.'

'Do not be sorry, Chloe. I tell you that I am sorry for not being the professional you needed me to be in that moment and I should not have made things difficult for you.'

'Everything worked out OK though,' Chloe told him. 'I mean it will work out OK no matter what because I will make it happen one way or the other so...'

'So?' he asked.

'So, can I ask? What happened with you and Kirstin?'

The words had barely left her mouth when the sleigh shifted sideways into a bit of a drift and suddenly they were going into a wooded section, tree branches spilling fluffy white snow onto them.

'You are OK?' Gunnar asked her as the sleigh drew to a halt in a clearing.

'Yes,' she answered. 'I just wasn't expecting that.' She shook the blanket, snow going up in the air between them, some falling and landing in Gunnar's hair.

'Hey!' he exclaimed, shaking his head. Next he was scooping up the snow from their laps and sprinkling it down on her relentlessly.

'Gunnar! Gunnar stop!' She wriggled in her seat.

'You begin this!' he answered, carrying on.

'And I will finish it,' she said, laughing. She grabbed a handful of snow, like a fat pancake, and planted it directly on his face. She giggled at the result, a big splat sticking to his stubble.

'I do not believe you did that,' he said. 'It was a wrong move.'

'Ooo, I'm so scared. I'm...'

And then, before she could say anything else, he had put the side of his face right to hers and pressed their cheeks together, all the snow transferring from him to her. She turned her face fast and that's when their lips collided. A mistake. Not meant to happen. Except... it was happening!

Chloe didn't know who had changed pace first but suddenly she was right up against him and their mouths were devouring each other, snow, skin, white hot heat amid the forest. And it felt incredible, intense, sexy, meant to be? She slipped her hands underneath his hat and pulled it off, fingers tangling in his hair. She was never like this. So forward, so giving in to all the feelings that were rushing through her. His mouth was open, his tongue teasing, tasting and she only wanted one thing. More.

And then... a tongue of a different kind licked Chloe's hand, making her jump in surprise. Gunnar held her and then they were joined in the sleigh by a husky puppy, eager to leap about exploring the spilt snow, their blanket, their laps.

'Hey there, little guy,' Gunnar said, stroking the dog on its head. 'You're a cute one.'

So was the man stroking the dog in Chloe's opinion. She swallowed as she looked at him, taking him in in yet another light. Strong, sensitive, kind to animals, always kind to her... And then those eyes found hers again and she couldn't stop the blush hitting her cheeks as all the intensity from their kisses rushed back full force.

Chloe stood, reeling a little, and then Gunnar took her hand, helping. But then, on her feet, and both of them quickly getting down from the sled, he didn't let go, but instead knitted their fingers close together.

'We should get the hot chocolates before they become cold chocolates,' Gunnar suggested, indicating a teepee-looking structure in the midst of the clearing ahead of them.

The puppy barked and seemed to concur. Right now she didn't need any chocolate at all. In fact, the only thing she needed was a cold shower.

41

The husky puppies had been adorable and one day all of them would be trained to pull the sledges like their older counterparts. Chloe had taken so many photos, of the dogs and of the idyllic setting. She could imagine a fire pit near the teepee, the staff of Sinclairz Chairs sharing mulled wine to warm up and having photo shoots with the puppies. She thought it was a complete bucket list experience, a memory to last forever. And, as promised, Gunnar had negotiated hard but respectfully on the price with the business owners. In Chloe's mind the dog sledding was already a 'must do' on her Sinclairz Chairs suggestion package.

'More thinking, *krúttio mitt*?' Gunnar asked.

They were back in his truck, leaving the dog sledding adventure behind, heading back towards Reykjavik. And, here in his vehicle, Chloe was definitely not only thinking about the celebration event, she was re-imagining those kisses in the sleigh. It had been the heat of the moment, but perhaps also a culmination of whatever this slow burn between them was. Because it was definitely there. However, something was telling Chloe to proceed with caution. How well did she really know Gunnar? And what exactly had transpired between him and Kirstin?

'OK,' Gunnar said. 'There is only one thing that we do now.' He sharply turned the wheel of the truck, taking a turn.

'What?' Chloe asked, hand braced on her door.

'When you need to think you must do this in the best place.'

'Which is?'

'You do not know this yet,' Gunnar said, taking his eyes off the road momentarily and looking at her. 'But, relax, because I do.'

'O-K,' she replied, tentatively.

'Do not worry. We drive only ten minutes. Then you will see.'

* * *

Gunnar took a deep breath as he pulled the truck to a stop a short while later. What was he doing? He was taking Chloe to somewhere he had only been with one person. His mother. It was a place so special to him that he had not been here since she had passed away. Was this a mistake? Was he acting on the same kind of intensity he had felt when he had kissed her in the sleigh? It had felt so perfect in the moment, when he had not allowed a chance to second-guess his emotions. And this was what he was still feeling now. Acting on impulse, or, more accurately, going with his gut instincts. And if he waited for his brain to overload him with other thoughts now, he would start to catastrophise.

'So, we are here,' he said, turning off the engine.

He looked at Chloe who was facing the window now. 'I don't see anything.'

He laughed. 'That is some of the point. Come.' He opened the door of the truck and stepped out onto the snow.

He heard Chloe gasp the second she saw what was up ahead.

'A lighthouse!' she announced like the type of structure was one of her favourite things.

'*Grótta*,' he said.

'Grotto? Like Santa's cave?'

'Yes, it is the word for "cave". Here it is best known for the lighthouse that still works, guiding the boats through this area of sea, the *Faxaflói* bay, and for the wildlife. There are many different birds here, gulls, Arctic terns but...'

'But?' Chloe asked, looking at him.

'We are not here for those.'

'No? The birds are sleeping?'

'I do not know what the birds are doing but... the stars never sleep. Look up.'

He didn't need to look up to know what was going to be there. He wanted to watch Chloe's reaction to the first time she saw the night sky in this place. She tipped her head back and then... complete silence. No gasp like when she had seen the lighthouse shining at the end of the peninsula, no sound whatsoever. He liked that. She was drinking it in, as if she was lost in thought. He moved closer to her.

'Come, *krúttio mitt*.' He pointed towards the lighthouse on the peninsula. 'The view is better down there.'

42

THE ISLAND OF GRÓTTA

The sky wasn't just speckled with stars, it was full of them. The near-black canopy was hanging like an unending dark curtain above the sea, the air fresh, the scent of salt water right the way through it, and Chloe had her back to the snow covered ground staring, seeing, but her mind empty of anything but the present.

'What do you see?' Gunnar whispered.

He was right next to her, lying alongside. She could feel the slight touch of his padded coat against hers but not the pressure of his body.

'A sky full of bright sparkling jewels,' Chloe told him, a contented sigh leaving her, on instinct, unconsidered, just there.

'A picture, no?' Gunnar said. 'Made by the greatest artist.'

'God?'

'If you like. But, I prefer "nature". A scientific fact, but open to interpretation.'

'Well,' Chloe said, shifting her body slightly closer to him until there was that actual connection. 'I can see The Plough.'

'Everyone can always see The Plough. Or as some call it, The

Big Dipper or the kitchen ladle. A friend of mine calls it The Grandmother's Spoon. She is crazy.'

'So, what different ones can you see?' Chloe asked.

'Well, *krúttio mitt*, I do not look for the constellations. I look for patterns of my own. Connecting the stars, then disconnecting them and connecting them a different way. I find that it helps my mind be free, you know.'

Chloe turned her full attention back to the sky and honed in on one particularly bright star. Where did she look next? What picture could she make?

'Right now I see a husky dog with very big ears,' Gunnar stated.

Chloe laughed. 'Now you're teasing me. You can't see a dog.'

'How do you know this? You do not trust that I have been stargazing for a very long time. That I know my way around the changing sky?'

'I believe you are a fantastic tour guide who knows his way around many Icelandic sites, but I don't believe anyone can see a husky dog up there.'

'Oh really,' Gunnar said, his tone a touch combative as he got into a sitting position. 'We need to fix this. Sit up.'

'What?'

'I cannot have you thinking that I am making this up. My reputation as a guide is at stake.'

She sat up and then suddenly his body moved. So swiftly, he shifted and moved right behind her until she was almost swallowed into the softness of his jacket and the firm, hard body that lay beneath.

'We need to be close,' he told her, voice soft yet edgily sensual. 'For you to be in the same line of sight with me.'

'OK,' she breathed, already feeling all the closeness and imagining so much more.

'So, follow the line of my finger, there.' He pointed to the sky, leaning her back into him so she was sat inside his embrace. 'You see this star?'

She concentrated, focussed on the tip of his finger, the star at its very end. 'I see it.'

'OK, so that is the start of the husky nose and then you go around here and up to its eyes, see?'

'I'm not sure.'

'Come on, you are not looking right.'

'Maybe because I'm not you,' Chloe suggested. 'You said that it was open to interpretation. Perhaps I don't see a husky dog but I see something else.'

'What do you see?' Gunnar asked her. 'Tell me.'

Chloe looked at the stars, all supposedly very similar but some of them, whether it was a trick of the light or of the mind, standing out just a little brighter than others.

'I see... the letter "v" like a string of beads making a necklace.' She pointed. 'There.'

'I see,' Gunnar said. 'But are they beads? Or are they teardrops?'

'Raindrops,' Chloe answered, letting her imagination roam. 'Or droplets from a waterfall. A necklace of nature.'

'It could be better,' Gunnar answered.

'You mean you're mad I don't see a dog?' Chloe said, with a laugh.

'No,' Gunnar said. 'I am not mad. But, what if the beads were not droplets. What if they were something else?'

'What do you think they are?' Chloe asked, turning her head a little to look at him.

'It does not matter what I think they are,' he said. 'Only what you think they are. Open to interpretation, remember?'

She looked back to the sky, her string of droplets. A strong, shining row of diamonds. What did they represent to her? And then, all at once it came to her.

'Dreams,' she whispered. 'The beads are dreams.'

'Very good, *krúttio mitt*. Very good.'

He drew her even closer towards him, wrapping an arm around her. She liked it. It made her feel special.

'You know, the only other time I came here I was sad,' Gunnar said.

'Why?'

'Because I knew my mother was dying.' He took a breath that Chloe could almost feel inside herself. 'I mean, I hardly remember a time when I did not think that she was dying because of how ill she always was but, when we came here, I knew it would not be long.'

'Did she teach you how to tune in to the pictures in the sky?'

'Many times,' Gunnar said. 'But when she brought me here, the way the sky is at this place, everything was more vivid – is that the word?'

'Yes,' Chloe answered. 'That's right.'

'I very much think she wanted me to have comfort from the universe here. To believe there is something else, if only pictures we create in our own minds to manifest what we might like our future to be.'

'I like that idea,' Chloe said, nestling back against him and feeling so completely at ease with it.

'So, tell me, what are the dreams on that necklace you see?' Gunnar asked.

She tensed a little now the conversational spotlight was back on her. What were her dreams? All of them. Not just the career she had put all her focus into when things with Michael had ended so savagely. What did she want from life? What did she truly want? She took a breath.

'To love and be loved. To feel that total balance with someone – both partners on the same page, trusting they are working towards the same goals.'

'That does not sound like a dream, *krúttio mitt*,' he whispered. 'It sounds like something everyone deserves.'

'It's not easy though, is it? Because as beautiful as life is, it can also be harsh. You know that, from losing your parents like I lost mine. From losing Kirstin, maybe?'

'I do not know if I ever had Kirstin at all,' he said with another sigh she could feel. 'Or, rather, if we ever had each other.'

'What do you mean?' Chloe asked gently.

'Well, like you say, it would be good if working towards the same goals allowed for the unexpected. Because life can throw in challenges and challenges should be faced together, no?'

Chloe thought about her and Michael. They had come up against a challenge, one of the biggest challenges, but instead of tackling that together, discussing, facing up to the reality of the issue of her infertility, they had both retreated. Then, before she had had time to process, to accept, Michael had run away.

'Maybe,' Chloe began. 'If two people cannot be completely honest with each other, about their thoughts and their innermost feelings, no matter how bad or sad that might get, they should not be together at all.'

As she contemplated on the sheer depth of what she had just said and wondered what Gunnar would make of it, he already had his answer.

'I think I agree.'

'You only think you agree?' She tipped her head back, wanting to find his eyes.

'I think,' he began again, 'that what holds people back from sharing that is pure and simple fear.'

'But no one should feel afraid if the space they've created is safe.'

'Ah,' Gunnar said, looking into her eyes now. 'I think that is a problem for the whole world, no?'

'So, what does the world do?' Chloe asked, transfixed with needing to know his answer.

'Trust, *krúttio mitt*. We have to trust.'

Usually a zillion thoughts would be firing off in Chloe's brain now but the only thing on her mind was him. This handsome, intelligent Icelandic man who she wanted to find out so much more about. It wasn't the time for any more words, it was time for actions to lead the way. She shifted herself in his arms, reached up, her fingers in his hair and drew his face towards hers. This kiss was hers to take and theirs to share under this sky full of stars.

43

GUNNAR'S HOME, THE OUTSKIRTS OF REYKJAVIK

Rubbing the sleep from his eyes as he made his way into the kitchen/living area, Gunnar looked at his watch. He was on time. A rarity and, in fact, he had slept so well. He smiled, eyes still only half open as he remembered the time spent with Chloe at the lighthouse, talking until late in the night, kissing with cold lips until they were the exact opposite, starting to trust in this beginning. And then... thump! He walked straight into something, had to stop himself from toppling over.

'*Fjandinn!*' he cursed, rubbing his shin.

Why was there a small sleigh in the centre of the space filled with goblin dolls, bulbous eyes fixed on him almost like the creepy characters from *Five Nights at Freddy's*. And then his focus was drawn to the rest of the space suddenly hitting him full force with its bright, garish coils of tinsel, lanterns, hanging stars and baubles, every single inch of wall decorated for Christmas. And in the corner was the old tree he had been putting there for as long as he could remember. Had Magnús got the tree down this year? It leaned to the left and no one could work out why. There were branches missing and the others had to be bent into the gaps so it did not look deformed. It was covered in silver and blue, red and white, spatterings of gold and lights that were flickering on and off then dancing in time like they were performing to a silent melody.

'Hildur.'

He said the woman's name out loud. She had done all this. With the help of Magnús. Hopefully with the help of Magnús as she had a broken foot she was certainly not resting!

'Hildur!' he called then.

It was odd that she was not up before him. If not here in the kitchen then in the bathroom before Magnús took it over for an elongated shower that took all the hot water. But, given the extent of the festive decorating that had taken place while he had been out, perhaps it was no wonder that she was having a lie in. Unless...

An uncomfortable sensation rode over him then and he started to make his way back down the hall. Hildur might be strong, but she was not a young woman, and she had a few health conditions. And now, this latest hospitalisation. The uncomfortableness began to turn into dread at the thought that this might be something other than extra sleep. He paused at her bedroom door, listening for sounds of sleeping, or, even better, waking. There was nothing, no sound at all, apart from the ticking of the clock Hildur kept on her bedside table. Nothing was wrong. His brain repeated that to himself over and over as his clenched hand wavered in front of the door. He just had to knock, Hildur would shout an annoyed reply and his heart would stop palpitating. What was he waiting for? He knocked. Nothing. He knocked harder. Nothing.

'Hildur!' he shouted, knocking for a third time. Still nothing. This time he didn't hesitate to open the door, worst case scenarios falling like a hard snowstorm, all of them involving

Hildur being incapacitated or worse. What he saw wasn't at all
what he had expected. Nothing. No Hildur slumped in bed, no
Hildur crashed out on the floor. No Hildur.

He didn't waste any more time in her bedroom. Closing the
door, he headed along the corridor to Magnús's room. Maybe
Hildur was in there. Don't panic. Everything is fine.

He knocked hard once and opened the door as he said the
name. 'Magnús, what is—'

He stopped abruptly when the bed he expected to see full of
a gangly boy was completely empty too. Unslept in. Now his
heart skipped all the beats and he had to stop fear rising up in
his throat. Something terrible had happened. No, it couldn't
have. Because that was an over-the-top reaction. There were no
signs of trouble in the house, only frenzied festive activity that
spoke of the two of them being OK throughout the evening until
it was time to sleep. But what had happened then? Had they,
God forbid, gone out into the cold for a walk? Hildur was barely
able to walk at all right now and Gunnar would like to think that
Magnús knew better than to be so stupid.

He moved, heading towards the front door. He needed to
check outside. Everywhere outside. The front and back gardens,
his shed, maybe even the woodland. Magnús's phone. He could
call him. And if there was no answer, he could locate him on the
Find My Phone app. OK, breathe. He picked up his phone from
where it was on charge in the kitchen and dialled Magnús's
number. It rang. Nervous anticipation filled him as he went out
of the front door to the garden, hoping to God that he didn't
hear the phone ringing from the outside. And then the ringing
stopped and the phone went through to voicemail. He ended the
call, anxiety squeezing his chest as he looked around the neighbourhood. Nothing seemed out of place. The thin layer of snow
on the ground with a few track marks where early morning

vehicles had already driven, the streetlights shining beneath a still dark sky, the bike belonging to his neighbour chained to their fence as always... He looked back to his phone as he stood in the cold, inappropriately dressed without a coat, and searched for Magnús's location. It spiralled, over and over until... nothing found. Now the pressure in his chest pushed harder. What did he do now? His family was missing.

And then his phone started to ring. An unknown number. He answered fast.

'*Halló.*'

His heart thumped in his chest as the voice on the other end of the call relayed information he was finding hard to take in. Gut-wrenching fear swamped his gut and, having heard enough, he raced back inside for his coat and the keys to his truck.

44

CHLOE'S APARTMENT, REYKJAVIK

Chloe was buzzing. She had woken up early and while Kat had snored, kind of peacefully, she had reviewed everything she had done so far in Iceland and put it into documents with detailed notes, pricing, timescales, pros and cons and everything she knew Michelle liked to have before they pulled it all together for final pitching purposes. She was also now three Icelandic coffees down and she was still daydreaming about the special time she had shared with Gunnar at the lighthouse.

'Is it morning?' Kat asked, sitting up in bed and looking like a cosy mess of bed hair and duvet.

'Yes!' Chloe announced. 'And we need to get ready because we are going on a trip!'

'Oh, wow, another one, so soon. I forgot you were an "all-in" kind of a girl who thinks every second should be filled with more steps than Fitbit can cope with.'

'You really forgot the last time we went to London for the day?'

'My feet definitely have the muscle memory ingrained; my mind is trying very hard to fight said memory.'

'Well, I need to find a couple more things to add to my proposal for Sinclairz Chairs so they, and Michelle, can see how much attention to detail I've put into this.' She closed the lid of her laptop.

'As supportive as I am being with your business endeavours,' Kat began with a yawn. 'I'm only interested in the details from last night.'

Immediately Chloe smiled, no control over it happening, all those beautiful feelings flowing fast like one of the Icelandic waterfalls.

'O-K, now I'm excited to know what's made you react with whatever that glowy, dewy, soft-focus, romance movie end pose was.'

'Well, it didn't start out great, but the ending was...' She sighed and didn't even recognise the sound herself. Who was she right now?

'And did you both have a great ending?' Kat asked, eyes bulbous like a bush baby.

'Not like that!' Chloe exclaimed. 'I mean... it's way too soon for that, right?'

'Is it? These days people are adding themselves to "free tonight" on dating apps and having sex with people they have absolutely no clue about.'

'Well, good for them,' Chloe said. 'But I don't work like that.' But should she? The kisses had been steamy, but she hadn't pushed for anything more and neither had he.

'So, if you didn't have sex, tell me, how did the not-talking the Icelandic language go at the meeting?'

Kirstin. And she was still no further forward in finding out exactly what had happened between her and Gunnar. She quickly filled Kat in on what she did know about the situation.

'Oh my God, I mean, what are the chances?' Kat asked. 'His ex being part of Sinclairz Chairs? That's insane. Or... fate.'

'Stop,' Chloe said. 'In a second you'll say it's the *huldufólk*.'

'Well, you have to admit it's a very strange coincidence. So, what happened between them?'

'I... don't know,' Chloe admitted, getting up from the table and beginning to gather things together for her bag.

'You didn't ask?'

'I did ask but he didn't altogether tell me.'

'Hmm, that sounds dodgy.' Kat got up from the bed, one arm out of her pyjamas.

'No,' Chloe said. 'I don't think it's that. He said things about "joint goals" and "the unexpected". I think it's painful for him.'

'And did you tell him about Michael? And how painful that was for you?'

Chloe dipped her head, would have put it inside the rucksack if she could. 'No.'

'Chloe! You need to let that out of you! And why not to Gunnar? The man who turned your face into mushy slushy.'

'Because,' Chloe said. 'I wouldn't know where to begin. And, you know, how do you just drop into conversation that you can't have children? This soon. In what can only really be a Christmas holiday romance.'

'But what if it turns out to be more than that? And you don't say anything and months go by and then—'

'And then he wants children I can't give him and leaves me,' Chloe filled in. 'Yes, I'm aware that, even if it's not a first date conversation to have, it needs to be had before anyone gets feelings.'

'And do you have feelings for Gunnar?' Kat asked like it was the last, life-changing-money question on *Who Wants to Be a Millionaire*.

Chloe's heart was thrumming a beat that couldn't be clearer. 'I feel something. And that's much more than I've felt since Michael left.'

'Then that's great!' Kat said, reaching out and slapping a hand of solidarity on Chloe's shoulder. 'We can work with that! I mean, obviously, you can work with that. So, tell me where we're going so I can dress appropriately for whatever this bound-to-be-too-many-steps outing is.'

'OK,' Chloe said, smiling at her friend. 'So, this is something I think Sinclairz Chairs are going to lap up because it hits so many "wants".' She inhaled fast and then slowly let the breath go bit by bit.

'OK, what are you doing? You sound like something from *Star Wars*.'

'We are going to do breathwork.'

'I know that. Because I've been doing breathwork over many kilometres since we got here,' Kat said with a shudder.

Chloe smiled. 'Not like this. Dress warm.'

45

MAGNÚS'S SCHOOL

Gunnar leapt from the truck and raced across the icy play space/car park at the front of the building, his heart hammering, his eyes on the roof. He reached a tape cordon he was going to break right through but his progress was halted by two police officers determined to make him stop.

'Let me go!' Gunnar yelled. 'I have had a phone call. My family is involved in this and no one is telling me anything!'

'You are?' one of the officers asked.

'I am Gunnar Eriksson. I am Hildur's... I don't know... but she lives with me.' He put a shaking hand through his hair. 'And I am Magnús Ólafsson's guardian.'

'I am afraid we must ask you to stay behind the cordon for now,' the other policeman instructed. 'For your own safety.'

'I do not care about my own safety! I care about the safety of my family!' Gunnar yelled, drawing the attention of the numerous onlookers.

'It is our job to keep everybody safe. Not yours.'

Gunnar could feel his blood becoming like lava. He had heard similar before, when the authorities had tried to stop him and others from going into the area affected by the volcano eruption. He hadn't listened then and he had saved Magnús. He was not going to listen now.

'OK,' he said, holding his hands up in some show of surrender as he backed up a little. 'OK.'

He waited a few beats, until he saw the policemen really drop their shoulders, dismiss him just long enough... and then he bolted. Sprinting underneath the tape, he headed for the door of the school and the way to the roof.

'You can't go up there!' the receptionist shouted at him. 'Wait! Stop! Somebody!'

Gunnar wasn't waiting. Because all he had been told on the phone was that Magnús was on the roof with an old woman and an old man...

Finally, at the top of the stairs he caught his breath. What was he going to find behind the door, on the roof of the building? He literally had no idea. But he knew, whatever it was, he had to be there, had to help sort out whatever was going on. He pushed on the door and the strength of the swing spat him out onto the roof and into the middle of one of the most ridiculous sights he had ever seen. Hildur, Magnús, and a man he did not recognise tied to a chair. It was like a scene from an awful movie.

'Hildur!' Gunnar exclaimed, walking forward. 'What is going on?'

'Stay back!' Hildur ordered. 'I told everybody to stay back.'

Gunnar stopped walking and held his hands up like he had for the policemen. He looked to Magnús who was holding something in his hands. Was that a pair of scissors?

'Please, will you tell this crazy woman to untie me?'

It was the old man speaking and, as he spoke, he shifted and rocked in the chair, every movement walking the seat closer to the edge of the roof.

'"Crazy woman"? Is that any way to talk to the sister of your late wife?'

What? This man was Hildur's brother-in-law? Gunnar refocussed. 'Magnús, please, come away from the edge.'

The boy shook his head. 'No. Hildur says this is the best way to make everything better for everybody.'

'And I am right,' Hildur said, nodding. 'All this talking and not listening. All this not getting to the heart of the matter. And, we would not be here on the roof if you had listened to me in the first place!'

What was going on? Gunnar was at a complete loss and someone needed to start filling in the gaps.

'OK, Hildur, tell me,' Gunnar started. 'Who really is this person and why is he tied to a chair?'

'This,' Hildur said, beginning to limp around the chair, each step bringing her nearer to the roof's edge. 'Is Bernard Lundgren.'

Lundgren. It took Gunnar a few moments to make the connection. Brigitta Lundgren – the girl that had been bullying Magnús.

'Hildur,' Gunnar said. 'What are you doing? Is this Brigitta's father?'

Hildur snorted then. 'No. Brigitta Lundgren's father would have had a heart attack on the stairs up here he's so fat and unhealthy.'

'Hildur—'

'I find that with all problems in life you should start by going to the very head of the family. To the "president" of the living ancestors, the elder, the wisest, the one who should be the moral protector of all those that go after him. Bernard is Brigitta Lundgren's grandfather and, at one time, he was married to my late sister.'

There was emotion in Hildur's tone as there was whenever she spoke about her sister, which was very seldom. But, being emotional was not an excuse for whatever this was.

'And so, Hildur, you have tied Bernard to a chair on the edge of the school roof and are doing what with him exactly?'

'We are making him listen,' Magnús told Gunnar with a nod of affirmation. 'And we did give him coffee from a flask.'

Gunnar closed his eyes. Could this get any worse? And what was he supposed to do? It was as laughable as it was terribly sad. His non-traditional family had felt that he had not done enough to help Magnús's situation and this is how things had ended up.

'And if he doesn't listen?' Gunnar asked. 'What are you going to do with those scissors? Cut off his ears?'

'No!' Magnús exclaimed in horror. And then his expression turned sheepish. 'Only cut off his beard.'

'Oh my God,' Gunnar said, exasperated. 'Hildur! What are you thinking?'

'I am thinking,' Hildur said, 'that how could someone my sister loved so deeply have gone on to teach his son that people with money and status in the community can get away with hurting good, soft souls who would never dream of doing wrong unless they are severely provoked.' Hildur plucked some things from a bag she was carrying. They looked like photographs.

'Hildur, you and I, we have always had a good relationship, no? What do you want me to do?' Bernard asked.

'I want you to look,' Hildur ordered, bringing the photo right up close to the man's face. 'And see that these photographs clearly show the nature of events at school. Your granddaughter taunting Magnús and Magnús finally *pushing*, *not* hitting.'

'I see, Hildur and I hear.'

'Then make things right,' Hildur said with fierce determination, waddling on her brace boot. 'Set the records straight. Tell your son who the true culprit of all this is – his daughter, your granddaughter. And, make certain that he withdraws the allegations to the police so Magnús's name is clear from any wrongdoing.'

'And if I do all this you will untie me? Get me off this roof and let me go back to my bed?' the old man said, still wriggling.

'Let us be very clear,' Hildur said, leaning a little into the man's space. 'I did not tie you to this chair. You did that for yourself.'

'Because you ordered me to. After you drove me here in a van.'

A van? Whose van? And Hildur was driving a van! With a broken ankle?

'I do not know what you mean,' Hildur said. 'How could an old woman with a broken ankle drive a van?' She shook her head and tutted. 'And if you, or any other member of your family would dare to suggest such a thing then you know what will happen.' She took the scissors from Magnús and made them open and close in quick succession. 'Snip. Snip. And, this time, I do not mean your beard.'

Gunnar had seen and heard quite enough. 'Hildur, come now, this stops now. Give me the scissors.' He reached out a hand.

'No!' Hildur roared. 'Not until he has given his word. Like a true Icelander. Like the man my sister always told me you were. A good man. An honest man.'

'I... give you my word,' the old man said, really beginning to shiver now and each movement rocking the chair, one leg perilously close to the edge.

Hildur moved then, pacing towards the edge of the roof and looking down at the people gathered below. 'Now hear this!' she declared like she was about to give a presidential speech.

'Magnús Ólafsson is innocent! He was a victim of a gross injustice and everyone needs to know that just because you are considered to have a different upbringing, with a family that is not born by blood, it does not make you a lesser human! In fact it makes you more human.' She spread her arms out wide. 'We are all born of nature! Made up of the particles of this Earth! We are all family! And, when you realise that, it becomes the greatest raisin at the end of the hotdog!'

With that familiar, yet weird Icelandic phrase delivered to the crowd below, Hildur turned back to Gunnar, Magnús and Bernard Lundgren, looking triumphant. And then she teetered, lost her balance on her injured foot and fell backwards from the roof.

46

REYKJAVIK DOMES

These dome constructions could be used as accommodation and Chloe couldn't help but think how cosy and snug and traditional they were. However, it probably wasn't right for Sinclairz Chairs. The group would want to be closer to the centre of the city, use the evenings to wine and dine after a day of adventure. Still, coming together under the luxury canvas, with views of Mount Esja, was perfect to practice some stress-relieving breathing. The group of ten – including Chloe and Kat – were on yoga mats on the floor, eyes to the see-through, sky-view ceiling, blankets over their midriffs, breathing in the scent of sandalwood, juniper and berries. She wasn't quite sure about the lying on the floor bit when it came to Sinclairz Chairs but, perhaps, a nice touch might be to have actual Sinclairz chairs here, harmonise the counteracting inner stress meditation with the therapeutic elements of the bestselling seats.

'Are they going to say the instructions in English as well as Icelandic?' Kat whispered from her position next to Chloe. 'Because I know you're fluent but I'm not.'

'Very funny,' Chloe replied.

'Seriously though, I will need to be told when to exhale because if I'm concentrating too hard anything can happen, including asphyxiation.'

'I will jab you with my elbow if you start to go blue,' Chloe answered.

Music began to play – a combination of pan pipes and slight guttural moaning and Chloe didn't need to look to know that Kat was side-eyeing her.

'Sounds like someone who added themselves to "free tonight" on Tinder and got a lot more than they bargained for,' Kat whispered.

'Sshh,' Chloe ordered. 'Or we won't hear the instructions in Icelandic or English.'

'Did he say it boosts immunity?'

'Yes.'

'So if I do this I don't have to eat disgusting green veg any more?'

'I don't think it works like that. It also improves sleep but you definitely don't need that.'

'Wow! Sore!'

'It also accelerates the metabolism.'

'Sign me up for the advanced course if I can eat more and not have to look up that Ozempic.'

Someone cleared their throat and after a quick glance to the front, Chloe saw it was their guided breathing tutor. They needed to stop talking and start focussing on the work.

Apparently, according to their instructor, the key to this was listening to your body's natural rhythm. It sounded so simple but the way you did it was super important. It had the power to change your brain power and unlock a wealth of benefits just by doing properly what the body needed to do anyway to survive.

In.

Chloe inhaled and focussed.

Out.

There was supposed to be no pausing between the inhalation and the exhalation. As long as you inhaled fully then you could exhale straight afterwards.

In.

Out.

Clearing the mind and aligning your body's natural actions with simple symmetry. Except not everybody's body performed 'natural' actions. Like hers. Unable to produce enough eggs regularly. Unable to have a baby.

In.

Out.

She was supposed to be clearing her mind, emptying her thoughts and concentrating on this simple pattern of life. Except she would never give someone life, never have a baby take its first breath while she looked at it with wonder and awe. And suddenly she felt more hollow than she had ever felt before. Like there was nothing inside her but useless empty space. Before she could even think another thought she was scrambling up from the floor and running for the door of the dome.

Only when she was outside did she inhale all over again, the fresh, clean, freezing Icelandic air coating the insides of her lungs. She looked out at the view – the mountain backdrop, the turf covered in snow all around, horses statuesque. She hadn't grieved for her loss. And some might say she had nothing to grieve. No one had died. No one had exhaled their last. But no one had breathed their first either. And no one would for her, not in the same way most women got, perhaps taking their fertility for granted. She had hidden the feelings away, thought she had no right to be so distraught, no reason to cry for those babies who would never be. But she had felt hurt, deep sorrow, real and truly painful, and it still ate away at her. Now, as she heard the guided breathing continuing from inside the dome, Chloe let the tears fall. Michelle would have a baby soon and, as delighted as she was for her boss, she knew that Michelle could never, ever really understand exactly how lucky she was. And then there was Michael's news. The man she thought she would be sharing parenthood with having a baby with someone else. It hurt. Hard.

'Come here.'

It was Kat's voice in her ear now and Chloe turned to face her friend, now standing alongside her and offering a look of comfort and as much comprehension as someone not in the situation could have. Eyes bursting with all the tears she should have shed much longer ago, Chloe fell into her friend's arms and wept.

'Absolutely no more guided breathing for you today,' Kat said, hugging her tight. 'I'm going to guide you somewhere much better and it will involve cake.'

47

LANDSPÍTALI HOSPITAL, REYKJAVIK

Gunnar had never seen Hildur look frail before. But here, in this hospital bed, her fragile skin the same colour as the pale white sheets, she looked every year of her however-many-years-old she was.

'Is she going to die?'

The question came from Magnús who was sitting on the other side of the bed, chewing his nails, hair flopping over haunted eyes, gaze going from Hildur, to the bag of IV fluids, to the contrasting spiral of tinsel weaved along the rail of the curtain that was closeting them from the rest of the ward. The boy was scared. Not just from what he had seen today, but all the things he had seen so far in his short life. He would not ever lie to Magnús.

'She fell from a great height.' Just the facts.

'I know,' Magnús said. 'But the firemen caught her in the life net.'

A miracle that they had. Someone had been watching over Hildur in that moment and he didn't care whether it was the *huldufólk* or pure chance, he was grateful that they were even here in this moment, Hildur's chest still rising and falling.

'They did,' he said, nodding. 'But, you know, it was still a hard fall. At Hildur's age, any kind of event like that puts a huge stress on the body and she has only just had her broken foot and—'

'And you have not said that she is not going to die,' Magnús interrupted. 'And all of this happening. It is all my fault!'

'Do not say that,' Gunnar ordered. 'It is no one's fault. Accidents, they just happen. You know this.'

'That is not what Hildur believes,' Magnús said, sniffing with emotion. 'Hildur believes that everything has a purpose.'

Gunnar shook his head. If Hildur wasn't lying in a hospital bed right now he would be cursing her for relaying her opinions and deeper meanings about life to Magnús for him to deal with in this moment.

'Hildur also believes that our entire home looks better when it looks like all thirteen of the Yule Lads have run in and puked up all over it,' Gunnar stated.

'Hildur said that if we do not have enough Christmas decorations the Yule Lads will leave only potatoes in our shoes.' He sighed. 'I told Hildur that because of everything at school I probably only deserved potatoes in my shoes anyway.'

Gunnar shook his head. 'Magnús, like I said, this is not your fault.'

'If I had not pushed Brigitta then none of this would be happening,' Magnús said. 'I should have ignored her. I should have tried not to let it get to me. I should have been stronger.'

'OK,' Gunnar said. He got up, picked up his chair and walked around Hildur's bed, putting his seat down next to Magnús. He clapped a hand to the boy's shoulder. 'Listen to me, Magnús. What is done is done. There is no point thinking of different outcomes or decisions we might have made in anything. We cannot change the past. The only thing we can do is learn from previous choices and use that knowledge to improve what we do in the future.'

'But the decisions I made in the past mean that Hildur's future is in this bed at the hospital,' Magnús said, eyes welling with tears.

'Not... my future.'

Gunnar and Magnús both jumped at the sound of Hildur's voice. The woman's eyes were opening a little.

'Hildur!' Magnús exclaimed, half-standing now and leaning close to her in an attempt at a hug.

'Magnús, give Hildur a little space,' Gunnar ordered, coaxing the boy back slightly with his hand.

'Sorry, did I hurt her?' Magnús said, now looking concerned.

'Stop... saying so much... when you are... really saying nothing at all,' Hildur said, paper-thin lips moving slowly.

'Hildur, do not try to speak. The doctor said you need complete rest and we do not have the results of your scans yet,' Gunnar stated.

'The... perfect situation for you,' Hildur stated. 'First I hurt my foot and cannot move. Now I... should not speak. What is left for me now?'

Gunnar's gut contracted with something close to joy. What was left for Hildur now was her humour. Still very much there and finding its way out even in this difficult situation.

'Do you want some water, Hildur?' Magnús asked, looking at the patient as if she might crumble into dust if he did not attend to her every need.

'That is what the bag is giving Hildur, Magnús,' Gunnar reminded.

'But... it is not... giving me coffee,' Hildur said. 'Gunnar, give the boy some *króna* and let him buy some from the machines.'

He got out his wallet and did as Hildur asked.

'Much sugar in mine,' Hildur said to Magnús before he headed for the door.

As the door closed and Magnús left the room, Gunnar knew the boy's departure had very little to do with Hildur wanting coffee.

'So,' Hildur said. 'Help me sit up so I can talk to you without... fear of choking.'

'The doctor said you were not to move.'

'The doctor is in charge... of my treatment,' Hildur said. 'He is not in charge of me. Either help or I will try myself.'

Hildur started to show signs that she was going to wriggle independently so Gunnar had no choice. He supported her, aided in moving pillows and getting her propped into a sitting position.

'You are OK?' Gunnar asked, seeing a flash of discomfort touch her face.

'No,' Hildur said, gritting her teeth. 'I need to know that you are going to finish what I started with regard to the Lundgren family.'

Gunnar shook his head. 'What would you like me to do? Cut off your ex-brother-in-law's beard or kidnap his son?'

'You do not agree with my methods,' Hildur said. 'Bernard knows me, Gunnar. Despite my needing to make a stand in a public way he was never in any real danger.'

'You are lucky that is also what he said to the police. And, you are even luckier that *you* were not killed!'

Hildur sighed. 'You are wasting words again, Gunnar. All inconsequential. And everything I would repeat again, exactly the same, even if I had hindsight.'

'Even you falling off the roof?'

'Even that,' Hildur assured him. 'Because you know I believe that everything happens for a reason, even if you like to pretend otherwise.'

'I do not know what you want me to say to that.'

'I do not want you to say anything to that. I want you to say that you will make sure that Bernard follows through, that the Lundgrens drop the police complaint against Magnús. That there is fair treatment. That Brigitta and her friends are held accountable for their bullying of Magnús that led to this whole situation. That that precious, sad little boy goes back to a school he once felt nurtured at and feels safe again.'

Gunnar tried to swallow away a large knot of emotion that was suddenly in his throat like a granite boulder as he listened to Hildur and saw her feelings etched on her expression.

'I will not be here forever, Gunnar.'

'Stop that.'

'No,' Hildur said. 'We always speak our truth in our home, no? I am old. That is the fact. But, today was not my day to die. Tomorrow? Who knows?'

'Hildur!'

'I am only saying that, while I am here I will do whatever it takes to support you and support your care of Magnús. And, sometimes, that support will involve something like what happened today and—'

'And, we agreed, that was crazy.'

'Actually,' Hildur said. 'We did not agree it was crazy. And, I thought long and hard about it and made a compromise. My original plan was much worse.'

Gunnar rolled his eyes in defeat.

'You need to stand up now, Gunnar,' Hildur continued.

'Sometimes you are too polite, too nice, too kind, too conforming.'

'What?'

'There is nothing wrong with being nice, Gunnar Eriksson. You are the most gentle soul I know and you teach Magnús so much kindness and respect but...'

'But? It is wrong to be kind and have respect?'

'No,' Hildur said stiffly. 'But respect must be earned and it must be mutually attributable. There should be no hierarchy for it.' She put her bony hand over his and clenched tight. 'You and Magnús are just as entitled to respect as anyone else. I know you both walk around thinking that you do not deserve great things, trying to work out when the next disaster is going to come along and take whatever you have left from you, but you cannot live like that.'

He opened his mouth to deny what she was saying, plead his case, but found he had nothing sincere to offer. In many ways she was correct.

'And, tell me,' Hildur began again. 'Are you still being too polite with the "except"? Chloe.'

He didn't know how to respond. Hildur didn't even know that he had seen Kirstin.

'Gah!' Hildur said, sounding exasperated with him. 'Gunnar Eriksson! If you like someone, tell them. Speak how your heart makes you feel. Say the words out loud. Because what good are feelings except to drive you insane unless you share them with somebody.'

'I know,' he admitted. 'I need to be honest and tell Chloe about Magnús.'

'Yes,' Hildur said. 'Good. And if that sweet boy is a reason to make someone run away from you rather than towards you they were not right for you from the beginning.'

He nodded and gave Hildur's hand a squeeze.

'OK, so, go and help that boy with the coffee machine because he will not be able to work it out on his own,' Hildur said. 'And if I am still alive when you both come back then it will be a good end to the day.'

Hildur closed her eyes and let an elongated sigh leave her.

'Hildur,' Gunnar queried, concerned.

'Go,' she ordered. 'I am resting, not expiring.'

With a smile on his lips, Gunnar got to his feet and went to the door.

48

SVARTA KAFFID, REYKJAVIK

The suggested cake treat had turned into soup. One sniff of the heavenly warming scent drifting from the small eatery and the thought of it served inside a whole rounded loaf of fresh bread, and Chloe's mind was set. Now, tucked into a cosy corner of the upstairs restaurant, loaves filled with delicious meaty soup, Chloe was starting to feel a bit more together.

'Well, I don't know about you,' Kat began. 'But I feel better for the soup benefits than I did for the breathwork.'

Chloe smiled. 'I don't think we gave the breathwork a real chance. It came highly recommended.'

'Be honest though,' Kat said, sipping soup from her spoon. 'Could you see Lincoln Sinclair lying on the floor of that dome panting in and out and thinking it was a vibe?'

'No,' Chloe agreed. 'But I could see him in a Sinclairz chair like a throne, leading the breathing class and relishing his staff worshipping him like the entrepreneurial god he is.'

'Wow,' Kat said. 'You really have thought about it.'

'I think I've thought too much about it,' Chloe admitted. 'And now my overthinking is starting to clash with the brief Kirstin gave me. Maybe I'm trying too hard. And maybe that's my life issue all round.'

'Now you're feeling guilty for trying too hard at your job?' Kat asked.

'At everything. Maybe even about trying to have a baby.' She wiped her mouth with a serviette.

'I'm not sure that's your fault. I'm pretty certain trying hard is what you're meant to do to make it happen.'

'I know but… when I wasn't working, it was my every waking thought and sleeping thought too and maybe that need pressurised everything.' She sighed, her whole body tightening as she thought back. 'And the longer Michael and I were living in that environment, baby-making being all we thought about, talked about, the greater the strain our relationship was under. And we stopped doing the fun stuff, you know.'

'That's quite normal as relationships progress though, isn't it? I mean, one moment you're having sex in the woods and the next you're fighting over who gets to tip the last crumbs of the Pringles tube down your throat.'

'But it shouldn't be like that,' Chloe said. 'Or maybe if it does get like that you can laugh together about it and shake things up a bit.' She sighed. 'Michael and I just stopped doing anything but having mechanical baby-making sex and while the hope that this would produce the perfect end result was getting us through, when it turned into a never-going-to-happen and we realised we'd wasted all that time, it was devastation all around and only highlighted how we had put too much emphasis on a baby and forgotten about the two people that were supposed to love each other.'

'And he didn't communicate afterwards,' Kat reminded her, tearing some bread from her bowl.

'Neither did I,' Chloe admitted.

'But, Chloe, you found out you couldn't have children. He only found out that he couldn't have children with you. It's a much bigger thing for you and he should have supported you through that.'

Chloe nodded, sipping some soup. 'And if he felt the way he should have felt about me, if he had truly loved me, then he would have.' She sighed. 'But I don't think either of us loved each other enough to get through the most difficult times. Maybe that was why the universe dealt me this situation, to let me know, to let us know that we weren't meant to be.'

'Exactly,' Kat agreed. 'Because otherwise, if you were a strong, solid partnership destined for a forever then you would have looked at other ways to have a family. Like adoption or fostering or whatever Angelina Jolie does.'

Chloe nodded. 'I know and, if I want to have a family one day, I will definitely consider all the options. But, it definitely has to be with the right person. Because it's one thing to be in a couple but it's quite another to be the solid foundation of a family.'

'Well,' Kat said. 'I think you will make a fantastic mum one day.'

'Really?'

'You mother me most of the time. Even my mother doesn't know how to mother me.'

'I'm going to take that as a compliment,' Chloe stated.

'It really is. And, if we're being completely honest, you mother Michelle too. I don't know how that woman created this business on her own but I know damn well that it wouldn't be as successful as it is without you.'

Chloe nodded. She was beginning to realise that she should have more confidence in her career abilities. She was driven and focussed but her one fault was perhaps driving so hard she passed a few traffic lights at amber along the way. Her passion for projects was second to none but she had to remind herself that these were not events for her, they were events for others whose wants and needs sometimes didn't want to be pushed in a direction she thought was better. Delivering what the customer wanted, not what you thought the customer should have, was paramount. And with that separation came a degree of released tension to some extent.

'Thank you, Kat,' Chloe said, reaching across the table for her friend's hand.

'What for? Being annoying? Turning up unexpectedly? Getting on your nerves talking about my mother's festive requirements being greater than Mariah Carey's tour rider?'

'No,' Chloe said, giving her hand a squeeze. 'For always being here for me no matter what. For jumping on a plane because you wanted to be with me when I found out about Michael and his new life.'

'That's what family does, Chloe,' Kat said, squeezing her hand back. 'And that's exactly what we are.'

The sentiment hit Chloe full force and she suddenly knew exactly what she was going to do.

49

REYKJAVIK BUS STATION

'Please, Erik, I know I am late but there is good reason and—'

It was the next morning and Gunnar hadn't slept. Despite being the most tired he had been in so long due to the drama of the day before, sleep had not arrived and, instead, he had spent the whole evening churning over everything in relation to Magnús, to Hildur, to Chloe. And every time he had moved he had knocked into another Christmas decoration because, when they had got back from the hospital where Hildur was to stay for at least a few days, Magnús had been instructed by said elder to continue the festive decorating into the bedrooms...

'Stop talking,' Erik ordered, half a cinnamon roll hanging from his lips as they stood in front of the line of buses.

'But, there really is a good reason, Erik, and I do apologise but—'

'I know your reasons, Gunnar,' Erik interrupted again. 'You do not need to apologise any further.' He put a hand on Gunnar's shoulder. 'My sister-in-law works at the school, remember? I know what has been happening with Magnús and the Lundgrens and what happened with Hildur yesterday.'

'You do?' Gunnar asked, relief filling his gut.

'I do,' Erik affirmed. 'How is Hildur?'

'This morning she called me to say she does not like the nurse with silver hair and the bread is too dry,' Gunnar said, shrugging.

'She is healing,' Erik remarked. 'Good. And Magnús?'

'The police will not be taking any matters further. There are no matters to take further with regard to Magnús after they reviewed the CCTV. And, as for Bernard Lundgren being on the roof of the school, he has claimed it was all his idea not Hildur's.' Gunnar sighed, knowing the truth but grateful for the outcome nonetheless. 'Brigitta Lundgren was to be suspended for a week, along with three other children, but Magnús asked the principal not to do this. They are all in the Christmas play and Magnús wants the show to go on so...'

'He is a good boy,' Erik said, nodding.

'He is,' Gunnar replied, feeling a little prideful. 'So, the bus is ready for the south coast tour? I will apologise to the customers for keeping them waiting. I will make sure they have the best time and—'

'No,' Erik said firmly.

Gunnar swallowed. This was the moment he lost his job. This was the next disaster to happen because things always came in threes. Hildur's accident. Magnús's issues with school. But, actually, Hildur had had a second accident and Kirstin had turned up and...

'You are on a different job today,' Erik said.

His relief at not hearing the words 'you're fired' quickly turned into curiosity.

'A different job? What route?' Gunnar asked him.

'It is a private tour,' Erik stated. 'You will take the luxury minibus. The customer asked for you specifically. She said she needed the best driver and the best driver was you according to your high ratings on Tripadvisor.'

As the information started to soak into him Gunnar looked across the icy car park to the luxury minibus and that's when he noticed someone stood beside it. Chloe.

'But what tour is it?' Gunnar asked Erik.

His boss laughed, cinnamon roll crumbs spilling from his lips as he finished the other half. 'She has paid a good sum, Gunnar. Just take her wherever she wants to go.'

* * *

Chloe blew out a breath that was thick in the air. It was freezing today, the snow a thin crispy carpet underfoot. But she was full of confidence about her new plan for the Sinclairz Chairs event and she was determined, by the end of this day trip, she was going to have told Gunnar her fertility story. It didn't need to be overthought, it didn't even need to be for any potential relationship opportunity purpose, it just had to be said. Her sharing her truth with someone.

'*Halló*,' she greeted, waving a hand as Gunnar strode towards her.

'*Krúttio mitt*, you wanted to see me so much you bought a luxury minibus,' Gunnar said, arriving with her.

'Oh, did I buy the whole thing? I still can't get the hang of the currency. I mean it was thousands of *króna* but I thought that was only for the day trip, I didn't realise the whole thing was mine now.'

'You would never fit it in your luggage on the plane,' he joked.

'Not the way you pack,' she answered.

He laughed. 'I loaded your case back up for speed not precision. But you know I will do a much better job at taking you on a private tour today. So, where are we going?'

'Let's start with the Golden Circle,' Chloe said. 'And see what happens after that.'

'OK,' Gunnar said. 'Then, please, your five-star transportation awaits.'

50

STROKKUR GEYSER

'So, there is no Kat today?' Gunnar asked as they walked from where he had parked the minibus to the start of this area of geothermal activity, crowds beginning to gather, all wrapped up against the cold weather.

'No,' Chloe answered. 'Kat said her feet were going to fall off if I made her walk all day again. But she will probably do just as many steps shopping for Christmas gifts in the town centre.'

'This is true,' Gunnar agreed, nodding. 'OK, so, what you need to know about this place is that Strokkur is the most active geyser here and it erupts approximately every five to ten minutes, shooting water around fifteen to twenty metres high. However, it can get even higher than that, sometimes to forty metres.'

'Wow, that's crazy,' Chloe said.

And then she screamed as something like an explosion happened and she put her hands to her ears and jumped in shock.

Gunnar laughed and took her by the shoulders, spinning her round to face the opposite direction. 'That was Strokkur!'

'I can't see anything,' Chloe said, eyes scanning the bubbling pools on the trail ahead of them.

'It is very fast,' Gunnar said. 'A few seconds, a powerful surge and it is all over.'

And Chloe was absolutely not going to deep-think the sexual connotations that were coming to mind right now...

'Well, you know, we will see in another ten minutes,' Gunnar said, taking his hands from her shoulders. 'Come, you will feel it get warmer when we are next to the water streams.'

Right now Chloe couldn't imagine it being warm at all here on the outside, but this was his island, he knew it far better than she did.

'So, I had a revelation about the event last night,' Chloe said, walking alongside him as they headed up the walkway.

'You did?'

'Yes,' Chloe said. 'I realised that I had been too focussed on delivering an action-packed showcase of Iceland when I should have been remembering what the event is for.'

'And this is?' Gunnar asked.

'It's an anniversary for Sinclairz Chairs. Ten years of being in business, building the company from that first chair prototype to now being one of the leaders in ergonomic seating. So, "celebration of achievements" is key.'

'OK,' Gunnar said. 'Good.'

'But, Lincoln Sinclair did not get here on his own. He might be the brains behind it all, but no man is an island. Good workers support him in every aspect of the business; they are the heart of Sinclairz Chairs and the reason it's still thriving. Some of his staff have been with him since day one, so I think it's going to be really important to make "family" a focal point.'

Gunnar nodded his head, looking deep in thought. 'Family is important.'

'Yes,' Chloe agreed. 'And it can take many forms. I mean, Kat is like the sister I never had and when your blood relatives aren't around any more, or actually even if they are, other people can be more important, closer.'

'I agree,' Gunnar said. 'It is not about how people are related to you, more so it is how they impact your life.' He took a breath. 'That is one of the reasons, the main reason why Kirstin and I did not work out.'

'Oh?' Chloe said.

'But, you know, at the beginning, when I should have been honest with her, I wasn't. So that was on me.'

Now Chloe felt a chill run through her. He hadn't been honest? He had been hiding something? What did that mean?

'I think, perhaps if I had been truthful at the beginning then things might not have deteriorated like they did.'

He sounded sad, reflective, like talking about this was hard for him.

'Gunnar,' Chloe began. 'Please, you don't have to tell me anything you feel uncomfortable about sharing because—'

'No,' Gunnar interrupted. 'This is not about "I do not have to tell you", Chloe. For so long I have been telling myself that I do not have to tell anyone at the beginning, that time will make a difference, but the difference has to start with me.' Gunnar sighed. 'Chloe, the reason Kirstin and I broke up was because a child was never going to be in her future.'

And that's when the geyser erupted again, shooting water up into the air as Chloe's heart went with it.

'Oh, wow, that was… so quick and spontaneous,' Chloe said, eyes filling up with tears, throat tight. 'And I missed it, wow, but if there's ten minutes right, I can… pop to the toilet.'

'Yes, but, is everything OK?' Gunnar asked, looking at her intently.

She nodded and did her best to channel BAFTA-winning actor. 'Absolutely, just need to, you know, use the facilities. I will be back.'

Not waiting for him to say anything else, she half-walked, half-jogged back the way they had started, all the while weeping on the inside.

51

KERID CRATER

Gunnar knew something was wrong. Not only because of his sense of sense, but because he had known Chloe long enough now to interpret her body language and read her signs. It was happening all over again and he hadn't even explained about Magnús and Hildur. When she had got back from the bathroom she had turned their conversation very much into tourist mode. He gave her information on the geysers, she took photos and videos and asked questions relating to her event-planning. It wasn't like it had been between them and it was hard to re-imagine how close they had been just the other night under the stars...

Now they were standing above this large volcanic crater lake made up of red volcanic rock and Chloe was snapping more photos and saying very little.

'So, this crater is not very old,' Gunnar said, moving alongside her.

'Really?'

'Yes. Only six thousand five hundred years.'

'That sounds old to me,' Chloe replied.

'But not when you consider how old the Earth is: over four point five billion years. If you believe science that is. The Bible would suggest that all the Earth is only as old as this crater but how reliable is a book that suggests that water can be turned into a wine and a baby can be born like magic.'

'Well,' Chloe said, turning away from the crater view to face him. 'Many people do believe that book. And Christmas will be here soon, the season celebrating the birth of the book's magic baby.'

'You are angry, *krúttio mitt*. Did I do something?'

Chloe sighed. 'I'm not angry.'

'Come on,' Gunnar said with a tut of frustration. 'We know each other a little now, no? I can tell that something is inside you and you want to shout it at me, but you are holding it back.'

She shook her head, but he knew she was lying. It was obvious and written right the way through her body language.

'OK,' Gunnar said. 'So, do not shout it at me. But why not shout it into the crater.'

'What?'

'Come,' he said. 'We will go down, close to the water's edge, into the crater and you will shout whatever you are angry at into its core. Maybe this will be perfect for your event. Your guests can shout celebratory messages across the water by candlelight or maybe something like... moments of truths. Reflection about the ten years that has passed for this company, the challenges they have overcome and plans for the future. Maybe a local choir can sing.'

'Are you taking the piss?' Chloe asked, hands on hips.

'What?'

'Making fun of me and the ideas I have? Like they're stupid.'

'No!' Gunnar exclaimed. 'No, I was being serious. It was

something I used to do with my mother. Please, let us go down to the water's edge.'

He held out his hand and wondered if she would take it, or whether he might never get to touch her again.

'OK,' she said, walking past him towards the trail.

Maybe he had his answer.

* * *

Chloe was unfocussed and that was the very opposite of what she wanted to be. This trip today had meant to be about her new vision for the Sinclairz Chairs event, but she had also wanted to take the chance and tell Gunnar her truth. But how could she now when the very reason that his relationship ended with Kirstin was because Kirstin didn't see children in her future. Chloe didn't just not see them in her future, she could not have them! This was the aged-however-old-the-universe-actually-was kicking her when she was already lying at the bottom of a crater.

But it was spectacular down here at the water's edge though, staring up at the red rock interspersed with vegetation covered in an icy sheen. Whether Gunnar had been serious or not, she could really envisage a choir and candlelight.

'The lake is partially frozen now,' Gunnar said, alongside her. 'When it is even colder and frozen harder, people will ice skate. You know, some people will probably try to ice skate now but that is crazy and could lead to death so we will not do that and I suggest that you do not add ice skating here to your event plans.'

One thing she couldn't see was Lincoln Sinclair in ice skates.

'So, if we shout something it will echo around here?' Chloe asked.

'You do not trust your tour guide?' Gunnar queried.

She wanted to trust him. She hadn't known him very long but the quality of their connection, the sizzling undertones and the almost soulful way their minds intertwined had begged her to carry on leaning into it. What had changed? Had anything?

'OK,' Gunnar said. 'Do not answer that. I will go first. To put you at ease.'

He cleared his throat and then put his hands either side of his mouth and shouted into the crater's centre.

'*Huldufólk!*'

It bounced back hard, echoing eerily and Chloe couldn't help but laugh at his word choice.

'What is so funny?' he asked her, smiling with his gorgeous eyes as well as his mouth.

'That you chose to shout something that you said you don't believe in.'

'It could have been worse,' Gunnar said. 'I could have shouted Santa Claus.'

Chloe gasped. 'You don't believe in him either?'

'In Iceland we have something a little different. We have the thirteen Yule Lads.'

'What?'

'They are characters that live in the mountains, in caves, that come to town at Christmas time to make mischief. In some stories they eat children and you will tell these stories so the children will have good behaviour before Christmas time. In other tales the lads just leave presents for people; these are sometimes nice and sometimes potatoes in their shoes.'

'Are you joking with me?' Chloe asked him.

He laughed. 'No, *krúttio mitt.* I mean, I do not know if the stories are truth at all, they are Icelandic fairy tales, but these are not made by my mind.'

She knew one story that was truth. Sad truth. Her lack of fertility reality. Maybe this was the time.

'If you like potatoes,' Gunnar said as Chloe moved a little closer to the water's edge. 'I guess finding them in your shoes is a good gift.'

She wasn't really listening to him now. She breathed the freezing air in deep and shuddered. It was like her body and her mind were both begging for some kind of release.

'You are ready to shout your truth into the crater?' Gunnar asked.

She sensed him standing behind her now, not touching her but close enough to make a connection if she wanted it. She had wanted it. Felt that giddy, excited churning inside when she was with him. Maybe just experiencing those kinds of feelings for someone again was enough, to restore her faith that life might not only contain career climbing, that there was a chance for something else.

'I'm ready,' Chloe said, teeth juddering.

With the deepest of inhales, as she closed her eyes tight, she shouted into the volcano, to the Earth and up high to the sky with every ounce of hurt and grief, but, most of all, with powerful acceptance.

'I CAN'T HAVE CHILDREN!'

And as her words echoed back at her, she snapped open her eyes, heart pumping, body re-awakening. Something in the universe felt like it had shifted, akin to the tectonic plates that had created this place. She listened to the reverberation of her words, felt it on the surface of her skin, then, determinedly, she let it sink in, almost welcoming the final acceptance of this reality. Then, when all was still again, when the only sound she could hear was the whistle of the wind above her own thudding heartbeat, she turned around and looked at Gunnar.

He had never looked more handsome to her than at this moment. That tall frame, so solid, those astonishing eyes fixed on her, unmoving, unperturbed but definitely absorbing. Usually now would be the time she would drop her eyes, or feel some kind of embarrassment for publicly admitting something so personal in such a way, but not today. Today she was owning this moment.

And then Gunnar did move. He wrapped his arms around her and he picked her up off the ground like she was weightless, holding her tight against him as if he wanted to transmit all that he had to her – strength, resilience, energy. Chloe closed her eyes and breathed him in, feeling like she was an over-emotional monkey clinging to a tree.

'I am here, *krúttio mitt*,' Gunnar whispered in her ear. 'Please know this. Feel this.'

She did feel it. And she so, so wanted to believe it.

52

A SECRET LOCATION…

Everything felt different and Gunnar could not explain it without wondering if the spirits of this island were absolute fact and not simply folklore. From the moment he had heard what Chloe hollered to the universe at Kerid it was as if something inside him had unlocked. Vulnerability wasn't weakness. Vulnerability was power. Why had he not realised that there was a chance for the greatest, strongest connection if you showed someone the parts you considered to be weaknesses?

He had held her for the longest time at the edge of the lake, until his biceps started to burn and then, when he had put her down, he had taken her hand in his and not let it go until they got back to the minibus. He knew then where he wanted to take her next and he could not have cared less if it fitted with any idea for the company event.

'This isn't the Blue Lagoon,' Chloe commented as Gunnar opened the door for her.

'No,' he said. 'It is not.'

'Is this a different spa?' Chloe asked. 'More exclusive?'

He smiled. 'Something like that. Come.' He held out his

hand and helped her down from the minibus, his backpack over his shoulder.

From the road it looked like there was nothing here but more rocks and turf, horses grazing to the left, not a house nor person to be seen, just the coastline ahead. But what lay only a few metres down this uneven land was pure heaven for the soul and that's what he knew Chloe needed.

'Is this where the Yule Lads hang out?' she asked as they walked. 'With their potatoes and ghoulish faces? I looked them up on the drive by the way, terrifying.'

'I am hoping that no one is here,' he replied, squeezing her hand.

A few more steps and then it opened up and the sight was even more special than he remembered. A thermal spa, circular, steaming, completely natural, like the Earth had created a precursor to the manmade infinity pools everyone craved. This wasn't the Blue Lagoon with its drinks' packages and bathing robes, this was just the healing hot water in its natural state.

'Oh my God,' Chloe exclaimed, gripping his hand. 'It's so beautiful.'

'It is,' Gunnar agreed, stopping with her to admire the view. 'It is one of the best places in my opinion because you are surrounded by everything that Iceland is. The Earth, the mountains, the sea, the sky and this gift of hot water.'

'A gift that no one knows is here,' Chloe stated. 'There's no one else here. We could be the only people in the world right now.'

They started to walk again.

'Oh, some people know it is here. Local people. My mother knew it was here. She used to walk here with her friends from school and play mermaids.'

'I wish we could go in,' Chloe said, sighing.

'What?' Gunnar asked. 'We are definitely going in.'

'But I don't have a swimsuit. I was going to hire one at the Blue Lagoon and...' She stopped talking and smiled. 'Oh, OK, I see. No one here, no swimsuits required.'

'*Krúttio mitt*, public nudity is completely legal in Iceland.'

'Is it?'

'Are you blushing?'

'No.'

She definitely was and it was causing a geothermal reaction inside him that really wasn't the reason for bringing her here. He needed to maintain respectful balance.

'You can leave your clothes on if you would feel easier,' Gunnar said, taking his backpack off. 'I have a towel. We Icelanders are always prepared for most things. The weather, the need to take our clothes off and swim.'

'Well then,' Chloe said, letting go of his hand and moving her fingers to the zip of her coat. 'I wouldn't want to go against any local traditions.'

'OK,' Gunnar said, taking off his hat. 'But we must be fast when we are naked, so we do not freeze before we get into the water.'

'That sounds like a challenge,' Chloe said, looking him in the eye.

He met her gaze, coat already halfway to being off and then both of them began tearing off their clothes in a bid to be the first out of them and in the water.

53

The water was beautiful and as it lapped over Chloe's shoulders and the back of her neck it felt like all her anxiety and stresses were being rinsed out of her by Mother Nature herself. It was so peaceful here with the mountains towering above them and the sea in front and below. Yes, a wilderness, but a landscape that also, somehow, gave off 'nurturing' and 'nourishing'.

She wasn't sure seeing Gunnar naked was giving off anything other than pure sex appeal though. As much as she had been hurrying to get out of her clothes, going quicker as each layer came off and more of her was exposed to the cold conditions, she had taken time to appreciate his fine form. Strong, muscular, looked like he could uproot a Christmas tree if needed. But she also knew how gentle he was, outside and in.

'You like massage?' Gunnar asked, swimming closer to her.

'Doesn't everyone?' she answered.

'I was asking only about you.'

She nodded, feeling both calm from the warm water, yet also softly bubbling with anticipation for whatever was coming next. 'Yes, I do.'

'So, turn around, rest your arms on the edge.'

He didn't need to ask her twice. She turned her back to him and positioned herself as he'd suggested. She was already feeling beautifully warm and relaxed but when Gunnar's fingers grazed her shoulders everything heightened ten-fold. Now she felt warm, relaxed and sexy...

'How do you feel after saying your truth to the crater?' Gunnar asked, hands caressing her muscles.

Her stomach fluttered in response to his question, a mix of nervousness and anticipation. 'I feel... that it was the right thing to do and it was the right time.'

'How long have you known?' Gunnar asked. 'If you don't mind that I ask.'

'No, it's OK,' Chloe said. 'It's been eleven months. I had a partner, we wanted to start a family together and it didn't happen.'

'I am sorry for that.'

'Don't be,' Chloe answered. 'I mean, I think now that there were many reasons it didn't work out for us, but the not being able to have children naturally together just wasn't what he wanted.'

She felt him slow down with his hands, ease his fingers over her muscles, soft then harder, her tendons aching with joy.

'And how did you feel about that?' Gunnar asked her.

'About not being able to have children naturally?'

'About your partner only wanting children who were born "naturally".'

She heard the quotation marks around the word 'naturally' and realised that no one had ever asked her that question before. The friends that knew had only ever asked her how she felt about her infertility, not Michael's response to it.

'I think it made me think less of him,' Chloe answered truthfully. 'The person I thought he was would have looked at other ways to create a family, if a family with me was what he truly wanted.'

She felt Gunnar's fingers stop massaging and she wondered if she had said something wrong.

'Turn around, *krúttio mitt*. Look at me.'

The warm water swirling around her, Chloe turned to face him. This handsome man who was starting to become more and more familiar to her. He was gazing at her now like she might be the most beautiful work of art. Precious. Special.

'Anyone who truly cares for someone will still care for them no matter how circumstances change,' he told her.

'You really believe that?'

'Yes, I believe that,' he re-affirmed. 'And, I think, if you do not believe that then you are sending a message that you do not believe in the truest, deepest forms of human connection. Empathy. Humility. Love.'

He looked so genuine, that he completely trusted this at his core.

'I want to believe it,' Chloe told him. 'But past experiences haven't reassured me.'

'Chloe,' he said, stepping right up to her, the steam rising from the water between them. 'We all have moments that shake us right through our centre, but the answer is not to let those moments devour your inner hope, your strongest resilience. The people who make you question everything you thought you believed about them are not the people who should be able to make you fall.'

As he said the words, he cupped her face with one of his huge hands and Chloe closed her eyes, leaning into his palm. It would be so easy to just rest here, to let go of previous baggage with Michael but...

She opened her eyes, looking at him. 'Gunnar, you said that Kirstin left because she didn't want children and now you know that I can't have them so the circumstances, they are no different for you.'

'I have not explained it very well,' Gunnar told her. 'Not from the start and not now either.' He took a breath. 'Do you remember Magnús? On the coach tour.'

She nodded. 'Your friend's son.'

'Except he is not my friend's son.'

'He's your son?'

'Not exactly that either but, yes, I am responsible for him. There are many volcanos on this island but, one day, there was an eruption no one was expecting. And when that happened, Magnús' parents, they were never found. Their house was destroyed... and I rescued the only person I could find that day – Magnús.' He sighed. 'He is the child that Kirstin could not see in her future with me. A child that already exists. One that I would do anything to protect.'

She saw the flood of love for the boy pouring out in his words and pooling in the depths of his eyes. He had made personal sacrifices to look after someone vulnerable who had lost everything he had. It was one of the most wonderful, selfless sacrifices and it only confirmed what an incredible, intricate person Gunnar Eriksson was.

Before she could think herself out of action, she put her hands in his hair and entwined her fingers with it, wanting to feel every strand on her skin. She ached for his lips to touch hers again, longed to feel his body on hers, every single inch. She drew his face to hers, grazed his bottom lip with her teeth.

'Chloe,' he rasped, feverishly.

'How do you say "I want you" in Icelandic?' she asked him, kissing a path along his jawline.

'*Ég vil þig*,' he told her, drawing her body tight to his.

She repeated it badly. Then: 'Sorry, I'm still not fluent.'

'It is OK, *krúttio mitt*,' he answered, lifting her up, her legs wrapping around his waist as they stood in the water. 'We can stick to body language if you want.'

She smiled, arms looping around his neck as she pushed her body onto his. 'Oh, I definitely want.'

He claimed her mouth then, backing her up against the side of the natural pool. And as Chloe gasped at his strength, demanding even more, their bodies began to move in perfect unison. In this beautiful moment she had never ever felt more alive.

54

Despite the chaotic nature of his life right now, with Magnús's school issues and Hildur in hospital again, Gunnar had never felt as purely content as he did in this moment. He put another piece of wood on the fire he had built beside the thermal pool from whatever they could gather and then his gaze found Chloe, bundled up in towels and his coat as well as hers sitting on a luxury blanket from the luxury minibus. What they had shared together he couldn't even put into words in his own head. It had been sexy, but oh so much more. They had moved with each other with such an intensity, from their touches, to their eye contact sizzling with desire, to the way he had felt like she was giving him not just her body but her soul too. He swallowed. It had never ever been that way for him before.

'I'm thawing out,' Chloe said as he went to join her on the blanket. 'Like a slowly defrosting Christmas turkey.'

He put his arms around her, drawing her close to his body. 'You are nothing like a Christmas turkey. You are so much more beautiful.'

He kissed the top of her head that was now wearing her hat and his and found her gloved hands, holding them tight.

'I won't put this place on the itinerary for Sinclairz Chairs,' she told him.

'You think it is not special enough?' he asked.

'What? No!' Chloe exclaimed, wriggling against him. 'That wasn't what I meant at all—'

'Relax,' Gunnar said, laughing. 'I am joking with you.'

'Well, good,' Chloe said, settling. 'Because I meant the exact opposite. It's too special for Sinclairz Chairs. That and the fact there's nowhere to get cocktails. Although I have brought in a mobile cocktail-making van for events before. And we could bring a loud band here on one of your buses and actually we could serve a whole banquet right next to the pool – we might need two buses to park here on the turf for all the staff and—'

In one quick move he tipped her sideways, then released one of his hands from hers and clamped it over her mouth and nose until all he could see was her eyes. What was lying there in those pupils staring back at him. Was she smiling now? Laughing? Something else? He knew she had been kidding with him.

'I know you do not mean that,' Gunnar said, his hand still pressed against her face. 'I see you, *krúttio mitt*. Ow!'

He let her go and she sat up, grinning.

'Did you bite me?' Gunnar asked, eyes wide.

'Only a little one,' she told him. 'Like the one you did on my shoulder. Kat will be asking questions about that if she sees it.'

'And what will your answer be?' Gunnar wanted to know.

'I will tell her that it was an injury.'

'Oh really,' Gunnar said, leaning closer to her again.

'Yes,' Chloe said. 'I will say that I went to do research... maybe a wood carving workshop or something that involved sharp tools or... birds of prey and—'

'You would rather say you were beaked by a falcon than say you were bitten by me? I am offended.' He folded his arms across his chest.

'Oh, Gunnar, no, I didn't mean it.' She rose up on her knees and put her arms around his neck, hugging. 'I know I said I know Icelandic to my boss but I'm really not a compulsive liar.'

'Really?' he asked. 'That is exactly what a compulsive liar would say.'

'Bite me again,' Chloe whispered in his ear. 'Make it look as far from a chisel shape as you can.'

He laughed and kissed her lips instead until they were again so wrapped up in the passion she started to shiver.

'You are cold,' he said. 'We should not stay here too long.'

'Just hug me warmer,' Chloe said, burrowing into him again. 'And talk to me. Tell me about Magnús and how long you've been looking after him.'

'The volcano, it was not expected to happen. And I know that these things do not follow a precise calendar, but the volcanologists can predict a close approximation. But not this time.' He sighed, remembering back. 'A friend, he texted me about the eruption, and I got in my truck and I drove there.'

'You drove towards the volcano?' Chloe asked.

He nodded. 'What was I going to do? Sit in my safe home and wait for news about the deaths of people, the loss of animals and nature?'

'Most people would have done exactly that or, I don't know, tried to help from a distance. Not put themselves in danger.'

'I think I was just confident that, knowing the area very well, having experienced eruptions before, it was my duty as an Icelander to try to help.'

'And there was Magnús?' Chloe asked. 'On the road? In a field?'

'Actually, Magnús was underneath a wheelbarrow. And he was terrified. He was covered in ash, he had burns, it really is a miracle that he survived.'

'So, you just took him to the hospital and then gave him a home?'

Chloe's outside perspective was making it sound like it had been easy but it had been anything but. It had taken Magnús weeks to get out of the hospital, longer to even speak about what had happened, and all the while, in the background, Gunnar was working with the authorities to be able to become his guardian.

'He was in hospital a long time and then the papers for me to become his guardian were taking even longer. I do not know if it was because I was a single man and that usually these things are done by a couple, but I decided I needed to ask someone for help for Magnús's sake.'

'Who?' Chloe asked.

'Someone else I should have told you about much sooner,' Gunnar said, sighing. 'Her name is Hildur and she is the most cranky, irritating, opinionated woman I have ever met. But she is also one of the wisest, kindest people I know too. She was my mother's friend and I fear she is someone my mother set the task of looking out for me after she died.' He paused before continuing. 'Hildur offered to move into my house and help with Magnús. She thought that having a woman in the home would make the paperwork on Magnús's guardianship speed up.'

'And was she right?' Chloe asked him.

He nodded. 'Yes, she was. She is right about most things. Except she is very bad with spatial awareness when it comes to roofs.'

'What?'

'It is a long story,' Gunnar said. 'Thankfully one that everyone has survived to be able to tell the tale of over dinner.'

'I don't understand,' Chloe said, looking bemused.

'I know,' Gunnar replied, holding her hands again. 'But I want you to. Will you come to dinner with me? To my home. Meet Magnús and Hildur, when she gets out of hospital.'

'Hospital?' Chloe exclaimed. 'Well, is she OK?'

'Yes, she is OK,' Gunnar said. 'But my life is currently a lot of drama. I will understand if it is all too much and—'

'No,' Chloe said. 'We aren't going to let honesty and the truth of things change how we feel towards each other, remember?'

'I remember, *krúttio mitt*,' Gunnar said, cuddling her to him. 'I also remember that you like it when I kiss you… here.'

He put his lips to the space just behind her ear and he felt her weaken against him like she had in the water before.

'I do like that,' she breathed. 'And do you know what else I'm going to like?'

'What?'

'You cooking me dinner,' Chloe told him.

He held her away then, looking at her, taking her all in, so beautiful bundled up in every item of clothing and all the layers he had to offer.

'Really?' he asked her.

'Really,' she replied. 'I want to meet your family.'

Family. Yes, it was. Unpredictable, a little scary, but real life. And undeniably a part of him he had now shared with someone he was starting to care so deeply about.

55

CHLOE'S APARTMENT, REYKJAVIK

Chloe woke up with a start. Her laptop was making noises as if she had set an alarm. She definitely hadn't and, looking at her watch, she saw that the time was 9 a.m. Not super early but she really should have been awake before now. She slid from her bed and padded to her laptop on the table, lifting the lid. Shit! It was Zoom and it was Michelle. Impromptu Zooms were never good.

'What's going on?' Kat groaned, rousing too.

'It's OK,' Chloe said. 'Go back to sleep. It's Michelle.'

'Is she in labour?'

Oh, God, she couldn't be. Could she? Her boss did do some unusual stuff when she was stressed or hyper or both but not usually unscheduled Zoom calls. However, no matter what it was, she had to answer. She teased her hair behind her ears, hoped she didn't have sleep drool around her mouth, switched the lamp on and then pressed to connect.

'Hello, Michelle. Is everything OK?'

'Chloe Bellamy, everyone. Everyone, this is my right-hand

woman, Chloe, who is currently working on a very auspicious event we are undertaking for a global brand.'

Chloe looked at the screen where her face was now inside a box. The absolute normal for Zoom, but the fact there were at least ten other faces in ten other boxes was not at all what she was expecting. How was she part of such a large meeting she knew nothing about and why had Michelle given her no warning? She was dressed in pyjamas that said, 'Dear Santa, Define Good.' She side-eyed the sofa to see if there was anything that could cover up her top. 'Hello, everyone.'

'Chloe, could you take us through the top tier wins we've had over the past year,' Michelle instructed.

Top tier wins. OK, she could guess at what that meant but she had never heard Michelle use the expression before. Did she mean the events that had gone the best? The most high-profile clients? The ones that had made the most profit? Right now she felt like she'd been woken up by Lord Sugar and was having to write a business plan on the spot in front of an audience she didn't even know. Who were these people?

'Chloe, did we lose connection? Is your mic turned off?'

And apparently Michelle was expecting instant answers and giving her no time to think. Well, thinking on her feet was what she had to do.

'Vixen Shoes,' Chloe said confidently. 'We choreographed their entire brand launch party. They wanted to showcase and sell the product whilst celebrating the conception at the same time. So we designed a dual-purpose event consisting of a fashion show and auction and then a canapés and cocktails party with everything relating to Vixen, the powerful mythical face at the heart of the brand's embodiment of female leadership.'

Silence. Blank faces. Did they want her to shut up or carry on?

'I... er... we've worked with a premiership football club,' Chloe continued. 'They wanted their board of directors to take part in a boot camp style fun day... and we also took the lead on the engagement party for Riley Stylus. She was in Season Four of *Love For Keeps*. No matter who the client is, no matter what they're celebrating or what specific requirements they have, we deliver an exceptional service each and every time.'

Still no one was speaking. Not even Michelle. Did they want figures? She could give them figures but it would take her a while to find things on her laptop; she couldn't just conjure up a spreadsheet in two seconds. And then someone did speak. It was a man's voice coming out over Zoom and Chloe chilled right down to the bone, colder than she had ever been before. He wasn't speaking English. And, although she didn't categorically know what language he was talking in, she could make a reasonably accurate guess by how it sounded. Icelandic.

The man with grey hair said his sentence for a third time and Chloe knew she had to do something, say something before the game was up.

Suddenly her phone lit up. A text message. Kat. Chloe looked over her shoulder and her friend was sat up in bed, phone in hand, giving Chloe the large eyes that said this was a message she really needed to read.

We can use AI. Chat GPT

Could they? Should they? Why was she even thinking about this? She should just tell the truth, right?

'Chloe? Are you still there? Or are you frozen?'

Michelle was waiting for her response more than the probably Icelandic man.

Another text from Kat.

> Ask him to repeat it again. In Icelandic that is 'endurtaktu það vinsamlegast'

What? Chloe had no idea where to even begin saying those words and she suddenly felt like a reindeer on an Icelandic road being dazzled by the bright lights of an oncoming speeding truck...

And then: '*Endurtaktu það vinsamlegast.*'

The robotic voice sounded tinny and super loud and one of the Zoom participants actually put their hands to their ears. At least the voice was female but, could it pass off as her? Shit! Her lips hadn't moved. There was only one thing for it or the game was up. She mouthed like she was a puppet.

Then the robotic voice said: '*Því miður er smá töf.*'

Another text from Kat.

> It means there is a time delay. Just keep mouthing after the robot speaks.

The man spoke again and Chloe looked at his image closely. Did he already have suspicion in his eyes? Know that this was all a ruse?

> He asked if you are enjoying Iceland

She knew the word for 'yes'. She also knew 'do you have wine' but that wasn't going to be enough. But before Chloe could think about whether to actually say anything or confer with Kat about how to respond, the robot voice was talking again.

'*Ísland er fallegt land. Og mér finnst mjög gaman að undirbúa spennandi viðburð fyrir afmælishátíð Sinclairz.*'

Chloe moved her lips and then she stopped fake-talking, a feeling of sheer dread shrouding her. She only really knew one word from that sentence and, at that moment, she knew, if the game wasn't up already, it was set and match now. Between Kat and AI, the cardinal business sin had just been committed and when Chloe's gaze found Michelle's in the centre square on screen, the look on her boss's face told a story all of its own. She was done for. She either left the meeting right now, tried to talk her way out of it, or she came clean...

'I'm so sorry,' Chloe said with all the professional confidence she could muster. 'I have to leave the meeting now. There's a planning emergency that I have to deal with. It was wonderful to meet you all and I hope I get the chance to talk with you again.' She waved a hand and pressed the icon to leave. Closing the lid of her laptop, she took a shaking breath. It was only a matter of time.

'What happened?' Kat exclaimed. 'Because I know I wasn't the fastest at getting the responses but I thought it was going OK.'

'It's OK,' Chloe said, shaking her head and feeling anything but alright. 'It was my fault. I got myself into this from not telling the truth at the start.'

'I don't understand,' Kat said, flapping about on the bed in frustration, all bed hair and chaos.

'You mentioned Sinclairz in whatever you got the robot to say last, didn't you?' Chloe said, putting her laptop down on the coffee table.

'I got it to say that "Iceland is a beautiful country. And I am very much enjoying preparing an exciting event for Sinclairz's anniversary celebration". Was that not OK?'

Chloe shook her head. 'You mentioned a client that no one is supposed to know we are working with. Nothing is confirmed yet. Nor does anyone know that Sinclairz Chairs are even having an anniversary celebration. And I have no idea who those people were. They could have been anyone. They could even have been from Sinclairz.'

'Oh my God,' Kat exclaimed, slapping her hands to either side of her face. 'This is all my fault! I'm an idiot! You need to call Michelle and you need to tell her that your imbecile friend, the one she never liked anyway, got you into this from the very beginning. Tell her everything, tell her you lied on your CV about speaking Icelandic because I told you to, say that not coming clean was my idea too and definitely tell her this fucking robot shiz was on me.'

'No,' Chloe said, her mind competing with taking immediate action to work out the best plan to salvage the situation or shutting down. 'No, it's fine.'

'It's not fine though!' Kat continued. 'Michelle is going freak, isn't she? And she freaks anyway about everything, and now this is a big thing and she's battling with third trimester hormones. I know about those because Esther at book club turned into an absolute witch about a month before she gave birth.'

'It's OK,' Chloe said.

She had actually said that sentence with utter calm and that took her by surprise. OK, so, in the moment, shock and horror driving her thought pattern, she might have given in to those initial feelings of panic. But now, her mind collating things together, offering her snapshots of her career thus far – good and bad – she was feeling like this might be a crossroads but, maybe, the exact place she needed to be.

'I feel so, so bad I might be sick,' Kat stated, hands in her hair.

'Don't do that,' Chloe said. 'Everything is going to be fine.' She crawled up the bed and put her arms around her. 'What you tried to do was a really, really nice thing. You coming here to Iceland was a really nice thing, Kat and I so appreciate you, I want you to know that.'

'I don't appreciate me right now. I think I've just made things worse for you and I should have stayed in the UK deliberating over gravy granules and fresh versus frozen sprouts.'

'No, you shouldn't,' Chloe insisted, squeezing her tight. 'You've always been there for me when it mattered most. Always.'

She felt Kat relax just a touch into her hug. She knew her friend steamrollered into things but that was the way she showed her affection. It might sometimes be misplaced or ill-timed but there was never a hidden agenda or any malintent, just pure and genuine affection driving her.

'I'm not going to answer any unplanned Zoom calls ever again,' Chloe told her. 'That's a lesson I've learned here.' She sighed. 'I've also learned that the best experiences aren't the ones with a dedicated VIP section you have to pay for.' Her mind returned to everything Gunnar had shown her on this trip. 'Sometimes the best things in life you really can get for free.'

'Amen to that,' Kat said, yawning as she lay back down in the bed. 'And I really don't care how you say that in Icelandic.'

Chloe took a breath, feeling lighter than she had in a long time. Perhaps today was the day for new beginnings.

56

GUNNAR'S HOME, THE OUTSKIRTS OF REYKJAVIK

'You are fussing,' Hildur stated, knitting needles in her hands as she sat working diligently on whatever she was making out of wool.

'I have not said a thing,' Gunnar stated, sipping at his morning coffee.

He really couldn't believe that Hildur was out of hospital and home so quickly. Even her broken ankle was no more broken than it had been before. A miracle.

'I am allowed to discharge myself, you know,' Hildur stated.

'I know,' Gunnar said. 'I just did not expect the hospital to allow you to do that past midnight or for them to organise your transport.'

'Did they forget to call you to let you know?' Hildur asked, not even bothering to hide her wry grin. He knew she had most likely told them not to contact anyone.

'I would have liked to have been here to help you, that is all,' Gunnar said.

'I am glad that you were not and that, instead, you were out with Chloe.'

He put down his cup before he dropped it. 'I did not tell you I was with Chloe.'

'But you were.'

'What I should have told you, if I knew you were coming back, was that Magnús had rehearsals for the Christmas show. Lena said he could stay the night. That she would take him to school this morning.'

Gunnar had had offers of all kinds of things in relation to Magnús since the drama at the school. Usually it would be something he would actively avoid. He was always the helper not the one who wanted to accept assistance.

'Good people want to help,' Hildur said. 'They just need a reminder sometimes.' She put down her knitting. 'And you are ignoring the "except", Chloe.'

'I am not ignoring her,' Gunnar said, an involuntary smile growing on his lips.

'Neither is your heart,' Hildur stated with a knowing nod.

He was nervous of his feelings though, tentative still, yet wanting to feel his way forward no matter how scary that might be.

'I would...' he began.

'Yes.'

Why did this feel so hard? His throat was dry and Hildur was looking at him like she might grade him on his conversational content. He just needed to get the words out of him and then it was done.

'I would like to... introduce you to Chloe. And Magnús of course.' He wet his lips. 'I have invited her to dinner.'

Hildur smiled, arms on the sides of the chair, looking like she was about to haul herself up into a standing position. And for someone who had fallen off the top of a large building such a short time ago it was far from recommended. Gunnar dived towards her, stood in her way, halting the progress.

'I did not ask the "yes" as a question,' Hildur told him, ignoring his efforts to prevent her from standing and doing it anyway. 'I said it because I knew this moment would arrive with Chloe.'

'That is wonderful,' Gunnar said mockingly. 'It is nice to know that you knew something about my world that I had no idea about. Who told you before me? The *huldufólk*?'

'You did,' Hildur informed him like it was a case of absolute fact. 'In the way you smile when you talk about her, in how you are softer with Magnús, able to tune in to your emotions again. You have not been that same way before. You were not ever truly that way with Kirstin.'

Gunnar knew it was fact. Somehow, in the short time he had spent with Chloe so far, he had found a raw connection that had grown quickly and deeply, without either of them really acknowledging the extent of it until now.

'Do not overthink it, Gunnar,' Hildur told him. 'Do not think that she has to get back on an aeroplane and fly to England. Do not think that Magnús is in a difficult time and perhaps this is something that can wait. Love does not wait. Love should not have to wait. Love, it comes through the door whether it is invited or not.'

He nodded and then Hildur leaned into him, putting her arms around him in the kind of warm embrace they didn't share very often.

'Gunnar Eriksson, it is time for you to live for you,' Hildur told him. 'The saving of the island and everyone else in it can be the responsibility of others for a while.'

'It cannot be your responsibility, Hildur, I know that much. I do not watch you for a short time and you are kidnapping people.'

'These are false accusations,' Hildur insisted. 'Bernard said he came willingly, the police have agreed it was so. Now, stop hugging me, we have a dinner menu to think about.'

'Oh no,' Gunnar said, making sure Hildur sat back down before he stepped away. 'You are not cooking anything. You are resting. Besides, I am still uncertain of how Magnús will feel to have Chloe here for dinner.'

'Magnús will be happy for you,' Hildur reassured him. 'He tells me sometimes that he wishes you were not so sad.'

'I do not want him to worry about me,' Gunnar stated. 'That is the last thing I want him to be doing.'

'Ah, Gunnar, whether you want him to worry or not, that is what comes when you are part of a family, no?' Hildur reminded him.

As always, she made an excellent point.

'However,' Hildur said. 'I am sure if you cook his favourite caramelised potatoes then he will be happy about anything. Food and ice hockey are what that boy lives for after all.'

'You are right,' Gunnar agreed. 'So, when do you think I should invite Chloe?'

'You are asking the wrong person,' Hildur replied, picking up her knitting needles again. 'I think that question should be asked of Chloe. Because do you still not know for how long she is staying in Iceland?'

Gunnar's heart contracted then. He still didn't know the answer. And as that realisation hit, he knew that whenever that time came it would be far too soon.

57

REYKJAVIK RÖST, REYKJAVIK

Chloe looked out over the sea from her seat outside this coffee shop with extraordinary views. Boats close in the marina and then the open water, its motion strong and sturdy today, dappled by the tiniest amount of winter sunlight seeping through the clouds. It was a bit like how she was feeling. Grounded but not motionless, steadfastly determined in her trajectory... Did she know exactly how the future would pan out? Absolutely not. But who did? Really? However, right now, it was enough to know that she felt ready to engage with life fully again, not bury everything else but her career aspirations.

There had been an email from Michelle waiting for her when she woke up but, for the first time ever, Chloe hadn't read it. Instead she had scheduled in a Zoom call with her boss and for once she was going to take the lead.

She saw the notification that Michelle had joined the meeting; it was time.

'Good morning,' Chloe greeted brightly as Michelle's face appeared on screen.

'Hello, Chloe, shall we skip the pleasantries and just cut to the chase here?' Michelle snapped. 'I have a mani pedi in thirty minutes. I don't actually know why we are having this meeting because I put everything I needed to say to you in the email I sent you.'

'Oh,' Chloe said. 'Well, I haven't had a chance to read that yet.' She took a sip of her coffee and willed its caffeine to keep giving her strength.

'You haven't read it?'

'No,' Chloe said. 'Because I spent this morning finalising the pitch for the Sinclairz Chairs anniversary event.'

'Oh, finalising the pitch for the Sinclairz Chairs anniversary event!' Michelle parroted. 'You mean the event you blabbed about in front of the chamber of commerce! Or, rather, not actually you blabbing, but some kind of weird alien voice that Lars said, and I quote, "sounded like Google Translate".'

Chloe cupped her coffee cup in both hands and let Michelle carry on.

'So, not only did you commit one of the ultimate business sins, talking about an event we have not even secured yet, letting other business people know there is such an event so they can tell any number of people about it and we can get more competition for the job, you got an app, or whatever, to speak Icelandic! Which says to me that you don't speak Icelandic and therefore you've never been able to speak Icelandic and you've been lying to me since the day your CV claiming to speak Icelandic arrived in my emails!'

Yes, that was pretty much what had happened. Chloe thought it was a fair summary of events and nothing that she hadn't been prepared for.

'I don't know, Chloe,' Michelle said, looking increasingly uncomfortable. 'I was beginning to think that I could really trust you.'

What? Chloe put down the coffee cup fast, almost sloshing some over the table.

'You were beginning to think you could trust me?' Chloe said, hurt flavouring the words.

'Yes, I mean, there are certain aspects of your strategy that need some careful moulding, but I thought this was something we could work through together in time and—'

'Michelle,' Chloe interrupted. 'Please think about what you're saying. Really think about it.'

'I have thought about it, Chloe. I thought about it all night long when I couldn't sleep because the creature I am growing inside me is hitting my bladder every five seconds like it's a fairground punchball game. I thought about how completely embarrassed I was about your behaviour in front of the chamber of commerce and—'

'Well, do you want to know what I'm embarrassed about? I don't expect you really do but, as this is my meeting, I am going to tell you anyway.' She took a breath and looked Michelle in the eyes. 'I am embarrassed that I actually thought you were more than just my boss. I'm embarrassed that I considered you to be my friend. Because I have worked so, so hard for you from the moment I started at the company. I have dedicated my every minute, no, more than that, my every second, not just to the company but to you personally. I have answered every call, every email, every late-night WhatsApp message about ridiculous things sometimes and I have never ever questioned anything you've asked me to do. I've just been there for you, dedicated, professionally and personally. And most of that isn't in my job contract, it's simply in my nature to be a nice person, to help, to support even when I was going through the most difficult of times myself.'

'Well, I—'

'And that's what hurts the most now,' Chloe carried on. 'To hear you bringing down my abilities when I have held you and this company up, created new opportunities, helped you build this business into the success it is today and you never even asked me why I was going in and out of hospital.'

There was quiet. No immediate response. Michelle sitting still just looking into the camera. Was she going to say anything? Was there any point to this anyway? Some people just couldn't see how their behaviour impacted others even if you tried to explain it.

'Chloe, why you were in and out of hospital is none of my business,' Michelle stated matter-of-factly. 'You made sure it never impacted on your work, I will give you that.'

Chloe sighed. It wasn't the response she had hoped for. 'As an employer, the full details aren't always necessary but, as my friend? As someone who has shared so much time with you and Milo. As someone who organised your mother's birthday presents every year?' She took a deep breath. 'Michelle, I was in and out of hospital because Michael and I were trying for a baby and it wasn't happening. And, what happened instead was I found out I can never have children. Yet, somehow, I don't even know how, I have been there for you and your family from the moment I bought you the pregnancy test.'

Emotion ballooned in her chest now and she looked past her laptop screen momentarily, sought solace in the sea again.

'Michelle, I am absolutely overjoyed for you and Milo that you're having this baby. But, I won't lie, it's been hard watching every second of your pregnancy – the sickness, the cravings, the seeing your bump grow and your skin glow and feeling those little feet strike out and kick. And it's been exhausting hiding my pain from you which is why I couldn't do it any more.'

'Chloe—'

'No, don't say anything now, Michelle. I know that I lied on my CV, that was stupid and unnecessary and I never thought it would ever come back to haunt me the way it has. And I also know I had plenty of opportunity to tell you the truth before I ever got on the plane to come here but, well, I chose not to. I also apologise for the robot voice stuff. That was Kat's idea. She was trying to get me out of a hole with the whole not speaking Icelandic thing and she made a bad choice. I will speak to whoever I need to speak to at the chamber of commerce and set matters straight, tell them my behaviour is not a reflection of you or Celebratey and—'

'Chloe, let me—'

'I am going to email you my presentation for Sinclairz Chairs. I think it's sensational. I think, if they go with us, they are going to have an anniversary celebration to remember with the theme being "family – we grow together". It encompasses the idea that traditional values can support new future visions, so it is very much being thankful for the very beginnings, but also preparing to get excited for all the success that is to come.' She took a restorative breath, but she was so positive that her idea for what the Sinclairz Chairs event should be was going to hit the remit and go even further. There was just one more thing to add. 'And the other attachment to the email is going to be my resignation.'

'Chloe, please, stop talking now and—'

'Now isn't the time for more talking, Michelle. I know this is an incredibly difficult period for you and it's not my way to leave someone in the lurch which is why I am going to work longer than my notice period, if you need me to. But, I need a break. I've not stopped to take stock of my life since Michael left. I just tried to work my way through it. And that can only work temporarily; after that you have to address things, or they just lie dormant waiting to crush you all over again when you least expect it. So, that's what I'm going to do. I'm going to take some time out for me.'

And, with those words said, she looked out at those rays of sunshine bursting through the clouds and knew, without doubt, she was making the right decision.

58

MAGNÚS'S SCHOOL, REYKJAVIK

Gunnar stood outside the school hall, looking through the small window in the door. Everything was dressed for Christmas now – a large tree by the stage, glittering in silver and white, tinsel and garlands hanging from the ceiling. It brought back memories of his childhood, but not only that one terrible night when he'd found out his father had died; now it evoked good thoughts, the remembered joy in simple pleasures. And there was Magnús on stage, in a puffin costume, flapping his arms and strutting in quite an accurate representation of how the bird moved.

'Mr Eriksson.'

Gunnar turned around and there was Mr Almr. '*Halló*,' he greeted. 'Is everything OK?'

'Please,' Mr Almr said. 'I think that is what I should be asking of you. How is Hildur?'

'Hildur is a force of nature stronger than an Icelandic storm,' Gunnar told him. 'Keeping her still to rest is not a job for those faint of heart.'

'I understand,' Mr Almr said. 'I have a mother exactly the

same.' He smiled, tucking the files of paperwork he was holding under his arm. 'I just wanted to let you know that Brigitta Lundgren will be leaving the school.'

'Oh?' Gunnar said, surprised.

'Her parents have decided she would be better suited to a private education.'

'Mr Almr, whatever has happened with Magnús, it was not our intention for her to feel excluded,' Gunnar said. 'Only for people to understand that everybody deserves to come to school and feel safe and an equal part of the community.'

'I know,' Mr Almr stated quickly. 'I am sure recent events have steered the Lundgrens into making this decision now, but I feel this was something they had considered before.'

'Does Magnús know this?' Gunnar asked him.

'No one knows yet and I would appreciate it if you kept this information to yourself for now. I just thought it might help settle Magnús maybe?'

Gunnar nodded. 'Thank you.'

Suddenly Magnús burst through the door, out of the puffin costume now, backpack hanging off one arm.

'Hey,' Gunnar greeted. 'Slow down.'

'I cannot slow down,' Magnús answered. 'I forgot some of the dance tonight and I need to get home to practice.'

'OK,' Gunnar said, waving a hand at Mr Almr. 'Let's get in the truck.'

Magnús ran for the door.

Inside the truck, with the heating turned up, Gunnar prepared to start the conversation he had been practicing in his head all day. He was nervous. He wanted to be doing the right thing. For everyone. But he also remembered what Hildur had inferred. That he needed to focus on himself for a while now.

'So, how is the show practice going?' he began tentatively.

'I told you,' Magnús stated, mouth around a chocolate bar he had plucked from his rucksack. 'I forgot some of the dance tonight.'

'I know you said that but you will be fine, you have some days and, Magnús, it doesn't matter if it's not perfect. It is a Christmas show, everyone will love it and applaud at the end.'

'Just because everyone's parents will clap at the end doesn't mean it shouldn't be as good as it can be,' Magnús told him.

He made a good point. 'OK, so, when we get back, do you want me to help you with... the dance?'

Magnús laughed hard then, chocolate almost spilling from his mouth. 'You want to dance?'

'I do not want to dance. You know how I am with dancing. But, I will dance to help you remember.' He smiled as he drove. 'Maybe if you see how bad I am you will think of that when you are dancing the routine and it will help you recall the movements.'

'It will make me laugh too much. And at the beginning of the show I have to be a sad puffin.'

Gunnar frowned. 'What kind of Christmas show has a sad puffin?'

'I am not telling you anything more because you need to wait to see it.'

Gunnar cast an eye over to Magnús, eating, playing with the strap on his backpack, and a feeling of happiness washed over him. He was so lucky to have this boy in his life. The tragedy of the loss of Magnús's parents would never be erased, but maybe Gunnar had been looking at the situation wrong. This wasn't just doing the right thing and stepping up for an orphaned boy, this was about building an alternative, bright future for them both. It wasn't about feeling obligated through circumstance, it was about choosing this path and this person because you cared. And he was beginning to care for Chloe too.

'Magnús, I was thinking, about... asking Chloe to have dinner with us sometime.' He swallowed, heart beating a little quicker.

'O-K,' Magnús said with a touch of what sounded like trepidation.

'OK?' Gunnar queried.

'Well, I do not know,' the boy said, fingers knotting with the backpack strap. 'Because if Hildur is cooking I would say it is a good idea but if you are going to try and cook then I think it would be a very bad idea.'

He smiled then. 'You think it would be safer if I took us all to a restaurant?'

'No,' Magnús said. 'Because she should come to our home. If there is a chance that... one day, maybe... she might become part of our family.'

The boy's words set off a whole cascade of emotions inside him, ones he didn't even realise he possessed. It was happiness, a little cautious perhaps, but definitely only the deepest sensation of positivity.

'You know that Chloe lives in England,' Gunnar reminded him.

'I know that she was sad,' Magnús stated matter-of-factly. 'On the tour, when we were at the waterfall.'

Gunnar nodded. 'You know how life can give good people difficult things to deal with.'

'Like with my parents and your parents,' Magnús said. 'Did Chloe lose her parents too?'

He nodded again. 'Yes, but there are also some other things that have made her sad too.' He paused for a beat before continuing. 'However, I do know that she also laughs very much, sometimes even at my jokes.'

Magnús groaned. 'You are not serious. Why?'

'Because some people find them funny.'

'Some people are stupid,' Magnús said.

'Hey!'

'But it does not matter if she laughs at your jokes if she is going to be sick because of your food.'

'That is not funny.'

'No, it is the truth!'

Gunnar laughed. 'OK, OK, so if Hildur cannot cook, and I will not let her cook no matter what she says, what do we do?'

'Takeout?' Magnús suggested.

Gunnar shook his head. 'No, Magnús, I actually think maybe... you and I should cook together.'

There was no response as Gunnar had to slow the truck down for a red traffic light and stop. Was Magnús not going to say anything?

'What do you think?' Gunnar asked him.

'I think,' Magnús began. 'That the last time we cooked together was the first time that I spoke to you after the volcano.'

He remembered. He hadn't been certain that Magnús would. That perhaps he might have chosen to forget.

'I know,' Gunnar said. 'It is one of my best memories of when you first came to live with me. The first word you said to me was "no". Something you have been saying to me regularly ever since.'

'You asked me if I liked cauliflower. What was I supposed to say?'

He smiled. 'We do not have to make cauliflower. You can help me choose what we cook.'

Magnús's eyes lit up. 'Can we make a traditional Christmas

dinner? If Chloe is going back to England before Christmas she will miss eating it with us so we should make that.'

Now Gunnar felt nauseous. It was no small task to cook the smoked lamb and all the trimmings. But Magnús's face was so alive with joy he didn't have the heart to dampen his idea or his spirits.

'You will help me?' Gunnar checked. 'Because it has to be good.'

'I promise,' Magnús said sincerely, 'that however it turns out it will be better than your jokes.'

'You really are taking every opportunity to make fun of me, aren't you?' Gunnar said light-heartedly.

'I will do it even more when you are practicing dancing with me when we get home,' Magnús remarked.

The light turned green and Gunnar drove off again. 'OK, Magnús. Smoked lamb, with caramelised potatoes and green beans.'

'Good,' Magnús said, nodding. 'And you need to buy a new shirt. Everything you have is too old. Again, like your jokes.'

As Magnús laughed at his own humour and turned on the radio, raising the volume as a Christmas song came on, Gunnar let this feeling of complete contentment sink down deep into his conscience. This felt good. Life was good.

59

TWO DAYS LATER

Reykjavik Airport

'Are you sure you have to go?' Chloe asked Kat, giving her friend the longest, strongest hug as they stood near the entrance to security.

'My mission here is complete,' Kat said, hugging hard back and then letting go and looking at Chloe with the most sincere expression on her face. 'I came here to make sure you were OK with the whole Michael Bali Babygate thing and then, I admit, it turned into "wow, isn't Iceland one of the coolest places I have ever been to" and also "wow, waterfalls are immense and I need to read more dark fantasy novels involving heroes choking heroines under those" and "wow, my best friend is the most resilient, amazing person I've ever known".'

'I agree about the waterfalls,' Chloe said, smiling. 'And Iceland really is cool and so cold today.'

'You need to agree about the last sentence too,' Kat ordered.

'I'm still learning about resilience,' Chloe admitted.

It had been two days since she had had her Zoom call with

Michelle and in that time it had been complete non-communication with her boss. As promised, Chloe had emailed the pitch for the Sinclairz Chairs event and she thought it was one of the best she had ever created. It was chic, it was chill and celebratory but it was also steeped in the tradition and importance of 'family', 'togetherness' and 'working as one to achieve united success'. There was a creating cocktails masterclass on a hotel rooftop, there was a private Northern Lights boat trip with traditional folk music followed by a DJ playing contemporary chill tunes until dawn. There was a unique combination of the south coast and Golden Circle tours by VIP minibus that Gunnar had helped her create and the husky ride was also in there – what better way to show teamwork than a band of cute doggies working together to pull a sleigh? Maybe Michelle had completely changed it. But, to Chloe, the success was not getting the Sinclairz Chairs job now, it was knowing she had done her best work, even if it would be the last pitch she ever planned.

'Stop thinking about Michelle,' Kat ordered as if she could read her thoughts. 'She will be knee-deep in designer baby paraphernalia and TikToks about preparing your pelvic floor.'

'I know,' Chloe said.

Kat rubbed her arms. 'Listen, if she's really crazy enough to accept your resignation and let you go and this is the end of things with her company then... the universe has other, much better plans for you.'

Chloe nodded. But it wasn't a reticent nod, it was one of pure conviction. She wasn't afraid of the future now, she was excited for it. Her job had been her much-needed safety net for so long, but now it was time to jump into life and trust that she would fly.

'And I know that I am going to be completely jealous of the smoked lamb that is coming your way later. Not a euphemism.'

'I'm more nervous about that than I am about anything Michelle is going to say or not say,' Chloe admitted.

'Nervous about a man cooking for you? I would lap that up while it's being offered. Not sure it happens that often unless it's a chef on *Sunday Brunch*.'

'Two men,' Chloe reminded. 'Don't forget Magnús.'

'Ah yes, the potential step-son.'

'Don't say that,' Chloe said.

She swallowed, nerves tingling. She hadn't known Gunnar very long but their connection had grown so fast and so strong and it was important enough to him to have her meet the boy he had been raising. It felt like a privilege to be invited into his home to share a meal and be introduced.

'And the old lady,' Kat added. 'The old ladies are always the ones judging. It's her you need to be nervous about, not the kid.'

Hildur. Gunnar had described her as someone with the whole Earth's wisdom but with the juvenile spirit of someone who did not let her age stop her from doing anything. Including falling from a roof apparently...

'Should I take a gift?' Chloe asked. 'I hadn't even thought about that. I should definitely take something, shouldn't I?'

'For the boy? Or the old woman? Is this sounding a little bit Disney Pixar right now?'

'I don't know. Maybe something for the house? For everyone? Or is that too impersonal?'

Kat squeezed her arms. 'Now you're worrying too much. Don't overthink it. It's just dinner at a guy's home with his almost-son and an overbearing Icelandic grandmother figure who will either be willing there to be a marriage or casting runes to try to find out your ulterior motives for her family.'

'Great,' Chloe said, shaking her head.

'Remember that very first Icelandic phrase I taught you?' Kat asked.

'Do you have wine?'

'Exactly. That is still all you need. Get a nice bottle of something, some sugary snacks for the child and you will be potential girlfriend of the month.'

Girlfriend. Was she on the way to becoming someone's girlfriend again?

'Now, let me leave,' Kat ordered, letting Chloe go. 'I have to head back to Winchester ready for my mother to arrive, along with her terrible world views and even more terrible wardrobe of sequinned outfits and a whole carefully curated schedule of "must-do" Christmas activities starting with making some cranberry-infused tea that is going to take years off me apparently.'

Chloe pulled Kat in for another hug. 'Thank you, Kat. For being here.'

'Thank you for having me and putting up with me and for taking me around some of this beautiful island. Now, go and explore the best part of it without me,' Kat said, grinning. 'That hot coach driver tour guide of yours!'

Hers. Gunnar was hers. But, in reality, was it even possible?

60

GUNNAR'S HOME, THE OUTSKIRTS OF REYKJAVIK

Gunnar couldn't remember a time when he had felt so nervous. It was just a Christmas dinner. Yet, somehow it felt like he might be making a feast that would be critiqued as if it was part of a cooking show where there was a prize. He pulled the *hangikjöt* – hung lamb – from the oven and set the tray on the side of the worktop to rest.

'That smells wonderful,' Hildur remarked as she hobbled into the space. 'Did you add the cloves like I said?'

'Yes,' Gunnar replied. 'Why are you not sitting down?'

'And did you glaze it like I showed you?' She leaned in over the meat dish, inhaling as if her sense of smell was going to answer the question for him.

'Hildur! Sit down!'

She waved a dismissive hand. 'You need to alter your tone, Gunnar Eriksson. You are about to have a lady friend in our home. We do not want her to think that you shout all the time at this poor, fragile, aged woman.'

'A poor, fragile, aged woman who I know for a fact was

standing on a stool to put more Christmas decorations up this morning.'

Hildur pulled a face. 'Did Magnús tell on me?'

'No,' Gunnar stated, turning his attention fully on Hildur. 'He said nothing, but I noticed there were more and now you have given yourself away. Hildur, I say again, please rest.'

'You are like an old worn song that has been overplayed,' Hildur said, stirring the bechamel style sauce he had prepared on the oven top. 'Ah! Music! We need to have music. What shall we put on? Something for the season? Or something romantic?'

As Hildur shuffled off to the smart speaker Gunnar took a minute to breathe. What was happening here? He was standing in his kitchen cooking the biggest family meal he had ever prepared in a house that looked like it could star in a Christmas movie. Glitter and goblins and a second decorated tree were all fighting for space, branches and garlands and baubles encroaching a little on the dining space he had set for four... And then he realised something was missing, or rather someone. Where was Magnús?

* * *

The taxi had pulled up outside a lovely looking wood and stone house set back from the road with a yard area at the front that seemed to be a pitch of some kind with a net at either end. It had an apex roof that seemed to be coated in snow-covered turf. Was this it? Chloe paid the driver and got out, feet crunching down on the icy ground.

'*Halló!*' a voice called.

It was then she noticed a boy in the front yard, an ice hockey stick in his gloved hands. He was wearing a bobble hat and a thick coat, joggers on his legs. Magnús. The last time she had seen him, on the coach tour, she had been led to believe he was the son of one of Gunnar's friends. Now he was someone she was being properly introduced to.

'*Halló*,' Chloe greeted, smiling.

'*Halló*, Chloe,' the boy said, a little nervously.

He was walking towards her now, through the small gate and out onto the road. As he reached her he whipped his hat from his head, displaying his blond flopping hair and gave a bow. 'I am Magnús. It is nice to see you again.'

When he popped back up, Chloe held out her hand. 'It's nice to see you again too.'

'I think you are very pretty,' Magnús told her.

She laughed. 'Oh, thank you.'

'Gunnar, he is, at best, only a six out of ten so—'

'Magnús!'

Chloe looked to the house and there was Gunnar on the top step, dressed in jeans and a navy-blue shirt, a tea-towel over his shoulder. She did not think he was only a six out of ten. She thought he was all the numbers and so much more.

'Chloe is here!' Magnús yelled. 'And I told her she is very pretty!'

'Magnús, come inside and wash your hands. Dinner is almost ready,' Gunnar called.

'He is very bossy,' Magnús whispered to Chloe as if Gunnar was close enough to hear. 'But he is also the kindest person I know.' He whispered even quieter then. 'But, if you do not like the lamb I have sweets we can share.'

'Oh, thank you,' Chloe said. 'Actually...' She put her hands into the bag she was carrying. 'I bought you something.' She took out the foil-wrapped Santa Claus and handed it to him. 'I hope you like chocolate.'

'I love chocolate,' Magnús said, his eyes lighting up like he had been given the world.

'Thank goodness,' Chloe said. 'I thought I might have to eat it myself.'

'We can share,' Magnús said, kindly.

'Hello, Chloe,' Gunnar greeted as he arrived next to them.

'Hello,' Chloe said, loving the way her stomach squirmed a little bit every time she looked into his eyes.

'I'm going inside,' Magnús announced, rushing towards the steps.

'Carefully! Slow down!'

Chloe watched Gunnar watching Magnús so protectively, making sure he made it into the house without slipping on the ice. And then he turned back to face her.

'Hello, *krúttio mitt*,' he greeted again, moving into her space.

'Hello,' she answered, her body enjoying the closeness as he leaned in for a kiss.

It all felt so natural now, like these moments were destined to be, like they had been written into her life plan and that all the things that had happened before had been to lead her to here. She relished the way his mouth made hers come to life before he ended the kiss and looked back towards the house.

'I am sorry,' he said. 'I was half-expecting Hildur to be at the window with a pair of binoculars.'

'Oh, wait, I think I see her,' Chloe said, putting a hand to her forehead in a seeking stance.

She felt Gunnar shift, head moving in the direction of his home. She laughed. 'Got you.'

He turned back to her, his expression far from light-hearted. For a second she wondered if she had said something wrong.

He held both her hands in his and squeezed them tight. 'Yes,' he said. 'You have.'

61

'So, tell us about your visit to Iceland,' Hildur said when they were all sat around the table feasting on the magnificent meal. 'Gunnar does not share details with me for fear that I will tell the whole neighbourhood and they will know his secrets.'

'Does Gunnar have secrets?' Magnús asked loudly.

'No, I do not have secrets,' Gunnar said, rolling his eyes. 'How could anyone have any secrets in this small house with such large personalities?'

Chloe laughed. She was adoring every single second of this event. From meeting the formidable matriarch with sparkling eyes, who could only be around five feet tall, to watching Magnús and Gunnar trying not to good-naturedly bicker with each other over serving up the delicious feast. There was no doubt in her mind already that this house was a home and it was made that way by everyone's unique differences pulling together towards their common goal – harmony.

'I apologise for these people,' Gunnar said to Chloe. 'I do not know how we got here but here we are.'

'Do not apologise for me, Gunnar Eriksson,' Hildur ordered. 'I am a gift.'

'Yes, you are,' Chloe said immediately. She smiled at Magnús. 'You both are.'

'She is pretty and nice,' Magnús remarked.

'You are encouraging them,' Gunnar said to Chloe.

'And you are not letting Chloe answer the question I asked,' Hildur said.

'Oh, sorry,' Chloe said, putting down her knife and fork. 'My trip here. Well, I work for an event-planning company and a client wants to have an anniversary long weekend here to celebrate a big business milestone. So I was sent here to see what activities would work, plan the schedule, make it bespoke for the client and work out how much it would all cost.'

'Nice, pretty and clever,' Magnús stated.

'You will make me blush with all these compliments,' Chloe told him.

'Not compliments,' Gunnar said. 'Truths.'

Now she did blush momentarily. 'You are too kind.' She smiled. 'Anyway, I put all the activities into a plan and I sent it to my boss and she will then review it, make some amendments maybe and then she will show it to the customer and they will decide if they like it or not. That's how it works.'

'Has your boss been to Iceland?' Magnús asked as he began eating again.

'No, actually and I think she was a bit jealous that I got to come here because it really is such a beautiful country.'

'Why didn't your boss come too?' Magnús carried on.

'Well, she couldn't fly,' Chloe said.

'She is scared to fly?' Hildur asked. 'I do not know why this is. How often do we see birds falling down from the sky? Flight, it is so easy.'

'She isn't scared,' Chloe said. 'She's just having a baby. When you are close to the time you are going to have the baby, you aren't allowed to fly in an aeroplane.'

The words had rolled off her tongue like they had no consequence but as Magnús launched into asking why pregnant women couldn't fly and Hildur started to explain in more than enough detail than was appropriate during a meal, Chloe felt a warm, strong hand find hers under the table. She hadn't told Gunnar that Michelle was pregnant and he understood. He now knew emphatically how challenging this last almost nine months had been for her. She squeezed his hand tight.

'So do they burst?' Magnús exclaimed. 'If they go into an aeroplane and the stomach is too big?'

'Ha!' Hildur laughed. 'If that was the case there would be many fat Americans bursting all over the world every other second!'

'Well,' Chloe said. 'I think if I eat any more of that... what did you call it?' She indicated the lamb that had been sliced on a large platter.

'*Hangikjöt*,' All three of her dinner companions said in unison.

'Yes, if I eat any more of that then I think I might burst.'

'This is not allowed,' Magnús said quickly. 'Because I helped Gunnar make a *lagkaka*.'

'What is that?' Chloe asked.

'It is a traditional Icelandic layer cake,' Hildur explained. 'We have made ours with rhubarb jam.'

'It sounds so delicious but, Magnús, you will have to eat more of it than me.'

'OK,' the boy said happily.

* * *

'I do not know why you are helping me to clear things up,' Gunnar said later when the meal was finished and Chloe had been taken to Magnús's bedroom by Magnús to help with the puffin dance practice.

'Why do you complain?' Hildur asked. 'I am sitting down. Pass me the platter to dry.' She reached out her hands, wriggling her fingers. Gunnar did as she asked.

'So... Chloe cannot have children,' Hildur stated.

Shocked, Gunnar dropped the glass he was holding into the washing-up bowl. 'What? How did you know?'

'Ah, Gunnar, still you doubt many things about me. I have told you of the strength of female intuition and I have told you about the spirits of this land; there is never anything that is unknown, just things that are untold.'

'It is not for me to tell you either,' Gunnar said. 'It is Chloe's story.'

'I understand,' Hildur said, nodding as she dried the plate. 'But you know that stories can change. Just like the story has changed for you over the years, and for me and for Magnús.'

'I know that finding out tonight that Chloe has had to work closely with someone through the whole of her pregnancy, seeing all those changes, wishing she could feel them for herself one day, must have been one of the hardest things for her.'

'Harder still that everyone expects you to be so happy about other people's joy all of the time,' Hildur remarked. 'We are always taught to be so polite, so loving and giving and caring and unselfish but sometimes, just sometimes, we need to also understand that one person's happiness can definitely invoke another person's sadness. Whether it is intentional or not.'

'She has kept her sadness inside for a long time,' Gunnar stated.

'Well, she does not need to be sad any more,' Hildur said with a nod.

'I think, when you get news like that, you are always going to feel sad about it in some way. Perhaps forever.'

'Forever is a long time,' Hildur said, passing him back the dry platter. 'But what does it really mean? Does it mean for the time we are alive or longer than that?'

'Ah, Hildur, another lesson about the spirits of Iceland?'

'Do you think Chloe coming here was a coincidence?' Hildur asked him like it was the craziest suggestion.

'No, I think that she had a job to do and that job took her to Iceland.'

'And the reason it was now? The reason that you met? The fact that you told me she had nowhere to stay and you could help? How did you actually meet? Did she just get on your coach or was there something else? Something a little more like... fate?'

Gunnar swallowed. They had literally fallen into each other, landed on top of one another when so easily they could have simply been allowed to walk on by.

'You know I do not believe in those kinds of things.'

'I know,' Hildur replied softly. 'But I do not think that matters. What will be will be and what is meant for us, well, no one can stop it from happening.'

With that said, Magnús came barrelling into the kitchen, puffin costume flapping out behind him. 'Gunnar, we need to get another ticket for my Christmas show. I asked Chloe and she said she will come.'

'OK, OK, calm down. I am sure we will be able to get another ticket,' Gunnar stated.

'If that's OK,' Chloe said.

She was stood behind Magnús now, looking a little hesitant. He didn't want her to feel that way, ever.

'It is more than OK,' Gunnar told her. 'I just... did not know how long you are staying here in Iceland.'

Chloe nodded. 'I know. I guess I don't even know that yet but, the Christmas show sounds like something I can't possibly miss and now Magnús has perfected his dance I need to see it with everyone in costume and find out more about these Yule Lads.'

She was staying for a few more days at least. Whatever was meant for him and the reasons behind it, Gunnar was grateful for whatever time they had before her leaving was inevitable.

62

GUNNAR'S COACH

'Hello, Chloe.'

'Hello, Michelle. How are you?'

As Chloe looked at her boss on the Zoom call she thought she had never seen her look so unput-together. Not that that was necessarily a bad thing. She knew that despite Michelle's confident projection, her boss was riddled with insecurities and sometimes it was those that made her act a certain way. But, it wasn't an excuse for her lack of appreciation and consideration. As the coach bumped up and down on their journey, thankfully with free and reasonably fast Wi-Fi, Chloe steadied the screen.

'You don't need to ask me that,' Michelle said. 'You shouldn't ask me that actually.'

'Is everything OK with the baby?' Chloe continued regardless.

Michelle nodded. 'Everything is fine. Perfect, they said at the last check-up. The head is fully engaged now. Apparently, that was supposed to make me feel joyful, but all I could think about was that one sex education class at school where they had a plastic pelvis and a Baby Annabell.'

'It won't be like that,' Chloe reassured. 'And you have the best doctors looking after you.'

There was silence on the call and Chloe wondered if their connection had been severed until:

'I am lucky,' Michelle stated with so much meaning, Chloe wasn't sure she had ever heard her say anything in that way ever before. And she wasn't quite sure how to respond, so she didn't. She just let Michelle's sentence have room to breathe and glanced out of the coach window at the scenery as they rolled by towards today's destination Gunnar had asked to be in charge of.

'I am so, so lucky,' Michelle continued, this time sounding bright, more upbeat, like this feeling was revolutionary.

'Yes,' Chloe agreed.

'And most of the time I behave like a raging bitch who is angry at the whole world with absolutely no reason for it.'

'Well...'

'And you can only say it's down to hormones for the past almost nine months of it. For the rest of the time... that's just been me being me and not appreciating anything. Like some privileged princess with no concept of reality.'

It sounded like Michelle had been getting deep into motivational podcasts – not necessarily a bad thing.

'Don't be hard on yourself,' Chloe told her.

'Why not?' Michelle asked. 'Why shouldn't I be hard on myself? You know, Chloe, everything you said to me was absolutely right. 100 per cent correct. And I know that for two reasons. One, because when you were saying the words to me I could feel them hitting those deep places inside we like to try to ignore. And, two, because you've never said anything to me that hasn't been 100 per cent correct.'

Chloe smarted in her seat. 'Well, apart from telling you I spoke Icelandic.'

'One thing,' Michelle said. 'One small thing that somehow I made into a huge deal. And made you feel you couldn't be honest with me about it.' She shook her head. 'Shocking. As is not only not treating you like my very best employee but not treating you like my equal or treating you like... my friend.'

'Well, in business I know it's hard to keep professional boundaries but—'

'But I did not support you as an employer, as an equal or as a friend when you were going through one of the hardest things anyone has to go through,' Michelle stated.

OK, this was definitely new and different behaviour from Michelle and Chloe wasn't quite sure how to react to it so, again, she let it sit.

'Chloe... the pitch for Sinclairz Chairs is magnificent.'

'Magnificent' was not a word Michelle used lightly. And Chloe felt that professional pride fizzing in her stomach. She wasn't just good at her job, she was magnificent.

Michelle continued. 'In the time you've had there in Iceland you've really put the work in. It actually made me want to resign as a director from this company and start working at Sinclairz Chairs so I get to experience this magical island you've described it as and all their work camaraderie the way you've put it together. You've made it sound like an advertorial for working with Lincoln actually.'

'Oh, have I?' Chloe said, frowning. 'I'm sorry if that's your take away from it, I—'

'Chloe, stop,' Michelle butted in. 'Nothing I am saying here is a criticism of any kind, OK? Nothing.'

Chloe swallowed. It was like some kinder, softer, lighter version of Michelle was pulling the strings now. It was unprecedented.

'You are not only an incredible employee, Chloe,' Michelle

carried on. 'You are an incredible person.' She took a deep breath. 'And I feel so much pride in saying that because I am so blessed that you work for me. But... I'm not sure how long that can continue.'

Chloe jolted as the vehicle bumped over a lump in the road and she had to steady her laptop as well as her heart. Michelle was going to accept her resignation. Well, Chloe had written it, meant it. But still, this was the moment her career as she knew it, as she had built it, was going to come to an end.

'You know what I'm saying, Chloe? Right?'

Chloe nodded. 'You liked the pitch, but I broke your trust when I lied on my CV and I breached ethical code when a robot voice told the chamber of commerce that Sinclairz were a potential client and all that is fact, despite the nice things you've said using "magnificent" and "incredible". You are going to accept my resignation.' She took a breath. 'So, what happens now? Do I just leave?'

'What?' Michelle exclaimed. 'What are you talking about? I don't want you to leave! But I understand your reasons for wanting to leave having worked with an unappreciative monster all this time!'

Did she really want to leave? Or did she just want things to change? Those questions could have fitted with so many scenarios in her life, but did she even have an answer?

'Chloe, where even are you right now?'

Chloe glanced out of the window at the scenery flashing by. It was snowing today, but lightly, like someone was up there in the clouds, sieving icing sugar on top of a glossy, mossy, rocky cake. 'I'm on my way to Husavik to see some whales.'

'I don't remember that being mentioned in the pitch for Sinclairz Chairs.'

It wasn't. This was something she was doing for her and

Gunnar. He had the opportunity to take this tour as the driver and she had remembered he had spoken about it when they were on the boat the first night she had seen the Northern Lights.

'No,' Chloe answered, simply. 'Not the main suggested itinerary. But, at the bottom of page six, you will see there are a few other options and this trip could be one of them.'

'Look, Chloe, no more beating around the bush. I want to be completely straight with you even if it means, you know, touching on my... oh God, I don't know if I can say the word...' She took a breath and panted like she might be about to push the baby out then and there. 'E... e... emotions.'

'That was very brave, Michelle,' Chloe said with utter sincerity. 'I'm very proud of you.'

'I need you, Chloe. Now more than ever. Because I cannot do this on my own and the only person I know who is as control freakish as me about this business is you. You are my safe pair of hands, the brains behind everything really and I never fully appreciated just how brilliant you are. But I want to now. Before someone else swipes you because they aren't as blind or as stupid as me.'

'O-K,' Chloe said, a little tentatively.

'Chloe, I don't want you to be my employee any more. I want you to be my partner. A partner in the business. Sharing the profits, working towards more growth, making plans to see Dress Code fold and go into administration... OK, maybe a bit harsh... but, Chloe, I think we would continue to be a dream team and I would promise to do better at collaboration than I have been, hopefully particularly when these hormones exit.'

Partnership. Chloe's dream. What she had been on the path towards since she had set her compass dial all the way over to the direction of work with no other points on the map. This felt like a defining moment; the snow clouds should have parted and a beam of light should have appeared like an angelic beacon spotlighting this transformative episode. Except, it didn't feel quite how Chloe had expected it to feel.

'Thank you, Michelle,' she said, a sense of unexplained ease about her now. 'I am really so honoured that you've said those things and made that offer to me and—'

'Well,' Michelle jumped in. 'Of course we can go through all the figure work and percentages and terms and conditions when you get back here for the Sinclairz Chairs meeting.'

Now a shiver ran through Chloe but it was definitely dread and not exhilaration. 'What Sinclairz Chairs meeting?'

'Chloe, I'm not going to email this brilliant work to Lincoln or his team. As magnificent as it is on paper, we need to sell this in person. And, when I say "we", I really mean "you" because you are the beating heart of this project.'

Her eyes were already on Gunnar, that driving side-profile from the seat she was getting accustomed to riding in. His blond hair pushed back behind his ears, a look of concentration on his handsome face as he navigated the road. She cared about him. Deeply cared. But what really happened next for them? There were no guarantees...

'The meeting is in two days,' Michelle said.

Now Chloe gasped. 'What?'

'We need to get this pitched with festive weather outside and a Yuletide backdrop inside. I've got Scarlet making the board-room into an Icelandic winter wonderland so if you can email her any more photos that can inspire her mood boards that would be sensational.'

Chloe didn't know what to say. Because if she left for the UK now she would miss Magnús's show.

63

HÚSAVÍK

'Today, we are hoping to see not just humpback whales.' Gunnar spoke to his happy band of travellers waiting to board the traditional Icelandic oak ship about to take them out of Skjálfandi Bay. 'But other kinds – fin whales or maybe even dolphins.'

Despite the excitement of the whales, a mention of dolphins always seemed to get appreciation. Except one person didn't seem to be fully engaged in his pre-tour patter. Chloe. She was gazing out over the bay like her mind was swirling with a million thoughts as her eyes grazed over the water.

'So,' Gunnar said, clapping his gloved hands together. 'We can get on board the boat now and the crew will give you further instructions.'

Everyone rushed toward the vessel, cameras already out of their bags, desperate to get the best seats or standing area where they could have the perfect view to capture a maybe once-in-a-lifetime shot. The only thing on his mind was easing whatever was going on in Chloe's. He stepped towards her, then, without overthinking, slipped his arms around her waist and drew her close into his body.

'Let us hope the whales do not mind snow,' he whispered close to her ear as the flakes continued to fall around them.

She snuggled into him and he relaxed a little, her head nestling close to his.

'You are OK?' he asked her.

'I am OK,' she answered.

But he sensed it in her voice. She was deep-thinking. 'Tell me, *krúttio mitt*.'

He felt her body tense first and then slowly release. He held her as she began to still, relax, simply breathe. And then she turned around to face him, snowflakes landing on her pinked cheeks. She was so beautiful, like a warm, radiant picture against the cold, rugged landscape. She was looking at him now as if there were a million things she wanted to say and he wished she would tell him, let him lighten her mental load. Then she slipped her gloved hands into his, giving them a squeeze.

'Let's get on the boat.'

* * *

It was even colder out on the water, but they had been provided with suits to lock their body temperature in and to repel the snow and it really did feel like they were at one with the ocean. As their boat guide gave information about the area and what they hoped to see, Chloe's mind was working overtime wondering what she was going to do about the new dilemma she was faced with. It was head over heart, something she had longed for versus unchartered territory and something she could never have envisaged coming along for her.

'There is Lundey, or, Puffin Island,' Gunnar said. He pointed ahead of them to a lump of rock sticking out of the sea then he passed her a steaming hot drink.

'Is this where we are going to see hundreds of black and white birds who look like Magnús's costume?' Chloe asked him.

'No,' Gunnar answered. 'We will not see any puffins today.'

'What?' Chloe said, confused. 'But it's called Puffin Island.'

'Yes,' he told her. 'But the puffins, they only come here for the summer months. To breed. In the summertime there can be up to three hundred thousand puffins here.'

'That's crazy,' Chloe said. 'So many.'

'Yes,' Gunnar said. 'And the island, it is only two hundred metres long and one hundred metres wide.'

'Can you go there? Walk on it?'

'No,' Gunnar said. 'It is owned privately. But we will go close on the boat. There are not only puffins there. There is much other wildlife too.'

She took a sip of her coffee and hoped it would warm her body and soothe the internal conflict too. But even Icelandic coffee couldn't work miracles...

'Chloe,' Gunnar said so softly. 'Do not think that you cannot tell me your truths.'

She leaned against the boat and turned a little to face him. 'Did you hear any of my call with Michelle?'

'No,' he said, shaking his head. 'I am a professional driver. My eyes were on the road, my mouth was telling the stories of the *huldufólk* and my ears were listening for the throwing up.'

Chloe laughed. 'There wasn't any of that.'

'On the way here,' Gunnar said, smiling. 'But, you know, after a trip on water, fish and chips and a long day.'

'Stop it.'

'I have stopped.'

Chloe took a breath of the salty snowy air and looked deep into Gunnar's eyes. 'Michelle offered me partnership.'

Her chest swelled as she delivered the news and she felt

excitement, joy and pride flooding her like it should have flooded her when she had first heard Michelle say it.

'Chloe!' Gunnar exclaimed, not hesitating to throw his arms around her and hug her tightly. 'This is the most amazing news! The moment that you so wished for in all of the world.'

And, just like that, her feelings changed, see-sawing instantaneously. Her body stiffened. It was not the moment she had so wished for in all of the world. That moment could never be achieved.

Gunnar let her go, stood back, knowing, feeling. 'Chloe, I am sorry. That was not what I meant. God, I am so stupid! The worst person! I did not think!'

'Stop,' Chloe said, putting a finger to his lips and pressing hard. 'I know what you meant and it's fine. It is what I wanted for so long. The thing I have been striving for, dreaming about, trying to manifest, it's finally come true.'

'But there is a problem?' Gunnar asked.

She nodded. 'Yes. I think. I don't really know. I'm just trying to work it out in my mind.'

He nodded now. 'There is much to think about.'

She looked out to sea now, as the boat began to move a little closer to the island, waves lapping at its base, snow covering the rocks. 'I suppose, when Michelle said all these amazing things about my work, about me, and then offered me the partnership, it didn't quite feel how I thought it was going to feel.'

'It did not feel good?' Gunnar asked her.

'It felt... OK.'

She couldn't believe she had actually voiced that. And how? How had her career dream changed from all she could think about night and day into an 'OK'. What did that say about the path she had set herself on for so long? What did it say about her future?

'You know,' Gunnar began, standing close. 'Sometimes when we have been very focussed on one thing for a long time we can be blinkered to everything else going on around us. Sometimes, dreams and ambitions they can be solitary places, places that we go to that feel strong and grounding and safe, always there to hold on to, our one purpose.'

'Yes,' Chloe said, nodding. 'Exactly that.'

'For me, this is Magnús,' Gunnar admitted. 'From the moment he arrived in my life he was the focus, the purpose. I did not think about anything else other than giving him everything I could to try to make up for everything he had had taken away from him.'

'And you have done an incredible job with him,' Chloe said.

'Maybe,' Gunnar replied. 'But, you know, that one thing or person or goal, it can hold you back from exploring other things, missing other moments in your life, or even finding a different road to travel to a destination you never had the time or the space to realise.'

'You have regrets about being Magnús's guardian?'

'No!' Gunnar stated passionately. 'No, not one regret for that. If the same situation would happen again I would do the same thing. But, I think I am beginning to realise that accepting responsibility for Magnús should not have meant shutting down every other area of my life.'

And that was exactly what Chloe had done with her work. She hadn't been able to conceive, which had made her relationship with Michael fall apart and all she felt she had left was her work. She'd needed something she felt she could excel in, succeed in, something that was totally under her control and something that wouldn't ever have to rely on someone else. Safe but oh so solitary... She gripped the handrail of the boat.

Gunnar put his hand over hers and interlinked their fingers.

'To be honest with you, I think the problem with most things is expectation.' He sighed. 'Other people's expectations, society's expectations, everyone doing the same things because people have done the same things for centuries. There is no room for personal expression, for deeper personalised thinking, for living without pressure, for living gently.'

Living gently. She liked that. She really liked that.

'Ah! Look!' Gunnar said, pointing ahead of them, his breath visible in the freezing air. 'I do not believe it! There is a blue whale! See?'

Chloe looked and there it was, a huge mammal swimming in the water. 'Is that rare?'

'Yes,' Gunnar said. 'They come only in the summer usually and, even then, they stay maybe a few days here to feed and then they leave again. In the winter this is not normal.'

She could sense his excitement and she loved how his thrill made her feel. And that's when it hit her. That's when it fully, truly, all-the-way hit her. She smiled to herself as she watched the blue whale submerge then pop up again and the other passengers started to 'ooh' and 'aah' as they took photo after photo. She wasn't going to take photos. She was going to drink this moment in for all that it was and all that it was telling her.

'Gunnar,' she said, squeezing his hand.

'Yes, *krúttio mitt*.'

'I like "not normal",' she told him.

'Me too,' he said, wrapping an arm around her. 'Me too.'

64

GUNNAR'S HOME, OUTSKIRTS OF REYKJAVIK

'So, are you going to tell me what is wrong?' Hildur asked later that night, looking up from her knitting. 'Or will you pretend you are reading that book for the rest of the evening?'

Gunnar lifted his head from the page he had re-read so many times and looked at his old friend. 'Are you pretending to knit?'

'Do not be stupid! Look! See how long the work grows!' She shook her needles and the wool attached to it that was forming a long train of something. 'Tell me about the story you are "reading".'

Gunnar closed the book, put it on the coffee table next to a display of pine cones Magnús and Hildur had painted silver, then leaned forward in his chair.

'We saw a blue whale today.'

Hildur gasped and put her knitting to one side. 'You saw a blue whale!'

'We know they are here but—'

'Not in the winter time,' Hildur said. 'Are you sure?'

Gunnar nodded. 'I am sure.'

'Then it was a spirit!'

'I knew you would say that.'

'But you tell me anyway.'

Gunnar shrugged.

'And because of this there is something on your mind.'

He sighed. 'Chloe had some very good news today. She has been offered partnership with the company she works for.'

'That is fantastic!' Hildur said, clapping her hands together. 'She is a very smart woman. I tell this from the moment we meet.'

'She is,' Gunnar agreed.

'But this is a problem,' Hildur said.

'No.'

'Gunnar Eriksson, I know you.'

'I do not know what to say,' he stated. 'It just feels like everything is repeating itself all over again.'

As he said the words he hated himself for feeling any kind of way about Chloe's work news. He should only feel complete happiness for her achievement and he did feel joy for her but, underneath it all was a horrible burning sensation that told him that as soon as he had begun to open himself up, be honest about Magnús, try to unlock that vulnerable personal side of himself, the universe was preparing to take it all away and shut it down again. And as all these thoughts revolved in his head, Hildur hadn't said anything, was simply looking at him like she was waiting for more...

'It is like what happened with Kirstin, no? She finds out about Magnús, she gets a new, better work opportunity, she leaves. It is the exact same pattern of events. I do not know why I expected anything else.'

'Have you said any of this to Chloe?' Hildur asked him.

'How can I?' he said, throwing his hands up. 'Why would I? I want Chloe to be happy. She deserves all the happiness given everything she has been through. And I am not the kind of person to say "but what does that mean for the beginnings of us"? We have known each other for such a short time. It is insignificant compared to all the time she has put into making her successful career.'

Hildur hauled herself to her feet and began to shuffle across the living area towards him.

'What are you doing?' he asked.

'I am coming closer so I do not need to shout,' she said, her arms brushing tinsel and baubles as she passed by the Christmas tree. 'There may be hugging.'

Gunnar folded his arms across his chest and retracted slightly. But he checked to make sure Hildur was on her way to safely sitting down beside him. And then she launched her tiny frame at him so he almost had to catch her and she held on tight with what he imagined to be the grip of a Norse god.

'You need to have faith,' Hildur told him.

'In God? In the spirits?'

'In Chloe,' Hildur said. 'And, in yourself.'

She let him go then, sitting down beside him and meeting his gaze.

'Chloe is not Kirstin. And you are not the same person that you were back then.'

'No?'

'No,' Hildur told him. 'Back then you were looking for someone to share a relationship with because you thought that is what you should be doing. You never really, truly opened yourself up to the possibility of love, you only partially unlocked the door and peeked out to see what was there.'

'I do not think—'

'I am right. You know this. Do not question it.'

Gunnar said nothing else.

'Kirstin was not the right person for you. And you knew that really, if you are honest. You knew how she would react to finding out about Magnús and, in the end, that is the reason you told her.'

Gunnar felt a squirming in his gut that said Hildur had seen right to the heart of the matter, as always.

'You were not ready with Kirstin. Kirstin was not the right person. The situation is not the same.'

'But Chloe will leave.'

'And you have known that from the very start,' Hildur reminded him. 'You knew that she was only visiting. Yet still you made time and opportunity to pursue something with her. Why?' She took a brief breath before carrying on. 'You do not need to answer that because I know the reason why. Because she is the right person. Because you are ready now, to unlock the door and step boldly out from behind it. No more peeking.'

He sighed. 'But she is still leaving.'

'Yes,' Hildur said. 'And you must let her go. No matter how hard that feels. Because if Chloe is the right person then she will come back. I have faith in her like I have faith in you.'

'But look at me, Hildur and look at the life I have. Chloe could find someone with more time to give her, not someone who spends hours on a coach every day and has a surrogate son to manage.'

'Ah, yes,' Hildur said. 'This is very true. And while we are on the subject of not being enough, why not wonder if she might be happier with someone who looks like Pedro Pascal?'

'OK, that was uncalled for.'

'People do not fall in love with a face,' Hildur told him. 'People fall in love with a feeling. That special something someone sparks in you when you are around them. That is what you have with Chloe. I believe that is what she feels with you.'

He so wanted to believe it. He wanted to hold the thought tight and imagine how much stronger it could grow given more time.

'And remember the blue whale?' Hildur said. 'You know what that signifies in mythology?'

'Wisdom,' Gunnar replied. 'But also solitude. I thought it was showing me how to get ready to continue to be alone.'

Hildur shook her head. 'No. In mythology a whale signifies "harmony", "courage" and "abundance". All good things.'

'I guess it depends what book you read,' Gunnar said with a shrug.

'But there is another thing a whale can signify,' Hildur continued.

'What?'

'Family,' Hildur said. 'Motherhood in particular.'

'What are you trying to say?' Gunnar asked her.

'I am not trying to say anything,' Hildur said. 'I do not have to. The spirits are doing all the talking. Loud and clear.'

65

THE NEXT DAY

Reykjavik Airport

'You have the cookies Hildur made you?' Magnús asked Chloe.

'Of course.'

'And the scarf she knitted?'

Chloe parted her coat so he could see that it was around her neck. It was terrible. There were dropped stitches and the colours were lime green and orange, but Chloe knew it had been made in double quick time for her as a parting gift. A parting gift. She didn't like that. She was going to make sure the parting was for as short a time as possible. She had holiday she could take and, yes, Michelle was about to give birth but they had to be able to work things out if she was going to be a partner in the business...

'Magnús, stop with all the questions, Chloe has a plane to catch.'

Gunnar, the voice of reason. The strong, solid, sexy man she had fallen for so quick and yet so intrinsically deeply. She looked at him now, taking him all in from his winter boots to the very tips of his beautiful hair.

'Will you be back for my Christmas show?' Magnús asked her.

She saw the look in his eyes, the hope, the preparation for disappointment, the swallow as he finished the sentence and got scared for her reply.

'Magnús,' she said gently. 'I promised you that I would be there for your show. I don't make promises unless I intend to keep them. OK?'

'OK,' Magnús said, nodding happily, a smile on his face.

'OK, Magnús, here, take this *króna* and get coffee,' Gunnar said, handing the boy some money.

Then Magnús threw himself at Chloe, wrapping his arms around her and hugging tight. The warmth there took her aback and tears were springing into her eyes before she could hold herself in check. It was the kind of hug she hadn't ever expected to experience.

'Bye!' Magnús said, running off towards the vending machines.

And then there was two. Just her and Gunnar, the way this visit to Iceland had begun but oh, how everything had changed in such a short space of time.

'I am sorry we do not have more time,' Gunnar said.

'In this moment?' she asked.

'In all the moments,' he answered. 'But specifically I meant the fact that we were fighting with Hildur so she stayed at home and soon you will have to board for the flight.'

'I know,' Chloe said. 'But, I will be back for Magnús's show. I have three days, right?'

'Chloe,' Gunnar said, shaking his head. 'It is OK.'

'What?' Chloe said. 'What do you mean? I'm coming back for Magnús's Christmas show. You just heard me promise him.'

'I know,' Gunnar said. 'And I know you will try your best to keep this promise, but you are going to be so busy. This is a big thing for you. The Sinclairz Chairs pitch, the partnership, a ba...' He paused for a second then continued quickly. 'And Kat, she will need you too if the stories about her mother are true.'

He had been going to say 'baby'. She swallowed and reached for his hands.

'And a baby is coming,' she said firmly. 'A beautiful baby is going to be born and Michelle is going to dress it in designer wear even though it's going to be sick even more often than your coach passengers.'

He nodded, squeezing her hands. 'Yes.'

'But I am still going to be back for Magnús's show,' Chloe said with all the conviction she had. She meant it. A hundred per cent.

'You need to go,' Gunnar said. 'It is OK, *krúttio mitt*.'

Except it didn't feel OK. Gunnar might be holding her hands but it felt like he was also holding back, or rather, perhaps letting go... Perhaps there was another question she needed to ask.

'Do you want me to come back for Magnús's show?'

Her heart was beating in her throat now and Gunnar hadn't immediately jumped to answer. Until:

'I think,' Gunnar began. 'That you must do what you need to do for you, Chloe. Less concern about expectation, remember? And you have worked so hard for this opportunity.'

She was shaking her head before she even knew she was shaking her head. What was happening here?

'I've worked hard,' Chloe stated. 'I will work hard to make sure we get the Sinclairz Chairs job but... I haven't made up my mind about the partnership. I told you that. I asked Michelle for some time to think about it. I have to be certain that I am choosing to take it for all the right reasons, not just because it's what I know and what has made me feel safe.'

'I know,' Gunnar said.

'But you're sounding like you don't know. Or that you... don't care. Or that when I talked about coming back you... didn't really believe me?'

He looked away from her for a second. It was long enough.

'You didn't believe me?' Chloe repeated.

'Chloe, it is not that.'

'Then what is it?'

Her heart was beating hard in her chest and her emotions were that horrible, groggy mix of frustrated and sick with dread.

'You must make your own choices, that is all,' Gunnar said in the most matter-of-fact tone. 'That is important.'

'I will make my own choices,' Chloe said, swallowing a lump in her throat. 'I just...' She let the sentence tail off because she didn't know what to say. This morning they had made love so tenderly, so beautifully that she had had tears in the corners of her eyes which he then kissed away. She didn't understand.

'Chloe—'

'No, it's OK,' she said, internally bolstering now. 'You're right. I have to board the plane.' She smiled. Fake.

'Text me when you land? Let me know you have arrived safely.'

She nodded. 'Yes.'

'Good.'

'OK, well, I guess I will go now.' She took a step away from him but if felt like it was really a gigantic leap. 'Bye, Gunnar.'

And then she turned away. She couldn't look at him any more because leaving was harder than she ever thought it would be. Because now it felt more awkward than ever. It hadn't been a holiday romance to her, one that ended in a weird conversation at an airport, not when she had been as honest with him as she had ever been with anyone, nor after he had introduced her to his family. As she started to walk, wheeling her case, clutching her bag, the urge to turn around was so strong and all the while of not looking she was wanting him to be there, spinning her around and kissing her hard and telling her how much he wanted her to come back. However, as the seconds ticked by, the journey to the gate had never felt so solitary. Finally, she got to the end of the corridor, where she had to make a turn. There was no denying she needed to see him one more time, commit his face to her memory bank. But, turning her head, all she saw was an empty spot. Gunnar had already gone.

66

KAT'S HOME, WINCHESTER, UK

'Chloe! You're shivering! Come in! Quickly! Mum! Get the kettle on!'

Apparently, even though she had spent so much time in Iceland, Chloe was not accustomed to the absolute soul-soaking rain of the UK or the amount of time you had to hang around outside in it for public transport connections. She had been quickly sodden from the moment she left the airport and it had continued on trains, buses and taxis until she arrived here at Kat's home, with no warning whatsoever, feeling bewildered and completely out-of-sorts.

'I... sorry,' Chloe said through chattering teeth. 'I should have called but thinking was hurting so I just... acted.'

'Oh shit, you're talking in riddles. What's happened?' Kat asked, unzipping Chloe's coat and taking it from her and then reaching coats down from her rail in the hallway and beginning to layer them up onto her friend.

'I... don't know. I got on the plane, but before I got on the plane, things with Gunnar just went wrong and I feel so stupid and I don't want to feel stupid I want to feel like I felt when things weren't going wrong with him and I have preparation to do for the Sinclairz Chairs meeting and I can't focus and—'

'OK, I've heard more than enough and there is only one cure for this. Mum! Forget the tea! Get the large bottle of Baileys out and three glasses. The big ones!'

* * *

'So, let me get this straight,' Kat's mother, Rula said. 'He has a son. And a woman he lives with. But she's not the mother of the son, or the grandmother, and she broke her ankle. But she didn't break her ankle falling from the roof of the school where she had kidnapped someone. And the son-who-isn't-the-son was being bullied because he was rescued from a volcano.' She looked at her half-empty glass of Baileys. 'Am I drunk, Katherine? Because this sounds like a film.'

'Don't forget about the sex in a secluded thermal lagoon,' Kat said, topping up Chloe's glass with the creamy alcohol.

'I didn't tell your mum that!' Chloe shrieked.

'And that I would have been even more interested in. Do you know, I once had sex in an igloo,' Rula announced.

'Argh! Stop! La la la la la la!' Kat said, slapping her hands over her ears.

'It wasn't with your father.'

'Is that supposed to make it better or worse because I don't know!' Kat exclaimed.

'I think the core take away from all this is that you like this guy a lot but you don't know what to do with that feeling. Am I right, Katherine?' Rula said, curling her feet up underneath her on the sofa.

'You are right,' Kat said, nodding. 'Chloe, you're being

cautious and I understand why but sometimes you have to let it all out.'

'Like when you've had a monstrous Christmas dinner and you undo your jeans and just let everything, you know, hang,' Rula added.

'But,' Chloe said, beginning to feel the effects of the alcohol. 'He's being cautious too. More than me. And this morning at the airport it felt a bit like he wanted to...' She swallowed, not really wanting to finish her sentence. 'End things.'

'No!' Kat exclaimed. 'No, I'm sure it wouldn't have been that. I mean, why introduce you to Magnús? That's not something you do lightly.'

'Unless,' Rula said, pointing a fiery red fingernail into the air, 'he's thinking, now you've got your big company partnership opportunity, that you're going to forget all about him and the short time you've had in Iceland.'

Was that what Gunnar thought? Chloe let her mind wander to the conversations they had had since she'd told him the news about Michelle making her offer. She had told him she wasn't sure about accepting, that she was wondering whether it really was the right move. But she hadn't made clear that that decision didn't affect the way she felt about him. Whatever she chose professionally wasn't going to impact on how she currently felt personally. She wanted to see where things went with Gunnar, navigate the distance situation whether she was Michelle's partner or not. Was he thinking she was making a choice between him and her career and she had opted for her career? Did he think the two things couldn't co-exist?

She gasped then. 'He thinks I'm doing the same thing Kirstin did!'

'What?' Kat said.

'Yes, I will echo that. What? And who is Kirstin? Was she the kidnapped person or the girl who bullied the not-really-his-son?' Rula asked.

'I have to go,' Chloe said, scrabbling up from the chair.

'Go where?' Kat asked. 'You've only just got here.'

'To the airport. Where's my coat?'

'What? Are you crazy? It's close to midnight now and I was going to get Katherine to whizz up a little cheeseboard and some pickled onions,' Rula said.

'Your coat is still drying, on the chair.'

Chloe was already heading to pluck it off and began collating everything she had brought with her. Was she crazy? Or was the crazier thing that she had even got on the plane in the first place? She'd been so focussed on the getting back to the UK to deal with Sinclairz Chairs she hadn't thought about reassuring Gunnar, and all he had seen was another woman walking out of his life after meeting Magnús.

'You don't have to fly back there tonight,' Kat said. 'Just call him.'

'No,' Chloe said. 'That's not enough.'

'But what about the Sinclairz Chairs pitch?'

'I know exactly what I'm going to do about that. But, right now, the only thing I need to do is get back to Iceland.'

67

REYKJAVIK AIRPORT

'...OK and here we are everybody. On behalf of my company, and of me and of the whole of Iceland including our magical *huldufólk* we wish you a safe journey to your next destination and we give you the greetings of the season. In Iceland, we say *"Gleðileg jól"*.'

It was the early morning and Gunnar smiled at his passengers as they began to disembark the airport transfer bus. And then his heart suddenly soared as he caught sight of a familiar coat. There was someone standing closer to the terminal building. A woman. Her hair was covered by a black beanie, but there was maybe something about the way she was standing? Could it be... And then the woman turned around. It wasn't who he had hoped. Hope. Did he even still have that after how he had been at the airport before she left? She had texted him that she had landed and he had 'liked' the message. Why had he only liked the message? Why had he said nothing? He knew why. Because he did not want to influence any of the important decisions she had to make about her future. That wasn't who he was. But, by saying nothing, was he making Chloe think he didn't care at all? The absolute opposite was true. He cared so much already.

'You need to get off the bus now.'

He jolted in his driver's seat at the sound of Magnús's voice right next to him.

'Magnús, what are you doing here? Why are you not at school?'

'I am on my way to school. Hildur has arranged a taxi,' Magnús said.

'And Hildur will be trying to climb these steep coach steps if you do not get out of the seat and come outside.'

It was Hildur's voice now. One look past Magnús and he saw the old woman was standing in the snow at the foot of the steps, wrapped up against the elements like a walking sleeping bag.

'What is going on? Why are you here?' Gunnar asked them as he got to his feet and hastened Magnús to get off the bus.

'Why are you here?' Hildur asked him. 'That is the question Magnús and I have been asking ourselves.'

Had either one of them or both hit their heads? He frowned at them. 'I work here. Today I am on the airport run. You know this.'

'And we also know that we cannot stand one more second of your sadness about Chloe leaving. Isn't that right, Magnús?' Hildur stated.

'It is right,' Magnús agreed. 'So, here is your bag.' He took the rucksack he was carrying off his shoulder and pressed it on to Gunnar.

'What is this?' Gunnar asked.

'This is an opportunity,' Hildur told him. 'Because it is the right thing to let people make their own decisions. But it is the wrong thing to let people make their own decisions based on inaccurate, or lack of, information.'

'I do not understand,' Gunnar said, swallowing nervously as he hugged the bag to him.

'You were not honest with Chloe,' Magnús told him.

'I do not know what you mean.'

'Like you are not being honest with that sentence!' Hildur exclaimed. 'Gunnar! You did not tell Chloe how you feel about her.'

'I am uncomfortable having this conversation.'

'I heard you,' Magnús said. 'You told Chloe you did not believe she was coming back for my show.'

His stomach dropped. He hadn't said that, had he? And Magnús had heard? 'I do not believe I said that. And Magnús, she made you a promise and—'

'And I believe her,' Magnús stated, pushing forward a defiant chin. 'Unless you have messed things up by pretending that you do not care.'

Had he done that? In his heart, he knew he had done that. Why? Now, when it was the most important time, had he self-sabotaged something that felt so good? So right.

'Take that look of pity off your face,' Hildur ordered, using Magnús's arm to keep her balance as she waddled forward a little. 'It is not too late to do something about it.'

'No?' Gunnar said, nervousness and dread bubbling inside him.

'No,' Hildur and Magnús said at exactly the same time.

'I should call her,' Gunnar said, putting the rucksack down on the ground and slipping a hand into the pocket of his coat for his phone.

'No!' Hildur and Magnús said together again.

'What?'

'No calling,' Hildur said. 'No texting or miscommunication. This has to happen in person. And that is why we have booked you a flight to the UK.'

'What?' Gunnar's heart almost stopped. This had to be a joke, didn't it?

'You should have an email with the boarding pass. It leaves in two hours so you have time to get a coffee,' Magnús told him.

'When you have picked your jaw off the floor,' Hildur added.

'Your passport is in the bag,' Magnús said. 'And some of your OK clothes. The best of bad choices.'

'You can go to Chloe. You can tell her how you feel and make certain that her decisions will be made with the knowledge she needs,' Hildur said firmly.

He didn't know what to say. His mind was racing as fast as his heart. Could he do this? Should he do this?

'What about my job? I feel Erik already wants to fire me.'

'Erik has arranged for Wolfgang to cover,' Hildur said. 'I have known Erik's grandmother for many years, Gunnar. And when a grandmother, or a grandmother figure, insists on something, you have to listen.'

His family were interfering. His family. He couldn't have felt more love for them in this moment. He stepped forward and drew both of them into his body for the kind of hug they had never had before. As mismatched as their heights and shapes were, it felt like the perfect blend and Gunnar became suddenly acutely aware of how extremely fortunate he was.

'If you want coffee you should go,' Magnús said, the first to extricate himself from the cuddle.

'And all this hugging is hurting my shoulders,' Hildur added, ducking out too. 'And they are one part of me that has not been completely destroyed by recent events.'

'OK,' Gunnar said, picking the rucksack back up. 'OK, I am going to England.'

He was going to England. Was this even real? But, as he

stepped up his pace, then turned it into a jog that developed quickly into a run, he had never felt more sure about anything.

And then, bam! A second later he was sprawled out on the ground.

68

Chloe felt like she was hallucinating. Either that or she had somehow time-travelled and was reliving her first ever moments in Iceland. Here she was again, flat out on the snowy ground, outside the airport building and there was blond hair and a padded jacket...

'I am sorry. I will just move my arm and I should be able to get up. One second.'

That voice. This couldn't be happening. 'Gunnar?'

Silence. Maybe she was imagining this whole scenario. Maybe she wasn't even awake. She had been totally sleep-deprived waiting in London overnight for the next available flight here. But then:

'Chloe?'

A few movements she felt beside her and then she saw him. Gunnar. Leaning over her, his blond hair flopping in front of his face, those blue eyes gazing intensely. So many thoughts and feelings started firing through her then, but the one that stepped to the front was, this is where I want to be. To love and be loved.

'Are you hurt?' he asked.

'Not like you mean,' she whispered.

'Let me help you up. Take it slowly.'

He put an arm around her and gently eased her off the ground and to her feet, brushing the snow from her coat. Then he picked up her cabin case and righted it. When there was no immediate need to attend to anything else he stopped moving and just looked at her intently.

'I hurt you, didn't I?' he replied.

'No, Gunnar, you didn't hurt me, you just confused me. But then, when I got to Kat's and I talked and I thought and I drank way too much Baileys, I realised that I'd confused you too.'

'Chloe,' Gunnar said. 'I want you to know that... the way I feel about you... there has been no one else... I have felt as strongly connected to in such a short space of time.'

'And I feel exactly the same,' Chloe said. 'And those feelings are so intense they are scary as well as exciting.'

'For me too,' Gunnar agreed. 'But, I realised, and Hildur and Magnús made me realise, I had made a mistake when you left. I was trying to give you space in your thoughts to make your difficult decisions with your work, but I should have let you do that knowing the honesty of my heart.'

'And I should have made it clear that I wasn't running away from you and Magnús and Hildur like Kirstin. Because I was always going to come back, Gunnar. For Magnús's show and for you. For us.'

'For us,' Gunnar said, in equal parts soft and sexy.

'Yes,' she answered. 'Because one thing you have helped to show me is how important it is to live and love all parts of my life equally. I've ignored my personal life for so long because I was too frightened to try again, scared that I couldn't be enough for somebody how I am and—'

'*Krúttio mitt*, you are everything and more to me. Just as you are. I want you to make your choice about the partnership knowing that whatever you decide, I would like to be right by your side as you step into a new future. I want to be... supporting you, dreaming with you, creating with you... together with you.'

Chloe's heart swelled as he held her face in his hands and looked deep into her eyes. She could see how emotional he was. She could feel how his words were moving him almost as much as they were moving her and she wanted to bottle that feeling, store it deep inside her and remember it always.

'I don't want to be together with you,' she told him seriously.

She saw his expression dip, the concern flash in his eyes and then she spoke again.

'I want to be together with you... and Magnús... and Hildur,' she told him.

She relished the smile he gave then, but not for long, because then his mouth was on hers and he was delivering one of those beautiful, full, deep, kisses that made her heart thump and her toes curl. And as he held her tight, hugging her close and then kissing her all over again, Chloe realised that Gunnar was the home she'd been waiting for.

69

MAGNÚS'S SCHOOL

Two days later

The school hall was magnificently decorated, sparkling and shining with Christmas décor as all the children took to the stage to perform the musical theatre piece about puffins taking on the role of Santa Clauses and Yule Lads and delivering gifts to everybody in time for Christmas Eve despite challenges of shipwrecks, pirates, bad weather and unseaworthy boats.

'Look at Magnús,' Hildur whispered to Chloe. 'He is the finest puffin of them all, isn't he?'

'He is,' Chloe agreed, taking photographs.

'You two are biased,' Gunnar replied. 'Everyone is doing an excellent job.'

'But Magnús is the best,' Hildur stated again.

Chloe slipped her hand into Gunnar's and connected their fingers. She loved holding his strong hands. If she could hold his hands for twenty-four hours a day and still be able to function as a normal human then she would do it. When she was holding his hand it felt like she connected with the world a little differently, she relaxed more, loved life more, remembered how special it felt to be part of something, part of someone else's life. And that's how it had been since she'd arrived back in Reykjavik. She was staying in a wood and stone house with the man she had fallen hard for, the most independent older woman she had ever met and an ice-hockey obsessed pre-teen who ate like a hungry wolf every hour of the day. And she was now a partner of Michelle's events business – their business. What she wanted in her life was new beginnings but also stability. Her fledgling relationship with Gunnar was a brand-new start and her work was her stability. The same foundation but with an added bonus, the promotion she had reached hard for. She had also set some important ground rules with Michelle. She had terms that were make or break when it came to her accepting the role. She was going to work hard, however she was not going be on call all hours of the day or night and she was going to work remotely as much as she could. And, right now, remotely was just a different word for 'Iceland'.

'Bravo!' Hildur exclaimed as the performance came to an end in a flurry of feathers, orange bills, exploding confetti canons and a crescendo of music. The old woman leapt to her feet and Chloe had to let go of Gunnar's hand to reach out and steady Hildur before she toppled into the aisle.

'Hildur,' Gunnar admonished. 'If you do not sit down you will be in that boot until after the New Year.'

'They can advise me,' Hildur answered. 'I will not listen.'

Chloe and Gunnar stood too, clapping the children and taking photographs of Magnús as he flapped his wings and turned in a circular dance and they made their way back off the stage.

Chloe's phone began to rumble in the pocket of her jeans. She pulled it out. Michelle.

'It's Michelle,' Chloe said to Gunnar. 'Do you mind if—'

'Go, *krúttio mitt*,' Gunnar said. 'Magnús has to get out of a bird costume and I believe the children are eating KFC before we leave.'

Chloe moved into the aisle, down to the exit and outside where light snow was starting to fall. Only then did she answer the FaceTime call.

'Hello.'

There was no response and Chloe tried to see what was going on on the screen. It wasn't Michelle's face, but what was it? There was a curtain... and some cloths and... then...

'Chloe, are you there?'

Michelle was almost whispering, a light, gentle tone that Chloe had never heard coming from her before. But it wasn't Michelle's face on the screen now, it was the face of a sleeping newborn baby, all pink and wrinkled and so tiny in a pale blue bodysuit and matching cotton beanie. Tears were in Chloe's eyes as she gazed at the cute bundle of perfection.

'Chloe?'

'I'm here,' Chloe replied quickly, her voice breaking a little.

'Surprise,' Michelle said, laughing. 'Actually, I don't know why I'm laughing, it's probably still all the drugs they had to give me to get through labour. I'm pretty sure some of my insides are on my outsides and I don't just mean Henry.'

'Aww,' Chloe said. 'You named him Henry. That's a lovely name.'

'It's Milo's dad's name. Believe me, if his dad was called Albert we would not be having this same discussion.' Michelle inhaled. 'But... he's perfect. Everything is OK with him despite being a little bit early and, you know, I am sure I will be fine too, once I've learned how to sit down again.'

'Congratulations, Michelle. I am so, so happy for you and for Milo.'

'Thank you, Chloe. I know it can't have been easy for you all these months.'

'No,' Chloe agreed. It hadn't been easy but, in some ways, having to face the facts of reproduction in such close quarters had been a baptism of fire and one that she had survived. 'But, honestly, I have no other thoughts or feelings other than I'm overjoyed for you. A brand-new little boy coming into the world is something so special to celebrate.'

'Oh and that's not the only thing we're going to celebrate,' Michelle continued.

The camera turned around and there was Michelle in a hospital bed, already somehow surrounded by lush blooms of flowers and cards, not a scrap of make-up on her face but looking as radiant as Chloe had ever seen her despite having just gone through a labour.

Michelle took a deep breath, eyes alive. 'We got the Sinclairz Chairs job.'

Chloe squealed and punched the air. 'Yes!'

Her yell drew attention from some people who were now leaving the school hall and coming out into the parking area, children still in costume.

'Did you doubt it, Chloe? Really? I mean, I know I wanted you back in the UK to do it but, what was I thinking, pitching it from Iceland, at the very heart of where Lincoln's wanting to take his team to celebrate the anniversary. It was perfect.'

Chloe smiled. It had been perfect. She had gone back with Gunnar to all the places she had put in the itinerary and filmed video clips describing everything she had written about so Sinclairz could see first-hand the beauty of the country and have a taste of the activities she had suggested. She had ended the pitch with a short live stream from the Sun Voyager statue near the water, the lights twinkling, the snow on the ground, a group of people singing traditional folk songs.

'Another success for the team,' Michelle said. 'And here's to many more of them.'

'I will definitely raise a glass to that and to the arrival of little Henry.'

'Chloe, there is one more thing I wanted to ask.'

Chloe's stomach dropped. Here came the test. Michelle had just given birth. She might feel on top of the world and be enthused about their new green-lit project but any second now she was going to realise exactly how much work there was to do and she was going to need every bit of help she could get. Chloe knew the 'one more thing I wanted to ask' was going to be 'when are you coming back'.

She pre-empted. 'I... don't know yet.'

'You don't know yet? What does that mean?' Michelle asked.

'Michelle, you shouldn't be thinking about this yet.'

'Of course I should be thinking about it! It's important!'

'I know it is, but we have Helene to cover the physical admin side of things and co-ordinate with the hosts, and I told you, I am going to make working remotely work. It's my priority to ensure that service levels don't slip and prove that freedom and flexibility can actually bring greater reliability.'

'Chloe, what the hell are you talking about?'

'The business,' Chloe said. 'Our empire.'

'Chloe,' Michelle said. 'I've given birth half a day ago. I know I'm the ultimate workaholic but even I draw the line somewhere.'

'Oh?'

'This isn't about work. I'm asking you if you will be Henry's godmother.'

70

THE SECRET LAGOON

The weather outside was frightful, but the secret thermal spa was more than delightful and as Chloe wrapped her naked form around Gunnar's she let her mind ease and her thoughts drift as he held her close and delivered sensual kisses to her neck.

'You are OK, *krúttio mitt*?' Gunnar asked her, hands on her waist.

'I am more than OK,' she answered, her fingers toying with the hair at his nape. 'I'm in a hot secret lagoon with a hot man.'

'Escaping an overexcited old woman and an overtired ten-year-old who ate a whole bucket of chicken to himself.'

'Our family,' Chloe stated, smiling.

'Our family,' Gunnar agreed.

'Is there room for one more, do you think?'

'You want to tell me something?'

It might not be the exact news that she one day had hoped to share with a partner but it was the closest thing to it and she had actually cried after Michelle had asked her.

'You know I told everyone that Michelle had had her baby,' Chloe said, arms around his neck.

'Henry,' Gunnar stated.

'Yes,' Chloe said. She took a deep breath. 'Well, what I didn't tell everyone was... Michelle asked me to be Henry's godmother.'

Even saying the words now made her super emotional and she tried to keep herself in check but failed. There were tears in her eyes again and, as Gunnar pulled her into his body, she knew he understood how she felt so completely.

'Chloe, tell me, how does that feel?'

'Wonderful,' Chloe said, tears spilling from her eyes now, unashamedly overwhelmed with him. 'Nothing else but wonderful.'

He held her tight as she cried, breathing into his wet hair, delighting in the sweet scent of him, feeling so completely content with life now. There was really nothing else she wanted other than more of what she now already had. She took a minute then lifted her head from his shoulders and gazed into his eyes.

'You know,' he said, pushing her wet hair back behind her ears. 'To be a godmother is like being a guardian. It is a big responsibility because someone has chosen you and you have then chosen to accept.'

She hadn't ever thought of it that deeply before but Gunnar was right. Michelle thought that Chloe was a person she wanted to help bring Henry up, to take care of his physical and emotional well-being. It was the ultimate honour and the only answer Chloe was ever going to give was a yes.

'The way you feel,' Gunnar continued. 'It is the way I feel when I decided to help Magnús. It is special. It is not like when you become a parent. Becoming a parent is obviously a choice, but not always, and then, the rest of that, it comes down to science. Being a guardian or a godmother, it has nothing to do with physical capabilities, it comes from the soul.'

'I like that,' Chloe said. 'So, you're saying that it's more spiritual.'

'I believe in the individuality of people. How they are made that way, who really knows? Some believe it is through God, others think it is evolution, some—'

'Think it is the *huldufólk* pulling all the strings.'

'Argh! Please, *krúttio mitt*, do not turn into Hildur. Keep that individuality I love about you.'

Love. He had used the word 'love'.

She smiled. 'You love that about me?'

'I love many things about you.'

'I love many things about you too.'

'I mainly love you.'

'I mainly love you too.'

He was looking at her looking at him and Chloe felt like her soul was on fire, burning brightly, and that Gunnar could see every leaping flame. And, as he took her in his arms again and captured her mouth with his, the skies above glowed with recognition that this one winter under the Northern Lights was only the very start of their happy-ever-after.

* * *

MORE FROM MANDY BAGGOT

The next utterly romantic escapist read from Mandy Baggot is available to order now here:

https://mybook.to/NewMandyBackAd

LETTER FROM MANDY

Are you feeling all wintry and cosy after finishing Chloe and Gunnar's story? I really hope you enjoyed this festive trip to Iceland and loved spending time with these characters. I'd love to hear what you thought of the book so why not leave me a review on Amazon or reach out on social media.

I visited Iceland in November 2024 with my child, Robin, as a celebration for them doing so brilliantly in their A-levels. We had the most fabulous time and many of the trips Chloe and Gunnar go on were to places Robin and I visited. Iceland is such a unique and beautiful country – if you do get a chance to visit I highly recommend it.

So, what's coming next? Stay tuned to all my social media channels and sign up to my Boldwood newsletter.

MANDY XX

ABOUT THE AUTHOR

Mandy Baggot is a bestselling romance writer who loves giving readers that happy-ever-after. From sunshine romantic comedies set in Greece, to cosy curl-up winter reads, she's bringing gorgeous heroes and strong heroines readers can relate to. Mandy splits her time between Salisbury, Wiltshire and Corfu, Greece and has a passion for books, food, racehorses and all things Greek!

Sign up to Mandy Baggot's mailing list for news, competitions and updates on future books.

Visit Mandy's website: www.mandybaggot.com

Follow Mandy on social media here:

facebook.com/mandybaggotauthor
x.com/mandybaggot
instagram.com/mandybaggot
bookbub.com/profile/mandy-baggot

ALSO BY MANDY BAGGOT

Boldwood

Boldwood Books is an award-winning fiction publishing company seeking out the best stories from around the world.

Find out more at www.boldwoodbooks.com

Join our reader community for brilliant books, competitions and offers!

Follow us
@BoldwoodBooks
@TheBoldBookClub

Sign up to our weekly
deals newsletter

Printed in Dunstable, United Kingdom

68291567R00202